W9-AFP-776

From an interview with Jodell Lee:

GF: Everybody knows that story, Jodell. That you discovered Wilder when you saw him win a race on a little out-of-the-way track somewhere way out there in the boondocks. You helped him hook up with your old friend Billy Winton's Grand National team, and now they're having a great rookie year in Cup racing. But it appears you have a special relationship yourself with the young driver.

Lee: I'll admit it. I see a lot of myself in the kid. A lot of Curtis Turner and Buddy Baker and old Fireball, too. He's good, but you know what else? He wants to win as bad as anybody I've ever seen. Lord, that boy loves to win! It's like he's driven by something almost supernatural to always put the nose of that racecar up front. He's the same way in cards or mumbly-peg or anything else. And if they raced refrigerators, I expect he'd be out there trying to win in one of the things.

Follow all the action . . .
from the qualifying lap
to the checkered flag!

Rolling Thunder!

Rolling Thunder
STOCK CAR RACING

ON THE THROTTLE

Kent Wright
& Don Keith

TOR®

A TOM DOHERTY ASSOCIATES BOOK
NEW YORK

NOTE: If you purchased this book without a cover you should be aware that this book is stolen property. It was reported as "unsold and destroyed" to the publisher, and neither the author nor the publisher has received any payment for this "stripped book."

This is a work of fiction. All the characters and events portrayed in this book are either products of the author's imagination or are used fictiously.

ROLLING THUNDER #8: ON THE THROTTLE

Copyright © 2000 by Kent Wright & Don Keith

All rights reserved, including the right to reproduce this book, or portions thereof, in any form.

A Tor Book
Published by Tom Doherty Associates, LLC
175 Fifth Avenue
New York, NY 10010

www.tor.com

Tor® is a registered trademark of Tom Doherty Associates, LLC.

ISBN: 0-812-54509-5

First edition: January 2001

Printed in the United States of America

0 9 8 7 6 5 4 3 2 1

This book is dedicated to the pit crews and everybody "back at the shop" . . . the true heroes of competitive, big-time stock car racing.

(Excerpt from an interview with legendary racecar driver and Winston Cup team owner Jodell Lee, published in Green Flag *magazine.)*

GF: Jodell, you've been in racing for over forty years now. You're over sixty years old. This is a grueling sport, even for the young guys out there. What keeps you going week after week in what has to be the most competitive sport there is?

Lee: That's easy. Every race we start feels just like the first one we ran, way back when, driving my granddaddy's car on a track they'd gouged out of a cornfield on Meyer's farm up the highway toward Johnson City. I get just as excited and my heart beats just as fast when they fire up those engines as it did that day, whether we're runnin' a little half-mile track or we're on the high banks at Talladega. If there ever comes a time it don't, that's when I go on back to Chandler Cove, Tennessee, and play with my grandbabies.

GF: But this is a tough game, even for the younger

folks. And you're one of the last single-car teams left in Cup racing. Can you compete with only one car and driver against Yates and Roush and Gibbs and the other multicar teams?

Lee: If I didn't think so, I'd hang it up today. I hate to lose and I'm not out there to finish in the back of the pack. And running against the big, well-funded teams does make it tough. Make no mistake about that. But it's always been that way . . . the most competitive game around. That's what makes it what it is. Whether you're running against Fireball Roberts and Richard Petty and Tiny Lund or Jeff Gordon and Dale Jarrett and Mark Martin, they're the best in the world and they have the teams to back them up.

That's what makes it so special when you somehow manage to sneak up on 'em and beat 'em. Maybe . . . just maybe . . . on that day and on that track, you and your driver and car and team are the best in the world. You hear me? The best in the world!

GF: Speaking of the drivers, who do you like nowadays among the new, young competitors?

Lee: Naturally, I like my driver, Rex Lawford. I'm just sorry we're not providing him with a better ride right now. Gordon and Stewart and Kenseth and Earnhardt's kid . . . they're all fantastic. There's probably some I don't even know about, too, out there somewhere on one of them little tracks, gettin' ready, learnin', bidin' their time till they can make a run. And then, there's Rob Wilder.

GF: Everybody knows that story, Jodell. That you discovered Wilder when you saw him win a race on a little out-of-the-way track somewhere way out there in the boondocks. You helped him hook up with your old friend Billy Winton's Grand National team, and now they're having a great rookie year in Cup racing. But it appears you have a special relationship yourself with the young driver.

Lee: I'll admit it. I see a lot of myself in the kid. A lot of Curtis Turner and Buddy Baker and old Fireball, too. He's good, but you know what else? He wants to win as bad as anybody I've ever seen. Lord, that boy loves to win! It's like he's driven by something almost supernatural to always put the nose of that racecar up front. He's the same way in cards or mumblety-peg or anything else. And if they raced refrigerators, I expect he'd be out there trying to win in one of the things.

GF: Well, Jodell, speaking of Wilder, we have to ask you about the rumors.

Lee: (*Grinning*) What rumors is that?

GF: That you may hire Rob Wilder away from Billy Winton to field a second team in the Jodell Lee garage. Or that you and Billy Winton may be talking about merging your operations.

Lee: You can't pay no attention to rumors.

GF: But we know your cousin Joe Banker builds engines for Winton's cars already. You all live within a couple of miles of each other up there in East Tennessee. And the man who's been in your pits since the very beginning, Bubba Baxter, seems to spend a whole lot of time these days over in the Winton Racing garage. We've even seen you watching several races lately from the top of Billy Winton's hauler.

Lee: I kinda figured y'all kept your eyes on the race out there on the track, not on the spectators and where they sit at.

GF: So is there any chance of Rocket Rob Wilder being behind the wheel of one of those dark blue Lee Fords next year? Or of Lawford and Wilder being teammates anytime soon?

Lee: (*Leaning forward, acquiring the trademark "Jodell Lee squint"*) Look, I don't know what might happen around the next turn in the racetrack. But I'll tell you this. All my life, I've fed off of being around winners. It's got to rub off. Curtis Turner and Little Joe Weatherley and Neil Bonnet were winners. So was the Pettys and the Allisons and Cale Yarborough and Bill Elliott and them. And so is this kid, Rob Wilder. Man, it rejuvenates me to be around folks like Rob Wilder. Folks that appreciate how special this sport is, how important it is to dedicate yourself to being the best that you can be if you want to stay in it. People that are driven to win. That's the way I've lived my life and that's the kind of folks I've always liked to associate with. My life has been all the better for being around the likes of them.

And someday, when finally I die, I won't have no regrets, 'cause you know what else? That old hearse they'll be using to carry my coffin down to the cemetery?

The way I figure it, that blamed thing is gonna be right up front, leadin' the pack on the very last lap I'll ever run.

And buddy, up front on the last lap is the only place I ever wanna be.

1

Swirls of tiny insects danced in the breeze, shoved along by a steady, insistent southwesterly wind. The gentle rushes of air provided little relief, though, in what was already becoming a hot, hazy Midwestern morning. Thunderclouds were already lining up impatiently in formation out across the distant prairie, not even waiting for the heat of the afternoon to give them impetus to begin marching in.

But this particular early August weekend was promising to be a hot one in other ways.

Cars and trucks were already lined up, streaming in from all directions as if answering some kind of homing call only they could hear. The small neighborhood of modest homes seemed almost to be shielding the giant speedway from those who would seek it. But the fans found it all right, tucked there in the middle of the neatly cut lawns, trimmed shrubbery, and towering water oaks. Hundreds of thousands of racing enthusiasts were converging on the facility and its rectangular ribbon of asphalt. Most of them looked on respectfully as they approached its magnificence, gazing in quiet awe at the massive shrine, at its hallowed ground, sacred for anyone who worshiped speed.

What had not actually been visible before suddenly appeared above the roofs of the houses and the mature trees like one of those thunderstorms building out on the horizon. Many of those who were heading her way would unconsciously pause and stare at the massive facility. Others scrambled for cameras. They would literally turn the corner and, suddenly, there it would be, hulking proudly before them. How could anything so huge have been hidden from them until they had gotten so close?

The intricate ironwork of her long, low structure formed an almost natural beauty, as if the speedway had been created by something volcanic, geological, not by the hands of men. The place had a profound gracefulness that seemed lacking in most of the newer, more modern racing facilities. And that's why even those who had visited often would usually pause reverently for a moment and stare at her, as if in worship, before heading on for her gates and turnstiles.

It was, after all, Indianapolis, a place whose name was synonymous with speed the world over, regardless of the language that might be spoken there.

Inside the place there was already a festive atmosphere, as joyous and high-spirited as could be found at any major sporting event. There were brilliant colors, fluttering flags, all kinds of music, exotic, enticing smells, and, of course, a patiently waiting but clearly excited throng of loud fans. And down there before them, the focal point of all that excitement, were two long lines of multicolored racing machines, stretched along the pit lane like a pair of rainbow-hued snakes sunning themselves while they awaited the command to roar to life and race away.

Soon, the men who drove those machines would duel with each other to determine who among them had what it would take at the end of the day to bring home the victory. Who would head the field for that last time as the cars eventually crossed the narrow strip of bricks that marked the finish line for any event that might be run here? Who would make the strongest case for bringing the trophy home from Indy? The verdict was still several hours from being rendered, and the jury of several hundred thousand people was prepared to witness the testimony.

The race crews were mostly oblivious to the crowd and the prerace ceremonies as they made a series of last-minute checks on their machines. One of the crews scrambled around a sparkling, bright red Ford that rested in fifteenth position, on the inside of the eighth row. The sky-blue highlights of the car's trim and numbers blended well with the dark blue logo of the machine's primary sponsor. The scripted letters spelled out "Ensoft," the name of one of the hotter companies in the computer software business, and the benefactor who paid good money to support this particular racecar and its team.

The vehicle's improbably young driver wore a bright red driving suit that matched his car perfectly. Despite the nervous anticipation that seemed to permeate the atmosphere of the pit road, the handsome, blond-haired youngster lounged nonchalantly against the side of the car, idly playing with his shoestrings. It seemed he might be about to take a leisurely drive to the corner market instead of climb into the car and race a flock of speed demons for four hundred miles at a breathtaking pace. But anyone who might glance his way knew exactly what this young man was about to do, despite the fact he was hardly halfway through his rookie season at this heady level of stock car racing. He had built a name for himself already. The media had quickly named him "Rocket Rob" Wilder, partly for how quickly he navigated racetracks, partly because he grew up near the "Rocket City" of Huntsville, Alabama.

The kid had quickly burst onto the scene the year before, almost winning his first big-time race at Daytona, all the time charming fans with his easygoing style, his quiet determination to win, and his Hollywood good looks. Now, midway through his rookie Cup season, the twenty-year-old had impressed even the toughest-to-impress observers of the sport. Although he'd not yet claimed his first win at this level, most of those in the garage and the media fully expected it to come any week and no fan complained if he pulled Rob Wilder's name in the office pool.

It wasn't just the car's talented, good-looking kid driver that indicated imminent success. The owner of his team, Billy Winton, had put together a fleet of racecars and a crew that seemed to get better each week, even as his driver gained valuable experience while racing against the sport's best.

The critics noticed immediately that Wilder relied more on finesse and a smart, heads-up driving style than he did on the push and shove that made many of his peers famous. Or infamous, as the case may be. Rob Wilder was already developing an impressive following among race fans, attracted by his magnetic personality, his youthful, self-effacing manner, and his skill at handling a machine traveling nearly two hundred miles per hour. And along the way he'd won the respect of those he competed against, too.

But if pressed, Rob would admit that it was all hard for him to fathom. After all, he was still a few months shy of being legal in most states. He found it difficult to understand why people would show up at a computer store or shopping center or at a race event and wait patiently in line for hours to meet him, to have him sign a photo or slip of paper. He had often dreamed of such a thing when he was growing up in Hazel Green, just up the road from Huntsville. But now that it was actually happening, he couldn't understand what all the fuss was about. He was only a young kid, a racecar driver who had never won a Cup race. A raw rookie who had been running potholed local tracks in a wired-together junker only a short two years before.

Sure, he had done a couple of national television commercials for Ensoft and people were always asking him to deliver his tag lines from the spots for them. Or they would recite back to him something he had said in a radio or television or newspaper interview, or describe in amazing detail some on-track incident he had already filed away in his memory banks.

Yes, it was heady stuff. Someone with a less even keel might have let it turn him. But Rob Wilder had two big advantages.

One was the coaching of his mentor, Jodell Bob Lee. Jodell had been a legendary driver and was now a successful team owner. Along the way he practically adopted the hard-driving, quiet-spoken youngster. It had been Jodell Lee who looked on one night as Rob won a feature race at a dusty little bullring of a track where the old driver was making an appearance. Jodell immediately recognized the kid's talent. He recommended Rob to his friend and former crewmember Billy Winton, who was, at the time, toying with putting together a full-time Grand National team. Along with his invaluable tips on racecar piloting, Lee also helped the kid deal with the pressures of off-track commitments and the adoration of fans, as well.

Rob's other big advantage strolled right up to him at that very moment and slid down to sit next to him on the pavement.

"I don't think I've seen this many people in one place since the last time I sat in a traffic jam for two hours on the Hollywood Freeway," she said, surveying the huge, colorful crowd that encircled them.

Michelle Fagan. She was a high-level executive, the vice-president of marketing for Ensoft, the Winton team sponsor, but she was also much, much more. Nowadays, Michelle spent far more time following Billy Winton's race team from track to track, overseeing the sponsorship tie-ins, than she did running the marketing department of the software giant. She could have hired someone to do these chores for the race team but she readily admitted she didn't want to do that. She had immediately come to love this rapid, loud sport once she had gotten a taste of it, as incongruous as that might sound for a California girl with a master's in business administration from U.C.L.A. A lady who, up until the car sponsorship deal, had only caught brief glimpses of stock-car racing while flipping between the business channels on her local cable television system. And a sharply focused executive who also just happened to have a high-tech bucking bronco of a company to try to tame.

"You know, Chelle, there's more people here to watch us run than there are living in Hazel Green and Huntsville put together?"

"You're nervous, then."

He snorted.

"Naw! All these parades and singing and stuff is just postponing my winning this race, is all."

"No. I think you're nervous. I believe I see your little hands shaking and you've got dry mouth and I believe you're on the verge of breaking out in hives. Yeah, Mr. Stock Car Boy, I think you're as nervous as—"

Before she could stop him, he dropped a handful of gravel down the back of her Ensoft-team racing shirt.

"Look out! Spiders! Bugs! Big old bugs!" he whooped and Michelle jumped to her feet and began a dance around the car, ripping out the tail of her shirt, trying to rid herself of whatever vermin Rob Wilder had dumped down her shirt.

And that little exchange symbolized Michelle's other primary task and maybe her greatest value to this team. Sure, she kept her hands full, arranging a staggering array of sponsorship activities for the car, the team, and the driver, scheduling interviews, overseeing tie-ins to advertising, setting him up to visit with customers, distributors, journalists, and Ensoft employees. She had to make certain her company maximized its multimillion-dollar investment in that bright red car and its attractive young driver. And all the while, she still tried her best, mostly by cell phone and fax machine and usually at a time offset by two or three hours, to keep up with her other duties back on the West Coast where Ensoft's corporate headquarters were located.

But by default, and at her own choosing, Michelle had assumed a far subtler role: that of confidant, co-conspirator, soul mate, baby-sitter, and best friend of one "Rocket Rob" Wilder.

Her relationship with the young man had evolved into more than a strictly business, sponsor-rep-and-racecar-driver association. It was a business relationship for sure, but it went far beyond that. Many in the garage and even on the team itself had trouble figuring out what the exact nature of their alliance might be. But they all knew too that it worked.

Michelle seemed to know exactly what to do or say to bring the young man back down to earth on those rare occasions when he got too full of himself. Or how to pull him back up when things didn't meet his own lofty expectations and he would inevitably get down on himself. It had not taken her long to realize that Rob Wilder expected to win every race he entered and that he would be severely disappointed when he didn't. But she seemed to have the knack to know what to do to get him over those small setbacks and back into a frame of mind to take on the racing world with his usual vigor and confidence.

"What in the world is going on here?" a tall, dark-haired man asked gruffly as he stepped from the other side of the racecar.

"Michelle's just having a conniption fit, Will," Rob answered, as straight-faced and innocently as he could manage.

Will Hughes was the crew chief on the Billy Winton car and a man not given to much foolishness. Especially minutes before the green flag was to drop. But at the same time, he, as well as Billy Winton, the car's owner, recognized Michelle Fagan's value in keeping their high-strung driver in a condition to race most effectively.

"Well, see that she doesn't do any damage to the car and try to steer her over behind the pit wall before she passes out," Will said, as calmly as if he were ordering a crewman to stack up a set of tires.

Hughes had first noticed Michelle's expanded value to the team the previous season when they were running the Grand National circuit. Rob had made the slightest of bobbles one day while qualifying. It was enough of a mistake that they had to start back in the pack even though they all knew they had the fastest car there. His goof-up was enough to send Rob into a blue funk, but Michelle seemed to know exactly what to say and do to get him over it. Sure enough, they notched their very first win there at the historic Nashville track. Now, with the more intensified pressure at the Cup level, Michelle's influence over Rob was even more valuable.

She was anxiously awaiting the start of the race now. Finally, she would be able to sit back and watch Rob circle the track and, for the first time since before six o'clock that morning, relax. She had spent a frantic morning shepherding a flock of guests that Ensoft brought in for the race. Part of that job had involved getting a semireluctant driver to the hospitality tent on time even though he would have preferred staying with the crew and the racecar and concentrating on the task at hand. But she managed to keep him smiling as he met and greeted the guests and posed for countless pictures and signed autographs for everyone there.

And there was another complication that cropped up that morning and threatened to throw the driver off kilter. Rob learned that his girlfriend, Christy, would not be able to make the race. She had planned to fly out from California for the race, the first time they would be able to be with each other in over a month. She was interning in the Ensoft legal department for the summer, taking a break, preparing for her first year of law school at Stanford after completing her prelaw studies at U.C.L.A. But the weather had conspired against them and the Ensoft corporate jet was going to have to stay in the hanger in San Jose until well after sunup. That meant Christy and the group of company executives wouldn't have time to make the race's early start.

That also meant more work for Michelle, entertaining the dignitaries all by herself. Besides, she had been looking forward to visiting with Christy, too. In addition to being Rob Wilder's girlfriend, Christy was Christy Fagan, Michelle's baby sister. Michelle had introduced Rob to her sister early in Ensoft's sponsorship of the red racecar and the two of them had hit it off immediately. They did make a striking couple, as the television camera crews had discovered immediately. They usually sought out the photogenic couple before a race and often trained the cameras on them, or fought to focus on Christy late in any race in which Rob was a contender.

Michelle had finally shaken the gravel from her shirt and was throwing Rob a mean look.

"If my sister was here, we'd gang up on you and whip your tail."

"Ooh, I'm so scared."

"You better be thinking about that car and how you're going to drive it."

"Shoot fire! The way this thing was running yesterday evening, the rest of them might as well head on home. Unless they want to race for second, that is."

Rob slapped the roof of his racecar for emphasis. He was about to say more when Will Hughes stepped around again from the other side of the car.

"Well, Cowboy, it's time to go racing."

Will had always called the kid "Cowboy," though he really wouldn't say why. The couple of times Rob asked him Will only shrugged his shoulders and changed the subject.

"It's about time!" With that, Rob stuck out his tongue in Michelle's direction, zipped up his driving suit, and slid one leg through the open window of the stock car. Michelle suddenly leaned over and gave him a quick peck on the cheek, then squeezed his hand. Rob felt the softness of her hand in his and he squeezed back. He allowed the grasp to linger before he finally let her go.

Rob slung the rest of his long lanky frame in through the open window and settled down into the custom-fitted seat. The padding hugged his body, leaving him little room to twist around in the contouring that was purposely designed to match his frame. He reached down and pulled the safety belts up between his legs, slid the padded shoulder belts into place, then snapped the center catch, fastening the belts together. Finally, he gave each belt a solid yank, making sure they were tightly fastened into place.

Rob inserted the earpieces for the radio into each ear, grabbed the short pieces of "one-hundred-mile-per-hour tape" off the dash, and used them to secure the tiny earphones in his ears. His helmet hung off a small hook attached to the roll bar. He reached for it and pulled it on, adjusting the chinstrap so it fit snugly but comfortably.

Outside the car, Will barked last-minute instructions to the rest of the crew, using his microphone and the radio net to make certain he could be heard over the noise of the crowd and the music and chatter from the speakers that lined the track. He glanced at his young driver as the kid slipped the steering wheel onto its column.

There was more than a little confidence in the young driver's manner, an assurance that sometimes bordered on cockiness. Will grinned. The young'un had every reason to be confident. He had a good, strong car beneath him. The engine, prepared especially for him by Jodell Lee's first cousin and longtime engine builder, Joe Banker, was capable of producing the power necessary to take the car to victory lane. This was the kind of track on which Rob felt most comfortable, wide, flat, with long straightaways ending in Indy's sharp, distinctive corners. And Rob Wilder was as gifted a driver as Will Hughes had ever seen. Sure, he still had lots to learn, but with the guidance of Billy Winton and Jodell Lee, he couldn't miss. If he continued to keep his head on straight, he would someday be a superstar.

That's why Will was here. He had worked with Jodell Lee's team when he first broke into racing, fresh from engineering school. But he had dreams of heading his own team, of applying his technical background, of winning lots of championships. His father had been a promising racer himself, but that promise was never to be fulfilled. Will Hughes saw his best chance to live his and his dad's dreams as the crew chief of Billy Winton's emerging race team.

Back inside the racecar, Rob was having his usual

prerace thoughts. He knew he could take this car to the front and keep it there. The only question was whether or not the racing gods would bless them long enough today so they could bring home the victory. Rob figured that as long as he did what he was supposed to do, only those things that were out of their control could keep them from being first to the checkers, from claiming their first Cup win.

He was so deep in thought that it took him a moment to realize the buzzing in his ears was Will Hughes calling him, asking for a final radio check before the command to start the engines. Rob reached his gloved thumb for the mike button on the steering column and held it down.

"I got a good copy on you, Will. Reading you loud and clear."

"What about you, Harry?" Will queried, glancing up toward the platform atop the grandstands where their spotter, Harry Stone, stood watching.

"Got you both five-by-five. You got me, Rob?" Harry asked.

"Any louder or clearer and you'll blow me out of this seat," Rob called back. He knew it would be much harder to hear the radio transmissions when the car was out there among the rest of them, yodeling at full song, but he would have no trouble understanding the commands they would pass on to him.

"Good. We're ready, then. Robbie, go out there and show them what we brought up here. I'd like to be drinking a little of that cold milk in victory lane when we get done this afternoon."

"I'm looking forward to that, too," Rob answered, then allowed the radio to go silent as he awaited the command to fire up the engines.

A renewed wave of excitement began to sweep the speedway as the national anthem's last strains echoed around the huge plant and the rest of the preliminary ceremonies wound down. All around the speedway the crowd stood, cheering and waiting. Many of them had been in this same place earlier in the year, in May, for the Indy 500. It was a different kind of racing but they didn't care. They had returned to admire the skill, the daring, the competitiveness of these men and their machines.

All the miles traveled, the price of the tickets, the endless wait in traffic, the search for one of the precious parking spots, the heat, hunger, and thirst were all about to be worth it. It would all be forgotten when the cars finally thundered to life and rolled away from a dead stop to get this relatively new racing tradition under way.

"Gentlemen, start your engines."

All the tension and hype of the last few days melted away along the pit lane as the scores of engines noisily came awake. It was finally time to go racing and everyone in the pits had a job to do, from the tire changers to the gas men, the crew chiefs, and the drivers. Most of them had been working full days since mid-week anyway, but all that was forgotten, too. All that toil was about to culminate in four hundred miles of superclose racing.

The crews scrambled around in their pits in what looked like total chaos, but they all knew exactly what they were doing as they made certain everything was prepared and ready and in its proper place. Behind the pits, the stacks of fresh tires sat stacked and mounted, ready to be bolted onto the racecars when needed.

Along the pit lane, the colored flags waved gently in the breeze. The fans lining the track stood already, cheering wildly, successfully drowning out the restrained grumble of the poised racecars. The cars and their drivers impatiently awaited the signal to move down the pit road and out onto the racing surface, trailing the pace car. Pictures were snapped, scanners set on the desired frequencies, and the headset radios dialed in to the radio broadcast. The fans with the scanners were treated to the last-minute checks between drivers and their crews before the cars rolled away to take to the famed speedway.

Before the command's last words were even finished, Rob Wilder reached over and pressed the starter switch with his gloved left hand. Without hesitation, the powerful Banker engine responded. Rob scanned the instrument cluster, making sure the amps came up as they were supposed to, then watched the oil and fuel pressure begin to register.

Nervous anticipation ran through his body as he studied the rear bumper of the green Pontiac sitting in front of him. With four hundred miles around the two-mile rectangle awaiting him, Rob was confident, sure he had what it took to drive this car to the front of the field. He pictured in his mind how it would look to the crowd when he sailed beneath the checkered flag, how it would feel to stand atop the car and take big, thirsty swallows of cold milk while the confetti flew all around him in the hot breeze.

The cars at the front of the line began to slowly move away. All the pageantry was now over. It was time to see who had the fastest car and who had the courage necessary to put it up front as they crossed for the final time the strip of bricks marking the finish line.

"Okay, Cowboy. Let's head 'em up and move 'em out. Time to get this show on the road!" Will called over the radio as he stepped back over the pit wall.

"Ten four!" Rob's voice crackled back as he eased off on the clutch, setting the Ensoft Ford loose, following in the green Pontiac's tire tracks.

Rob Wilder was about to compete for the first time on the storied asphalt of "The Brickyard." Right now, he wasn't sure what was pounding harder, the pistons in the Ford's engine or the heart inside his chest.

2

Rob was surprised by how the massive grandstands around him appeared now that they were crammed with fans. All the way down the pit lane, fans were jammed into place everywhere, filling either side of the track. The scene was nothing like he expected, even though he had seen it on television many times before. It certainly looked different from this angle! So far in all the practicing they had done, he had driven past an endless expanse of mostly empty, tiered gray bleachers tucked up under the overhangs with only a scattering of people watching. Now they were full of spectators, a swirling, continuous sea of color, stretching all the way around the circuit.

The car rolled easily on the track's smooth surface as the long line of racers dipped down into turn one together for the first time. Rob was impatient, wanting to go on and stomp on the accelerator instead of running off these first few pace laps at half-speed. He forced himself to keep his emotions in check, though. He was driven to drive fast, an instinct as strong in him as survival. He was only truly at peace with himself when he was steering this racecar at speed. Any other time, he was, at least on some level, longing for the chance to once again slide behind the wheel and race.

Thankfully, the pace laps wound off quickly, and, even though he couldn't actually hear it, Rob could sense the frenzy of the crowd growing with each trip around the two-mile-long track. Finally, the lights on the pace car were doused, signaling they were about to make the last trip around before the green flag waved.

Rob checked his shoulder harnesses one final time to make sure they were snug. He twisted the wheel back and forth, scrubbing the tires clean of whatever debris they might have picked up during the pace laps. He certainly did not want to go sailing off into turn one for the first time, only to have the tires lose traction beneath him and send him skating toward the already battered wall. That could ruin a driver's day in a hurry!

"Easy on the start, kid. No hurry. Just thread your way up through the field."

Rob felt a chill run down his spine. The words he had heard, or imagined he heard, had not been on the radio at all. Not Will Hughes in the pits or Harry Stone up on the spotters' platform.

It was the eerie disembodied voice that seemed to ride with him sometimes, coaching him, telling him what to do when he faced crucial moments in a race. Rob had long since accepted it though he had no idea what or who it might be, or even if it actually existed. The only person who seemed to believe him was Jo-dell Lee. The old driver didn't seem surprised at all. Instead of ribbing him like the others, he seemed to know immediately what the kid was talking about.

"Whatever it is . . . ghost, imagination, your own intuition . . . you oughta listen to it, Robbie," Jodell had advised. "If it works for you, listen to the old boy."

And so he had, and it had gotten him through more than one tight spot. Still, sometimes he had to wonder if he was losing his mind, listening to and obeying weird voices when he was all alone out there in a hurtling racecar. That was the reason too that he rarely mentioned it to anyone other than Michelle. She seemed understanding yet puzzled whenever he brought it up. He tired of the catcalls he took from Billy, Will, and the others whenever he told them he'd heard them again.

Now was hardly the time to be worrying about it, though. The cars were closing down for the start, sweeping into turn three. Rob tightened up closely onto the back bumper of the Pontiac, leaving himself literally inches off its rear end. He studied the row of cars stretching out in front of him and plotted his first moves when the green flag finally waved. He also steeled himself in preparation for whatever unexpected occurrence might suddenly happen ahead of him.

Someone might miss a shift coming up to the start. An anxious driver might rush something and suddenly get sideways ahead of the balance of the field. It happened occasionally and the start of the race was the most likely time for it.

Still in two orderly lines, the cars rolled smoothly through the wide arc of turn four, then headed for the long front straightaway. Still idling at half race speed, they approached the line where the green flag waited. It was already being held high in the right hand of the starter, who stood on the narrow flag stand that jutted out over the edge of the outside retaining wall. With his left hand, he motioned for the leaders to wait, to hold back, to avoid jumping the start.

Behind the two lead cars that paced the field, the rest of the competitors stacked up tightly, every single one of them eager to jump ahead, to take their shot at the leaders. And at this point, the moment before the green flag flew, every one of them was convinced he could win this race.

Rob Wilder was no exception. He itched to jump on the hammer, ached to show what his car could do when it ran at speed with all the others. Slowly, the cars approached the stripe, the tension building in the cockpit of each of the racers. Rob tried to concentrate on the flag he could barely see up ahead, to anticipate the start, to find whatever slight edge he could get on his competitors from the very beginning of this contest.

Then, suddenly, the flag began to wave, and it seemed every driver in the field danced on their gas pedals at the same instant. The radio circuit was full of screams of "Green! Green! Go! Go!"

The cars actually seemed to pause for a moment and then, as if chained together, they suddenly shot off toward the seemingly flat first turn, steadily gaining speed. The turn itself most resembled a tunnel formed by the grandstands that would run the length of the outside of the straightaway and along the back of the pit lane.

Rob Wilder was thrown roughly back into his seat by the surge of power from the mighty racing motor beneath his Ford's hood. But he hardly noticed as he focused on getting a run on the car in front of him when they headed down into turn one. He thought he might actually have a shot at gaining a spot before the first cars were even up to full speed.

Rob gripped the wheel tightly as his car crossed the starting stripe and beneath the waving green flag. He yanked the wheel down to the inside, already pulling out of line as they roared off for the first corner. He managed to get a front fender up alongside the

Pontiac before he was forced to get out of the gas, tapping the brakes as he set the car up for the quick run through turn one, then across the short chute to turn two. Zooming out of two, Rob once again tried to get a run going down the long backstretch. The Pontiac bobbled ever so slightly coming out of the turn, but that was all Rob needed to duck down to his inside, making the pass cleanly.

That accomplished, Rob set his sights on the next car in line as they steered through turn four, still not even one full lap into the race.

The cars shot perilously toward the outside wall as they exited the corner, taking as wide a line as possible all the way through the rectangular turn. The crowd seemed to gasp as car after car appeared to sail within an inch or two of the treacherous wall. Then, almost instantly after narrowly avoiding a clash with the barrier, they all attempted to get themselves into a single-file line as the entire field charged down the front stretch between the two rows of writhing grandstands. The cars seemed to be engulfed by a tunnel of eddying colors as the fans still remained standing, cheering.

Up front, the leader and the second-place car were already starting to put some distance on the rest of the field. Third and fourth place still raced side by side, neither driver able to get the advantage on the other. The next dozen or so cars ran in a single-file line behind those two, but with each one jockeying, scrambling, for one of the precious positions on the inside line. Rob Wilder held one of those positions and was running hard to protect it.

While the cars behind him were sparring for their own spots on the track, Rob sized up the next car in line ahead of him, watching how he drove into the corners, how he exited them, where he ran on the straightaways. His own mount felt good beneath him, the engine singing a throaty song as it produced all the power he needed. There was a slight push in the front end, though, as the Ensoft Ford exited each corner. The car wanted to veer outward, toward the concrete retaining wall. Rob wrestled with the steering wheel each time through the turns, trying to make the car follow the way the track went. But the car seemed to have a mind of its own, defying him, trying to head toward the wall with Rob doing all he could to catch it.

"We got a little push coming off the corner," Rob informed Will Hughes after a few laps.

"She'll loosen up as the track gets slicker. In this heat, you'll be skating all over the place before you know it."

"I hope so. I about knocked down the wall coming out of two last time."

"Remember, we set her up for long runs. Get some wear on the tires and she'll come right on in," Will reminded him. But he also understood his driver's frustration and concern. A racecar driver wanted the car perfect from the start, able to get all the speed and handling he needed from the get-go. Rob was no exception, but he did understand that a car's handling would change dramatically as the race wore on and track conditions changed. Still, Will worked to teach him the patience it would take to one day become a great racecar driver.

"Ten four," Rob answered, still concentrating on the car in front of him.

Rob continued his charge to the front, picking off the car on the backstretch, then getting another in the center of turns three and four. After only nine laps he had managed to crack the top ten.

As he made the final pass to claim tenth place, Rob smiled. The car was plenty strong. And Will had been right. The handling was slowly starting to come around, too. In a few more laps, he figured he would have the best car at Indy, and all that stood between him and the point was a little time and a few laps.

Michelle Fagan watched as much of the action as she could see from her spot down along the pit road. The track's layout made it difficult to actually witness much of the race from there. About all she could see was the section of track straight in front of the pits, and that was only a few seconds as the cars shot past. Instead, Michelle found a spot in the back of the team's pit, watching the television monitor hooked to the back of the pit wagon.

Still, she knew much of the race action would take place in the pits so she passed on a chance to watch the race from a better vantage point. Even now, she took her eyes off the screen and watched the tire specialist check and recheck the stacks of tires that stood there next to her. The over-the-wall crew stood poised next to the low barrier that separated the crewmen from pit road, ready to dive over the top at a moment's notice like a platoon of marines taking a beachhead. They knew a caution flag could wave anytime, or that Rob might need to make a quick unscheduled dash onto pit road and they had to be ready.

Michelle had come to love the excitement of the action in the pits. Sometimes she marveled at how much she enjoyed the more subtle aspects of the sport she had hardly known existed a couple of years before. Now, with Rob charging toward the front, she could hardly wait for the first pit stop so she could watch the ballistic ballet the crew performed at least five or six times each race day.

Will Hughes was busy. He carefully timed each lap and compared the results to the figures on the clipboard he always carried. He was satisfied with Rob's times so far. Only the lead car was turning the track any faster and that was by only fractions of a second. With the cars now beginning to spread out around the track, Rob should be able to use the speed advantage to continue his march to the front of the pack. The longer they got into the race on this set of tires, the greater his advantage should become. That's precisely how they had planned it. The car had been set up so the handling would start a bit off center but would come in on the longer runs. While the times on the Ford were now getting marginally slower, Will noticed with a smile that they were not falling off nearly as much as the other cars with which they were racing.

He glanced over at Donnie Kline just as Rob's bright red Ford shot by their position, even then taking over the eighth position. Kline was a big man, his shaved head shining in the hot sun. He was the team's chief mechanic and directly charged with the car's handling setup. Will showed Donnie a smile and a nod to let him know how satisfied he was with how the car was now getting around the track. Donnie gave a wave to the rest of the crew, who were now pumping fists into the air and cheering Rob's latest move up in the running order. To a man, they were on a high, excited by the prospects of having a fast, competitive car here at Indy. Each of them had worked hard, grueling hours since well before the season had begun in Daytona in February. They had gotten better each week, more competitive with each race they got under their belt. Now they could take pride in seeing how this rookie team had come together and the broad grins on their sweating faces confirmed it.

As they crossed the strip of bricks for the twenty-fifth time, Donnie began canvassing each crewmember to make certain he was ready for the first scheduled pit stop when it came. He barked orders over the radio, making sure each crewman was in the proper position, ready to go over the wall, and that he had whatever he was supposed to have when he did. A fresh set of tires sat lined up, ready, next to the "carriers," the two men who would tote the tires over the wall with them even as Rob screeched to a stop. Air wrenches were checked and double-checked, making sure they worked properly. A certain tension seized them all now as they stood there, poised, awaiting the call to make the team's first pit stop at Indy. They knew how crucial their performance would be.

Rob had little time to think about the pit stop. His only thoughts were on the bumper of the blue Chevy that he was now trying to chase down so he could take seventh place. Three car lengths separated the two of them as they dove into the corner. Rob stepped on the brakes and felt them begin to bite as he used them to help set the line that the car would take through the corner. The steering wheel vibrated slightly in his hands as he sawed it back and forth. He could feel the car's body try to keel over as the g-forces exerted their ever-present power, but she held her line and shot through the corner as Rob got back into the gas coming out the other side. The push was still there, though less than before. Still, it gave Rob an anxious moment when he wondered if the car would turn enough and in time to avoid making contact with the outside wall at the exit to the turn.

Rob then called on the extra power that always seemed to be there in Joe Banker's engines as he tried to close the gap to the Chevy. He jammed his foot hard to the floor, trying to squeeze every last ounce of muscle out of the screaming engine. He chased after the car ahead, using the relative calm of the straightaway to glance at the track ahead through the Chevy's windshield. He noted the distance to the next couple of cars running ahead of them then brought his concentration back to the Chevy itself.

He drove deep down into the next corner, closing in on the car he was chasing. Only a car length separated them now as they raced through the center of the turn and on into the short chute, one driver doing all he could to take over the other's position, the other driver just as determined to not give it up. Hands and feet worked in expert coordination as each driver pushed his respective car right out to the ragged edge. The slightest slipup would push the car over that fine line that separated a successful lap from total disaster.

Rob listened to Will Hughes calling the laps out to him on the radio and the occasional "Inside," or "Clear high," from Harry, telling when there was traffic above or below him on the track. He tried to block all else from his mind as he pushed his machine to the limit, not only of its own capabilities but of rational physical possibility for such a heavy object in motion on a closed course.

Ahead, the front cars began to encounter the slower cars at the tail end of the field. All across the radio nets, drivers were begging for a caution flag to allow them to pit so they could adjust their ill-handling cars. But silently, every one of them prayed it would not be him who was involved in the accident that would lead to the yellow flag they all so desperately needed.

On the other hand, Will Hughes would have been perfectly happy to run under green all day. He was well pleased with the times Rob was posting on the stopwatch so late in this long run at full speed. Many of the teams were expecting cautions early in the race and set their cars up accordingly. Now, their gamble was costing them. Will, however, figured the race would follow the pattern of the others that had been run at the famed "Brickyard," that it would have long runs of relatively caution-free racing. That's why he and Donnie had set up the Ford the way they had.

The lap count approached forty and some of the cars running at the back of the field were starting to get themselves lapped. Thirty-fifth place, then thirty-second, and, finally, thirtieth all fell a lap down to the leaders. But that created a problem for Rob Wilder. Time and again, the slower lapped cars got in Rob's way as he tried to move closer to the leader.

At forty-five laps, he was running in fifth position, bearing down on the Ford that was keeping him out of the fourth position. But now he decided to use the gaggle of lapped cars to his advantage. He used a couple of them for picks, like a basketball shooter dribbling around a teammate to take an open shot.

The handling of Rob's car finally was near perfect, the persistent push almost gone now when he drove through the corners. This allowed him to get a smoother run through the turns, to get in the gas a fraction of a second quicker each time. With the car running easier through the turns, Rob was able to seriously pressure the racers ahead of him.

Coming off turn two, Rob was able to get his nose under the left rear fender of the fourth-place car. He raced hard down the backstretch, all the while looking ahead at a couple of lapped cars. A glint of silver in the sunlight ahead caught his eye then. Rob's stomach fell and he gritted his teeth.

The lapped car to the inside was the silver-painted Pontiac of Stacy Locklear and Rob was going to catch him within the length of the straightaway. Catch him and have to deal with him.

Stacy Locklear was one of the sport's unabashed troublemakers. He was convinced that rough driving and risk-taking was the way to success on the Cup circuit. If there happened to be a crash, Locklear was usually somewhere around it, and more often than not he had contributed to the cause of it. The sad thing was that Locklear's team usually provided him with a good ride and he possibly had the talent to be a decent driver if he would only channel his abilities in the right way.

At Martinsville in the spring race, an unyielding Locklear had spun out Rob as he was chasing down the leaders late in the race. And despite his efforts to avoid him off the track, Rob had more than once suffered verbal barrages or stare-downs from Locklear in the garage or in the pits or even once at an appearance. Most of them were conveniently out of earshot of anyone else and especially the Ensoft crew. Rob knew the barbs were likely rooted in jealousy, that they were Locklear's crude way to try to intimidate the rookie, but try as he might to ignore him, Rob still sometimes allowed the guy to get under his skin. More than once Rob had checked up just before losing his cool and doing a number on the cocky so-and-so's head.

One thing that helped Rob keep his cool was the wisdom of Jodell Lee, who often explained to him how a driver was expected to handle himself on and off the track. The subject of Stacy Locklear had inevitably come up.

"Don't let somebody like that jackass get to you, Robbie," he lectured. "Them that lacks talent sometimes tries to make up for it with guff. Best thing you can do is pretend he don't exist off the track and try to stay out of his way when you're racin'."

And those were the words Rob was thinking about as he closed the distance to Locklear's car. The silver car was involved in its own battle with another of the lapped cars, the two of them racing as if they were on the last lap, going for the win. Rob studied both of them, carefully deciding where he would go if the two cars suddenly wrecked in front of him. That certainly seemed like a possibility the way they were dueling with each other. For any other driver on the circuit, Rob would not have been considering an escape route. With Locklear, it was a good idea to do that exercise every time he found himself near the reckless driver out on the track. With such a terrific run going, Rob tried to drive smoothly as he approached the two cars, hoping he could make a quick, clean pass and then be on his way to cruise on past the leaders.

In no time, Rob ran right up on the back end of

the two cars and was preparing to pull around them
as they exited the next turn. Rob used the superior
handling of his Ford to quickly make a run to the
inside of Locklear coming off the fourth turn, then
relied on the awesome power of the engine to outrun
the two cars down into the first turn. When Harry
Stone yelled "Clear" over the radio to let him know
he had made a clean pass on the two cars, Rob pulled
back into his line. Only then did he glance in his
mirror to make sure Locklear wasn't going to try to
give him a shove in the center of the corner in an
attempt to spin him out. That was a typical move for
him when someone dared to outdrive and pass him.

Locklear's car was obviously pushing badly in the
corners. That's why he was already a lap down and
that kept him from being able to keep ahead of the
rocket ship Rob Wilder was piloting this day. Rob
quickly put several car lengths' distance on him as
the three of them raced off turn one and into the short
chute that separated it from turn two. By the time Rob
cleared the second corner and hit the backstretch,
Locklear's silver Pontiac and the other car were fad-
ing quickly in his rearview mirror.

He breathed a sigh of relief. Too many bad things
seemed to happen when Stacy Locklear was in the
vicinity. The rearview mirror was the best place for
the likes of him.

Twenty car lengths ahead of him now there was a
familiar black Chevrolet and it sat in third place. Rob
set about tracking him down but he knew catching
him would only be half the battle. He would definitely
have his work cut out for him when he eventually
attempted to make the pass on the wily veteran, a
driver who seemed to take it personally when someone tried to go around him.

"Okay, Cowboy, we're getting inside the pit window. The leaders are looking like they're gonna pit
in three laps. When you see them break for the pit

road, follow them on in. We'll call the stop."

"Ten four, Will. Make sure I get a cold drink," Rob responded calmly, as relaxed as if he were making an order at a fast food drive-through window. But he *was* thirsty. Now running out of the heavy traffic, he was more and more aware of how hot it was inside the car.

"We'll have you a drink but you have to make it quick. We don't plan on taking long to get those four tires changed. Track position is key here and we don't want to give up any of what you've earned."

"I'll follow the others in," Rob answered, never taking his eyes off the track ahead of him.

Two laps went by as Rob cut in half the distance between himself and the black car running in front of him. Michelle watched the crew scramble as they prepared for Rob's entrance onto the pit road the next time by.

Out on the track, Rob set his line in turn two, getting a clean run through the corner. As the car shot out of the turn onto the back straightaway, he was suddenly aware of the sweat dripping down his face and into his eyes. He was practically suffocating from the heat inside the cramped cockpit of his racer. Static crackled in the earpieces of his radio.

"Bring her in this time around," Will was calling. "Remember to watch the RPMs on pit road. We don't need the officials to give us a speeding ticket."

Speeds were limited on the pit road for the safety of the workers in the pits. Anyone who broke the rule would be penalized and it was often enough to snatch away from an offender any hopes he might have had for winning the race. Since the racecars didn't carry speedometers, engine RPMs at the legal speed were calibrated before the race started so the drivers would know how fast they could legally go when pitting.

"This time by. Ten four," Rob confirmed.

"We're doing four tires and gas and a quarter round

of wedge out of the right rear. Okay, guys, we need a good fast stop here under the green flag."

"You hear him, boys," Donnie Kline added as he clutched the big jack in his arms, ready to jump over the pit wall. "No mistakes now! No mistakes!"

The crew all lined up next to the wall as they strained to catch sight of their car swinging down off the track and onto the long pit road. Rob came up off turn four and followed the front three cars down onto the pit lane. Most of the front-running cars followed along behind them, each wanting to pace his own stops to those of the leaders.

Rob quickly slowed his car as they charged down onto the pit lane. He glanced down at the tachometer, making sure the RPMs were below where they were supposed to be. He searched for the Ensoft signboard among all those that were waving and bouncing up and down on the ends of the long poles that held them out over each team's pit stall.

Will guided him down the pit road toward their stall, located about two-thirds of the way down the lane, well past the start/finish line.

"Ten stalls out," he called. "Make sure you stop on the marks. We don't want you too close to the wall."

Rob didn't reply. He had spied the fluorescent number "52" hanging off the end of the long pole. He pointed the car toward the stall, braking hard but not too hard so he would make sure he stopped in the right place. It was a difficult transition from the flat-out speed on the track to the controlled bolt down the pit lane. But if he didn't get stopped in time and slid through his stall and across the white line that marked the end of it, he would be forced to back the car up before the crew could begin working on it. That would cost them valuable seconds in the pits.

While the car was still a couple of stalls away, the crew leaped over the wall with Donnie leading the charge around to the right side, the jack held out before him like an offering to the racecar.

He and the front tire changer were already in place as Rob slid the car to a stop. Smoke drifted from the superheated brakes. Donnie jammed the jack under the Ford at the midpoint under the driver's door and gave it a hefty pump. The right side of the car immediately hopped up off the ground and the two tire changers went to work.

Paul Phillips was at the right front, zipping off the flying lug nuts with a shrill whine of his air gun. The tire carrier rolled a fresh set of rubber into place as Paul yanked off the old one. He flipped the spent tire over onto its side then grabbed the new one. He hefted it up into place and quickly tightened its lugs onto the wheel's studs. The nuts had been glued into place on the tire so they would be ready to tighten down.

It was all part of a carefully balanced routine between each of the members of the over-the-wall gang. Each man had a specific job to accomplish in as few movements as possible. A tenth of a second shaved off during the stop could mean picking up considerable distance once he was back out on the track. And with track position so important, every spot that could be held on to or picked up during a pit stop was one more that didn't have to be raced for out there on the track.

The crew finished smoothly with the right side of the car and rushed around to the left. The gasman was already stepping in with the second can of gas, hoisting it up to the filler cap. The gasoline gushed out of the can into the fuel cell that sat in the trunk area of the car.

While all this was going on, Rob kept the engine revved slightly so as not to stall the car as he waited. He accepted the bottle of ice water that was pushed at him through the gap between the doorframe and the window net, all the while keeping his mind on how he would leave the pits as he squirted a stream of the cold liquid into his mouth. He wished it had been a yellow-flag stop so he would have had time to receive a rag to wipe away the sweat that was coursing down his face.

Maybe next time, he thought.

Donnie was already sliding the jack beneath the left side of the car. He watched the gas man and both tire changers, making sure they got every last drop of gasoline in the tank. All the while, he was thinking how proud he was of these guys. He had come over from another garage because he thought Billy Winton was building a potential championship team around the "52" Ford. Donnie had helped to carefully select each of the crewmembers, had worked all winter training and rehearsing them, and now, finally, they were gelling into one fine bunch. He couldn't help but grin as he watched them work.

Once the tank was full, the gasman backed away, his signal that he was finished, that the car now had all the gasoline it would hold. A half-second later, the two tire changers tightened down the last of the lug nuts. Donnie watched them carefully so he could drop the jack the instant they were finished.

Rob already had the car in first gear, ready to go. The bouncing of the car when the jack fell was his signal to tear off, and Rob jumped on the gas pedal, let out the clutch, and twisted the wheel to the right as the car began to roll away. He tossed the water bottle out the window as he pulled away, not giving any quarter to the cars that were charging up behind him as they all fought for position coming off the pit road.

He quickly worked his way up through the gearbox, ever mindful of his speed as he crossed the white line at the end of the pit road. Once past it, though, there was no more speed limit and he hammered the gas down to the floor, roaring back out onto the race-track. The cars that had not yet pitted zipped past him on the outside as he blended back into traffic.

Rob brought the car up to speed, trying to keep the black Chevrolet within striking distance as the two of them raced off into turn three. The "3" car had made as good a pit stop as the Ensoft team had, leaving it with the same ten- or twelve-car advantage it had had before the stop. The cool water he had inhaled during the stop had refreshed him, even if he'd only had time to take a couple of draws on the bottle. He licked his lips and swallowed hard. Barring a caution period, it would likely be a while before he could get more to drink.

But now it was once again time for Rob to push everything out of his mind, his dry throat, the heat, the discomfort, the numbing vibrations, the super-heated air. It was time now to chase down those leaders a quarter of a straightaway ahead of him. He squinted that way and went after them while Will patiently called out the times every time he flashed by their position on pit road.

After a few laps, though, Will had a new bit of information to relay. He changed the call to nothing but the interval between Rob and the leader.

"One-point-seven this time by. Oh, and the leader is about to catch some traffic," came Will's call. That meant that Rob was one-point-seven seconds behind the leader. That was down from a one-eighty-five the last time by.

The kid was flying. And he was gaining ground on those who stood between him and the honor and glory he so desperately craved.

But he was too busy to reply to Will's regular, emotionless transmissions on the radio. He concentrated on hitting his marks as he approached each turn. He tried to drive as smoothly as possible as he closed steadily in on the black number "3" Chevrolet that was still holding on to third position.

Rob gritted his teeth and smiled. He could feel his confidence continue to grow as Will called out the seventy-lap mark. He had just closed in tightly on the rear bumper of the "3."

The crew, though, was missing the excitement of Rob's attempt to take third position. They were working quickly to restock the pit after the last stop and to get into position for the next one when it came. The empty gas cans were loaded onto a wagon and hauled off toward the gas pumps to be refilled. The tire specialist checked the temperature across the face of each tire, then wrote down the findings to be relayed to Will Hughes. Likewise, the wear was checked to determine how the surface of each tire was playing out. That information too went directly to Will.

Michelle had intently watched the scramble in the pits as the team finished changing the left-side tires. It looked to her as if Rob were already moving before the jack ever allowed the car to set back down on the pavement. Everything about the stop was timed down to fractions of a second. She still marveled at the carefully choreographed motions that made up every pit stop. It almost reminded her of the intricate moves she learned when she competed in high school and college gymnastics. A slight bobble there could cost points too, but there was no teamwork like what went on in racing. And certainly not nearly the raw, undeniable danger.

She was forced to step out of the way as the steaming tires were passed back to the tire specialist at the back of the pit. She watched the expression on his face as he took the temperatures across the surface of the tire. She had learned early on that the best way to tell if the news was good or bad in the midst of all the noise and confusion was to watch the faces of these men. This time, the tire specialist cocked his head sideways and made a face that said, "Pretty good."

Ideally, the temps would be uniform on the inside, middle, and outside of the hot tire's surface. Michelle watched as he next measured the amount of rubber left on the tire. With little more than a couple of thirty-seconds of an inch of rubber on the wheel, tire wear was critical no matter what track they were running. She marveled at the care he took as he measured the depth on each tire, then followed it up by checking the air pressure that had built up in each one, studying the hot rubber like a doctor perusing a patient's X ray.

Again, he all but smiled. It would be good news he would be sending over to Will Hughes. She relaxed and returned to the television picture to watch as Rob tailed the black car so closely that they looked like one conjoined machine.

The teams started out each run with a much lower air pressure in the tires than what they wanted to have at the end of the run. The heat buildup in the tires caused the air pressure to rise as the heated air expanded. Everybody tried to underinflate the tires at the start of a run, knowing that the heat buildup over the length of a long series of laps would slowly raise the air pressure to, hopefully, the desired level. The downside to this was that an underinflated tire ran the risk of having the cords separate and that could lead to a dangerous tire failure. For that reason, the drivers were instructed repeatedly at the start of a run to take it easy on the tires until they were hot enough to bring the air pressure up to where it was supposed to be. A tire damaged early in the run didn't usually show up until much later when it would finally come apart. If it happened suddenly, a driver could find himself abruptly headed squarely for the fence, or spun around with the entire field bearing down on him as he helplessly watched them approaching.

Rob left the tire-pressure worries to Will. All he wanted to do was run the car flat out all the time. The hardest thing he had to do as a driver was to take it easy on the car and her tires. He, like most drivers, wanted to smoke the tires through every corner. With the hard compound tires he grew up racing with back on the short tracks around home, taxing the tires was rarely the issue. It often was here. Tire management was one of the few things that gave Rob difficulty at this level. While he was regarded to be a smooth driver, he had still been known to burn a set of tires completely off the car. He was still trying to learn the subtle differences that showed up in the handling of the car if a tire wore in a way the team and the driver did not expect.

Rob figured he could do most anything with a car. If it wasn't handling right, he only pushed it a little harder, becoming one with his vehicle. He seemed to have an innate sense of precisely how the machine would respond to his commands, how it would behave on the track.

That's what had led many observers to tell him that he reminded them of drivers from the golden days of racing. The old-timers on the circuit were always tossing around comparisons between this hot young driver and legendary competitors like Jodell Lee, Little Joe Weatherley, and Fireball Roberts, men who often seemed as much a part of their machines as the fenders and engines.

Coming off turn four, Rob swung down low to make the pass on the "3." The black car moved over in an attempt to block, just as Rob expected. But then he suddenly gave the kid room and let him shoot on by. The seven-time champ was merely acknowledging that he knew the kid had a faster car at this point in the race and he would let him by this time with no attempt at blocking him. Later in the race it would be a totally different story.

Rob cleared the black Chevrolet, then honed in on the second-place car, another Ford that ran only half a second in front of him. Will continued to call out the times that confirmed that Rob was consistently running as fast as the leader. Once he caught him, there would be one fine race for the packed house to behold.

Will fully expected Rob would do even better as the tires began to wear down later in the run. But so too would the leader if they were set up similarly.

Now, Rob no longer actually needed to hear the interval called out to him over the radio. He could count the car lengths down himself as he closed in quickly on the back of the blue and white Ford.

But as he closed in on the rear of the second-place car, he knew this next pass would be much more difficult than the last one. The two cars were evenly matched in the way their handling was set up. Rob held the edge with the power of his motor, but passing was difficult on the flat track. He would have to wait for the slightest slipup or opening to get around and into second place.

Rob had already begun to size up his opponent as he closed those last few car lengths. And he was looking for the opening that could come immediately or scores of laps down the way as he pulled up on the rear bumper of the Ford. The two of them raced down the long front straightaway and practically every fan in the place watched, anticipating the upcoming duel.

Rob looked inside and outside, probing for an opening as they approached the entrance into turn one. The driver ahead of him pulled down tightly against the white line that ran round the inside of the corner. He was clearly not willing to allow this rookie driver any opening on the inside. There was another group of three or four slower cars they would catch on the backstretch. Rob hoped he would be able to use some of those cars as a pick in an attempt to get past the other guy. The kid tested his competitor to the inside again as they navigated the short chute between turns one and two.

The two cars crossed over the tunnel to the infield as they raced for the second corner. Rob pulled to within half a car length of the back bumper of the blue and white car as he concentrated intently on getting through the corner smoothly. He tried to pressure the driver ahead of him, hoping to cause him to make a mistake, no matter how slight. Rob would only need a fraction of a second to make an opening for the pass once he got any kind of a niche.

The cars swung through the second corner nose to tail before shooting down the long backstretch past the lush green of the golf course that lined both sides of the track. Rob eased to the inside as the other Ford pushed high, toward the outside wall. The driver tried to cut down on Rob to block him but his bright red car was already there. Rob got the nose of his car up alongside the door of the other car midway down the straightaway, then he urged his Ford on as the two of them raced for the far corner.

Diving into the turn, Rob pulled almost even as the two cars raced side by side. He wrestled the wheel to hold his line straight and true, keeping the car down as low on the track as he could, allowing the driver of the other Ford plenty of room to race on the outside. But the other driver realized that he was caught out there in a much less desirable spot. He struggled to hold on to his car while maintaining his position.

But it was inevitable now. Coming out of turn three, the Ford on the outside bobbled. The driver still fought to hold on to the car while trying to hold his speed. The cars actually touched for an instant, a puff of white tire smoke signaling where Rob's right front made hard contact with the wiggling car to his outside.

The two cars separated and Rob finally pushed

ahead, boldly but cleanly taking possession of the spot. Their brief but jarring contact was quickly forgotten as Rob concentrated on chasing down the leader, who was now running only a bit over a second ahead of him.

Will Hughes resumed calling out the interval as Rob started to reel in the first-place car. He continued to push his own racer hard through the corners, confident in the fact that his was the fastest car on the track, at least for the moment.

"Outside! Car on the outside!" Harry Stone called over the radio as Rob caught up to a group of cars that were running together. The leader had just jetted on past them to put them a lap down, but in working his way around those slower drivers heading into the corner, the leader had been held up briefly.

And that was just enough for Rob to close the remaining distance.

The kid didn't say anything in response to Harry's warnings. He kept his eyes and his mind on cleanly clearing the slower cars, then on dealing with the leader.

"Leader, next," Will called, still not bothering with the interval. Rob now pulled up on the back end of the multicolored Chevy. The leader was a young man too, but he already owned several championships. He wasn't likely to panic when he realized the rookie in the red car actually caught him, nor did he care that the upstart kid might have plans to drive right on past. And young, handsome, and soft-spoken or not, everyone knew this particular driver would not cut Rob Wilder and the Billy Winton team any slack at all out there, especially in a pass for the lead.

Rob looked low through the next couple of corners for an opening that just wasn't there. He peeked to the outside, but that was a hopeless route, as well. The outside line had been running a tick slower for everyone all afternoon long. He tried to get a run off each of the corners, but the driver in the multicolored Chevy would have none of it. Every time Rob thought he saw a sliver of an opening and tried to make a run at it, the leader expertly but cleanly blocked him.

Rob fought off his growing frustration. He had the faster car. Why couldn't he drive on past this guy and lead this race? The sweeping, relatively flat banking in the turns favored the leader, though.

But then, as he watched the Chevy, Rob could see him begin to slide a bit in the corners as a result of the pressure being put on him from behind. Rob knew if he kept it constant, the leader would eventually succumb, pushing up in the corner, and he could finally slip right on past him. He had to fight the urge to drive smartly up to his bumper and give him a slight nudge to clear the way. That might be appropriate on one of the smaller tracks. And Rob even managed a smile as he realized that if Stacy Locklear were in his position, he would likely go right ahead and pull the move here, regardless of the consequences. But that was not Rob Wilder's driving style. He knew that in some other race on another day the situation would be reversed, and he hoped the young champion would remember how cleanly Rob had raced him this day. He would certainly remember it if he spun him into the wall!

Back in the pits, Will studied the monitor at his feet, watching as the kid dove high and low, struggling to make the pass. He desperately wanted to call out instructions to the kid, to urge him on, but reluctantly he kept quiet. He knew his young driver was concentrating intensely and that he was doing exactly what he was supposed to do. And he was doing it very well. He would make the pass when the time came. Of that, Will Hughes could be sure.

Will couldn't help it. His chest swelled with pride. Leading the race at Indy was a big deal for any team or driver. But for such a young team, and one led by

a rookie driver, it would be a giant step toward le-
gitimizing their ascension into the top echelon of the
sport.

Rob's second-place finish back in the spring at
Martinsville caused a lot of the doubters to reluctantly
give the kid and his team credit. A string of top-ten
finishes after that reinforced their position with the
last of the skeptics in the garage who looked on the
good run as a fluke. These guys from East Tennessee
were for real!

The Ensoft team was no longer overlooked by the
fans, lost somewhere in the back of the garage, passed
over by the reporters on pit road. They were already
a legitimate story in this year's Cup campaign.

Now, should they take the lead here in Indianapolis, no one could possibly look past them again. This
skinny, good-looking kid could drive a racecar. He
was the real deal. Everyone knew he had decent
equipment, though not quite the equal of some of the
other well-funded multicar teams. But theirs was not
among the top sponsorship packages on the circuit,
the ones who seemed to find themselves at the top of
the point standings year after year.

True, there were already rumors of other teams trying to lure the amazingly talented young driver over
to their garage for next year. It was well-known that
the only contract Billy Winton, the team's owner, had
with his young charge was a handshake and an understanding of what they both wanted to accomplish.

Rob certainly wasn't thinking contracts at that moment, though. He was trying to find a route around
the multicolored Chevy so he could take over the top
spot. He despised being this close to the lead and
having to wait for an opening so he could make his
move.

The cars dove into turn one and Rob noticed once
again that the rear end of the leader's racecar seemed
to kick out on him. This time, though, it was much

more pronounced. Rob made a mental note and would be ready to pounce if it happened there again.

This was precisely the kind of racing the fans in the stands had come to see. Good, clean, close racing, where the quality of the machines was matched only by the skill of the men who guided them. The vast audience watching the show on television would be enjoying what the multiple cameras were showing them too. Indeed, the booth announcers were full of praise for the young blond-headed challenger, the not-much-older former champion, and the exquisite sparring they were doing with each other.

Rob worked his hands and feet in a rapid display of athletic coordination as he expertly worked the pedals and twisted the steering wheel. His brow furrowed in concentration, he watched for the slightest sign of a mistake, all at more than a hundred and sixty miles per hour. The effects of the heat and fatigue he felt earlier in the race were miraculously cured now, wiped away by this chance to finally take the lead he was so certain he deserved.

The lead car crossed over into turn two, struggling, doing all he could to hang on to his car-length lead. But try as he might, he couldn't seem to shake the bright red Ensoft Ford that now filled up his rearview mirror. For the young leader, this was nothing new. He was accustomed to leading races, comfortable being chased by others, supremely confident in his own abilities. He knew the rookie behind him was driving a faster car. With the way his own car was handling, it was also likely that it would only be a matter of time before the rookie got by him. That is, if the rookie had enough guts to attempt the pass and the moxie to pull it off. The young champ knew it was his job to make it as difficult as he could as long as he could for the kid behind him.

Rob watched as the back end of the leader's Chevy skewed slightly once again in the center of turn two.

The slight back-and-forth motion would have been practically imperceptible to anyone else but it was plenty obvious to a racecar driver. Rob knew what the movement meant. The leader had a loose racecar, his racer's back end wanting to twist around on him as if it were determined to try to pass the front end. It would be a continuing fight for him to hold the car down on the track and still maintain speed.

Still, the two of them raced hard down the backstretch, rumbling closely together down toward turn three. Rob managed to get a slight run on the Chevrolet, easing down to the rainbow-colored car's inside.

Rob breathed in the familiar scents of a hot racecar. There was the usual aroma of overheated paint, burning oil, hot metal. But there was something else. What was that? Burning rubber? He shrugged it off as he chased the leader down into the third turn, now mere inches off his back bumper. There was plenty of hot rubber out there, all right.

He relied on the superior handling of his Ford to hold his car down tight to the inside. The leader was trying to do the same thing, trying to block the red car's path. But his racecar wasn't handling nearly as well and he had to fight to try to hold the position.

Once again, the back end shot loose for an instant, forcing the leader to have to wrestle with the steering wheel as he struggled to keep the car beneath him. As they roared through the center of the turn, the leader's car kicked out even more as the two of them raced for the same spot out on the track.

For a fraction of a second, the opening was there, and Rob was expecting it, ready to pounce. The slight kick upward in the center of the turn was all Rob needed. He maintained his line almost impossibly low on the track, almost to the bright green grass. The nose of his car shot by on the inside of the Chevrolet, giving Rob a tantalizing taste of the race lead. The former champ knew this brash young rookie had him now. There was no point in fighting it, maybe losing the car completely and sacrificing his chance at a decent finish and lots of points. He could fix the car on the next stop and take back the lead later. Still, it was with reluctance that he gave up the fight and prudently allowed Rocket Rob Wilder and his red car to sail on by.

But the young former champion had to smile as he tucked his car in tightly behind Wilder. The kid had shown the savvy of a veteran in making that pass, the patience of a seasoned driver in waiting for the perfect opportunity to take his shot. A typically overeager rookie might have used a fender or a shot in the rear to try to get around him and maybe would have ended up putting both of them into the wall instead. It was a favor he would return to the kid one day should the situation be reversed and he had the chance to put a pass with class on the youngster.

Heck, the way these two cars were running, he would most likely get his chance before the checkered flag waved in this race.

Once past the Chevy, Rob began to steadily pull away from the former champ, putting several car lengths on him by the time they had circled back around to the first turn.

"Leader," came the monotone voice of Harry Stone, informing his driver that he had just taken over the top spot, just in case he hadn't noticed.

"Leader! Leader!" Rob screamed to no one in particular but loud enough to rival the throaty scream of his racecar's engine. He finally keyed the microphone as he hit the front straightaway and he almost matched the calm of Harry's voice when he said, "Ten four."

He was leading at Indy. Leading at Indy! He let out another whoop before settling down to drive on.

"Good job, Cowboy. Way to take her to the front," Will called out on the radio as he watched Rob's number go up on the scoreboard as soon as he crossed the start/finish line. "Now be smart and keep her there till this thing's over."

"I fully intend to," Rob said sincerely.

Whew! He was leading at Indy!

Now, they would have to pass him if they wanted the lead back. And there was no way on God's green earth that Rob Wilder was going to surrender the point now that it was finally his.

No way!

3

Easy as pie."

Rob said the words beneath his breath, still a little giddy from the ease with which he made the last several passes and the final move to the front. But the celebration was over. The rapid approach of turn one quickly brought his focus back to the here and now and the task at hand.

Charging through turn one, he again caught a strong whiff of burning rubber in the cockpit. Couldn't be his car, though. She was handling so well and neither Will nor Harry had said anything on the radio. Likely one of the cars he had just passed had a tire rubbing or a belt slipping.

At that moment, Harry was busy watching the next group of slower cars ahead of Rob and calculating how long it would be before he caught them. He missed the slight wisp of smoke from the Ford's right front as the tire on that side hit its maximum stress point in the center of the corner. The television cameras didn't catch it, either. They had temporarily lost interest in Rob Wilder and were focused on what had become a furious battle for second. The third-place Ford had finally caught the multicolored Chevy. As those two cars raced furiously for the position, most eyes focused on the fine battle they were staging.

Rob was more than satisfied with the way that the car was handling as he pressed it through the next corner. She was running superbly, and especially for such a long green-flag span. He could keep the car right down on the white line that ran all the way around the inside of each corner. He was leading the field, still putting distance on the second- and third-place cars every time around the big track.

"You got a half second on 'em, Cowboy. We got fifteen laps before our next stop," Will called out.

"Car's perfect. We don't need to change a thing," Rob shot back quickly, loath to give up even a moment's concentration.

"Keep it up!"

"This car is so good. I hardly have to push her at all."

"Just be smooth and patient with the lapped cars."

"Don't worry," Rob answered, allowing the conversation to drop as he focused on the corner that was rapidly filling his windshield.

He set the car's line precisely the way he had in each lap so far as he came upon the transition from the backstretch to turn three. He twisted the wheel to cut the arc of the corner in a perfect display of practical geometry. He dove low as he raced into the turn once again, got on the brakes, dropped the nose of the Ford as it charged into the corner.

There was the smell again, hot rubber, intruding like an unhappy memory as he came up off the corner and onto the short straightaway before the car shot into turn four. He was briefly in the gas before braking again through turn four.

"Will, I thought I saw a little smoke coming off the right front, but I'm not sure. See if you can see it on the monitor," Harry Stone called, being certain to make the transmission on the team's second radio channel so his cautionary observation wouldn't alarm or distract Rob. Until they were dead sure there was a problem, they didn't want to break Rob's concentration as he paced the field.

"I didn't see anything but I'll look next time by," Will reported.

"Ten four, Will. Let me know when you want to pit him. Looks like most are looking at fifteen to twenty laps more."

"I think we'll short-pit him, bringing him on in twelve to fifteen laps out. He's running so good I think we can maybe pick something up on the others. Our tires are not falling off as bad as everybody else's are."

Michelle got antsy every time the network cut away from Rob to focus in on other cars all the way around the track racing for position. She stood cheering, though, as he cleared the lapped traffic blocking his way. Then she would cringe every time he got close to one of the slower cars, crossing her fingers until he safely cleared them.

She looked up to catch a glimpse of him in real life as he rocketed by their position on pit road, then immediately returned her gaze to the monitor to watch as he progressed on down into the first turn. Then, he was approaching another group of lapped cars, likely about to catch them somewhere in turn two.

Michelle smiled broadly as she thought of the exposure her company was getting as their car paced the field, showing the way in such a prestigious event at one of the most famed speedways in all of motorsports. She could visualize the photos on the sports pages tomorrow of their car leading the pack off into one of the turns. Or the video clips from the race that would be shown later that evening on the highlight reels on the sportscasts.

The Ford was flying as it once again reached the end of the long front straightaway. Will Hughes twisted around in his seat, trying to keep the car in sight before it disappeared down into turn one. Theirs was still the fastest car on the track. They were very consistent from lap to lap. If they could keep this pace, they were going to put a lot of good cars down by at least a lap before they made their next pit stop. If they could whittle down the number of cars on the lead lap, it would certainly work to their advantage later in the day, and especially if they got a rash of late-race caution periods. Whatever might happen later on, the fact remained that they were setting a torrid pace for this early in the race.

Rob was feeling surprisingly comfortable in the car now. The biting tightness of the seat belts digging deeply into his shoulders was all but forgotten. The rivulets of sweat running down the inside of the front and back of his driving suit were now unnoticed. The back of his mouth felt as if it were stuffed with cotton from breathing the hot air blowing through the hose from the cool box and into his helmet, but he didn't mind at all.

It was amazing what a few laps at the front of the pack at a place like this could do to make a young driver forget his miseries. Leading and winning were all that mattered to him, and now he was literally living his dream. It was a time like this that made all those other Sundays bearable. The days when the car was off a tick and he struggled to keep up. The races when it seemed he was dragging a sled full of anvils behind the red Ford. The contests when those openings to the lead never materialized and the run to the front was nothing more than a fervent wish.

No, times like these made it all worthwhile. The times when he could take the car to the front against the very best and then drive off and leave them in distant pursuit. Those were the moments that Rob Wilder lived for.

Now, as he rocketed off toward turn one, everything seemed to unfold in front of him in drawn-out slow motion. The bright colors of the grandstand seemed to swirl and blur and wave him on as he approached the entrance to the corner.

"Hang on tight!"

"Huh?"

The voice came out of nowhere. Rob glanced quickly around the cockpit as he set his line going into the corner. What was the voice telling him? He'd heard it often enough now to know to listen to what it told him.

Rob took a new grip on the wheel as he tapped the brakes and started to twist the wheel to steer the car into the corner. He felt the brakes begin to bite, dropping the front of the car down, the nose sitting down on the track the way it was supposed to do. The g-forces twisted the body of the car over on its axis as Rob pushed it hard toward the center of the corner.

Then, he stared through the turn, sizing up the couple of cars running up there in front of him that he was rapidly closing in on. The cars he would soon leave in his exhaust when he ultimately put a lap on them.

"BOOM!"

The percussive explosion reverberated through the cockpit.

The car jumped out from under Rob as if some giant hand had slapped it sideways and toward the wall.

Rob didn't have time to figure out where the sound came from. Instinctively, he jammed his right foot hard on the brakes while he tried to find the clutch with his left to keep the engine from stalling. The steering wheel jerked sharply to the right, ripping itself from his grip and sending the car shooting directly toward the outside wall as if it were being drawn there by some awful, powerful magnetism.

Rob hardly had time to realize what was happening, much less make any attempt to try to steer the car away from the wall. The tremendous velocity and momentum the car carried coming down off the front straightaway into the corner propelled the car straight into the concrete retaining wall.

There was that awful fraction of a second between when the tire exploded and when the car made severe contact with the wall that Rob realized the inevitability of what was about to happen.

"This is going to hurt," he thought as he fought the car all the way.

"KABOOM!"

The car slammed virtually head-on into the wall, still hurtling along at almost one hundred and eighty miles per hour when it did. The sound of the Ford's impact with the solid, unmoving concrete reverberated off the steel framework of the massive grandstands, drowning out all the other sounds around the speedway for an instant. The clamor of the collision instantly quieted the crowd.

The car trailed a long stream of tire smoke since Rob had stood hard on the brakes in a futile attempt to slow the car down. The sickening contact with the wall in the middle of turn one instantly crumpled the entire front end of the car, compacting it like an accordion. The jolt was so vicious that the Ford came to an almost immediate stop where it hit the wall. The gray smoke from the tires mingled with a new boiling, black, oily cloud of smoke that billowed from beneath the hood. Tiny tongues of flame licked at the underside of what was left of the hood of the car.

The fire, fed by oil from the ruptured cooler, grew bigger until it had engulfed the right front of the car. Cars . . . all the racers in the field . . . streamed past the crumpled, motionless red Ford, seemingly oblivious to the mess resting against the wall, to the smoky fire that was clearly intensifying, fanned by the air off their machines.

Will was watching the scoring monitor at his feet after Rob disappeared from his view and into turn one. He clearly heard the boom when the car shot into the outside wall. The sound of the impact echoed all the way down the front stretch and along the pit road. Then, when he looked up, he could see the large cloud of smoke from the crash. Before he even had time to react, to consider the possibility that it might actually be his car that was the source of all that noise and hellish smoke, he heard the normally calm voice of Harry Stone, but this time he was shouting over the radio circuit.

Will Hughes cringed at his words, at the message they relayed.

"Bad crash! Our boy's in a bad crash!"

Will jumped to his feet, straining, squinting, trying to see all the way down toward turn one.

"Robbie? Robbie! Talk to me, buddy!" he pleaded into the microphone suspended at his lips. He struggled to keep the growing sense of panic out of his voice. But the thick plume of smoke was worrying Will, and he replayed the *whoomp* of the impact in his head. The silence over the radio was telling, too. He could feel a lump begin to rise in his throat. "Anything, Harry?" he shouted.

"Fire, fire, fire!" Harry chanted. "Robbie, you need to get unbuckled and get out of that thing. She's burning real good under the hood on the right side."

"What's going on, Harry?" Will queried, doubtlessly asking the question each of the Ensoft gang would like answered. The word "fire" was one no race crew wanted to hear. Nothing worried a driver more than being trapped in a burning racecar. "Is he out of the car? Can you see him moving around in there?"

Harry ignored Will's question and studied the car through the lenses of his binoculars. From his spot he could see the flames boiling from under the hood and already starting to climb up the left side of the car. Smoke poured from the cockpit, obscuring the inside of the car where its driver would be. Maybe conscious, maybe not.

"Robbie, we need to get out of the car. It's on fire," Harry called, the urgency obvious in his voice. In the back of the spotter's mind was the realization that either Rob Wilder knew the car was on fire and was unable to get loose, or he was out, unconscious, unaware of the danger he was in. "Where's that fire truck?"

What had seemed like hours had actually only been a few seconds short of a minute. The other cars in the field were just now slowing to take the caution flag back at the start/finish line. Until the other cars on the track slowed down and cleared the wreck, the safety truck could not cross the track to the wrecked car.

With the fire, every second counted. And there still was no sign of Rob Wilder coming out of the car.

Michelle watched in horror as the network replayed the footage of what caused the wreck in the first place, as the camera focused in tightly on the Ensoft Ford as the puff of smoke from the right front documented the exact moment when the tire blew. The Ford immediately jerked wildly to the right and shot head-on into the outside wall almost directly in the center of the corner. The impact of the crash stopped the car cold.

But it was those first fingers of flame that brought Michelle's hands to her mouth, that forced a gasp from her throat. She could feel her knees begin to shake as she watched desperately, waiting for him to come climbing out the window, stomping angrily, just as he had the few times before when she had seen him caught up in crashes.

But this had been different, unlike any wreck she had witnessed so far. Even her unpracticed eye could tell that the car hit the wall awfully hard. And there was a fire. What had been only a few flickers of flame was quickly becoming a good-size blaze and, in the span of only a few short seconds, was growing, threatening. All the while, the camera was zooming in on the car, the announcers repeating how desperately they wanted to see the kid come bouncing out of the car. But the absence of any movement inside the smoke-filled machine told the viewers what the announcers were unwilling to say.

Michelle wiped tears from her cheeks as she watched the screen and waited. A glance at the worried faces of Will, Donnie, Paul, and the others confirmed that she had reason to be concerned. These were guys who seemingly never got scared, not even in a sport as treacherous as this one could be.

Then she caught Will's eyes, saw the abject horror that lurked there, and her stomach fell. The realization hit her with an impact as hard as anything she had felt in her life.

There was a chance, an awful chance, that Rob Wilder was badly hurt. That he was slumped over unconscious in that fiery racecar. That he might be in real trouble out there.

She slumped back onto her director's chair and did something she had not done since she was a little girl.

She raised her eyes to heaven and prayed.

4

Rob Wilder had jumped hard on the brakes more out of instinct than anything else when he felt the tire give way and the car jerked away from him and headed straight toward the outside wall. There was no time to really react, not even for someone with almost supernatural reflexes like Rob's. There was only a split second between the tire blowing and the beautiful red racecar plowing head-foremost into the unforgiving concrete retaining wall.

One moment the car was sailing along at a hundred and eighty miles an hour, leading the race, its pilot beaming with pride and smelling victory. The next instant there was nothing but blackness. Deep, sweet blackness.

Then, the youngster was floating, chasing stars across a night sky like elusive fireflies. It was an almost pleasant experience as he romped like a happy child in the warm darkness.

But then he was suddenly aware that he was having

trouble catching his breath. And what air there was burned his throat and lungs mightily when he sucked it in.

Still he was reluctant to leave the enveloping, comforting security of the surrounding blackness. It was eerie, unlike anything he had ever experienced before during his tumultuous upbringing. Somehow, inside the embrace of the warm darkness, he felt all the love he had been denied while growing up. He suddenly seemed free from the insecurities and lack of balance that had plagued his childhood.

Then, there was a constant, strained buzzing sound in his ears and it didn't seem to want to go away. Why wouldn't it hush? Why wouldn't it simply leave him alone, allow him to hang there limply in the seat for just a few more minutes? It had been such a long, tiring day so far. It would be good to relax a bit, let the blackness soothe his aching body, nurture his pained soul.

But the buzzing got louder and gradually he began to sort out the various sounds. Some were coming through the earpieces and he slowly pulled the words out of the fuzzy distortion. Something about "fire." But the words seemed so distant, not even from this planet. He tried to shake his head, to clear away the indistinctness that had seemed to settle in all around him, but his helmet now felt so heavy he couldn't move.

"Get out!"

He heard the voices yelling at him, familiar voices, but the words they were screaming made no sense at all.

Rob tried again to suck in a deeper breath of air but his lungs didn't seem to be working yet.

Oh, well. He'd try again some other time.

He had no way of knowing that the impact with the wall had knocked the breath out of him, his chest crushed by the safety belts while doing their job, keeping him restrained in his seat. Now, as the breath slowly came back to him, something else was interfering with his ability to breathe. He was choking, gagging, as he became aware of the black smoke that filled the inside of the racecar. But try as he might, he still could not catch his breath or clear the fog that seemed to have so effectively settled in and made itself at home inside his head.

He found himself floating again across the black sky. All he wanted to do was simply close his eyes and relax. If he could only manage that, he knew everything would be okay. Now, at peace with everything around him, he was ready to let his consciousness slip away again, to escape the buzzing noise, the relentless heat, the distant, unnerving distorted words, and the choking air.

The growing wall of fire was not a part of his dark, secure world.

But just then, he felt what seemed to be a sharp slap to the side of his head. Groggily, he glanced up as best he could but he couldn't seem to see anyone. He choked again on the thick smoke as he once again fought for a clean breath of air.

"Get out of here, kid! Wake up! Climb out now!"

The voice was much clearer than the others had been on his radio earpieces. Those faraway words were still there, buzzing like a swarm of mad bees, like a thousand voices, all talking at the same time in different languages.

But this latest voice was different, loud and clear, cutting through the panicked chatter filling his ears as it urged him to action.

"Fire! You have to get out of this thing!"

Rob could now taste the oily smoke on his tongue and the air around him seemed to have grown infinitely hotter.

Smoke? Heat? The voice had mentioned fire. Maybe he should try to move.

When he opened his eyes, the black smoke that filled the cockpit was so thick that he could hardly see anything through the faceplate of the helmet. Though it took all the strength he could muster, he managed to reach up with his gloved hands and fumble with the quick-release buckle to the safety belts. As he flicked it open, he glanced to his right and saw orange flames licking hungrily through the open window.

There was a moment's panic then as he struggled with the tangle of belts and hoses that had him tethered to the burning car. And his hands and arms seemed unwilling to obey his commands, his fingers numb, frozen, or asleep. But somehow he finally freed himself and lunged for the fastener to the window net. He wasted precious seconds fumbling for the release with his deadened fingers before the net suddenly dropped away and his escape route was clear.

By now the flames were scorching his skin and singeing his hair in the few spots his suit didn't cover. He tried to pull himself up from the seat and out the window but a sharp, searing pain shot up his left leg from the ankle, the sudden intensity of it keeping him from using it at all. The steering wheel had his right leg hung so he had to call on his unresponsive hands again to try to work with the catch and take it off the column. The gloves and the tingling in his fingers made the catch tricky to open and Rob's panic increased dramatically.

There seemed then to be a real chance he would burn up in the red racecar before he could get himself freed from its grip.

Finally, though, the wheel was loose and he almost took the time to lay it carefully up on the dash as he usually did. But then he thought better of it and flung it out of his way. He again reached for the window to pull himself out. It seemed the flames were raging now, searing hot, and the smoke was still so thick he could hardly see anything.

He was holding his breath now, the air too dirty to get a good lungful at all, but his chest was wracked with spasms from all the smoke he had inhaled already. He knew he had to get out. He half crawled out the open window, then dropped through the flames to the pavement and somehow managed to roll away from the burning car.

He hurt all over. Hurt as bad as he ever had in his life. Hurt so bad he couldn't even pinpoint where all the pain came from. But he was out of the car, away from the flames.

Now, if he could only breathe. Try as he might, he couldn't seem to get air into his lungs, and he felt the blackness begin to claim him again.

How odd that he had managed to get out of the blazing racer, yet he would die right there on the asphalt from lack of oxygen. He coughed and choked and tried to suck in enough air to keep on living. He desperately wanted to live long enough to get something to stop the awful pain that seemed determined to eat him alive.

Will stood on top of the pit wagon like a general in the midst of a losing battle. He barked orders and called for information but there was nothing but confusion all around him. No matter what he tried he could not bring order to the chaos. He needed answers and he needed them now. And worse yet, he was unable to see what was happening down there in turn one through all the smoke.

The one person who could see what was going on was Michelle, thanks to the graphic pictures on the television monitor in the back of the pit. The camera had zoomed in close on the smoking heap of twisted metal, on the growing inferno along the car's right side. The flames had now started lapping up the left side too, toward the driver's side window.

She wondered where the safety trucks were and why they weren't already out there, helping Rob out of the burning car. The last of the strung-out field was only now straggling by the wreck site and that kept the fire trucks stuck in their respective parking spots behind the wall until it was safe for them to roll out. All the while the flames seemed even more hungry, more determined to claim all of the red Ensoft Ford before they would be sated.

Through her tears, she hardly noticed that most of the crew was now gathering behind her, straining to see on the screen what was going on down there in turn one. Fortunately for them, they could not hear the announcers' grave pronouncements and speculation as to the condition of their driver.

Finally, thankfully, the safety trucks were rolling toward the wreck even as the front of the car seemed to become fully engulfed in flames. The trucks skidded to a halt as their crews jumped over the sides and raced toward the fire. The first man to get there dropped his fire extinguisher and was forced to stop and retrieve it. He bent to pick it up just as Rob came sailing out the open window of the broken racer as if propelled by someone still inside who might have given him a boost out. Then he rolled away from the searing heat, smoke pouring off him as if he, too, might actually be ablaze.

In the pits a small cheer rose as the Ensoft crew saw their driver come flying from the smoke-filled cockpit, through the flames, out the window, then tumble down onto the pavement trailing a cloud of smoke after him. The fireman got the extinguisher on the flames and went to work quickly, doing his best to smother the raging fire.

Rob still couldn't tell how far he had rolled from the car and it made sense to get up and run. He could still feel the scorching fire, even through his driver's suit. He tried to climb to his feet, to run farther away

from the car, but when he stood, he could put no
weight on his left foot. Awful pain engulfed his entire
leg. He tried to hobble out of the way but could only
stumble and drop to his knees, still not far enough
away from the car to truly be safe.

He felt hands under his arms then. A couple of
safety crewmembers lifted him up, locked their arms
behind his back and beneath his thighs, forming a
relatively utilitarian chair, and carried him over to
where an ambulance was just then screeching to a halt
at the bottom of the track.

"You're gonna be all right, soldier," one of them
said.

"Try to breathe deep, Rob," the other advised.

Rob was fumbling with the strap securing his helmet, somehow assuming getting it off his head, the
mask off his face, would make it easier to find some
clean air somewhere. His helmet usually offered ref-
uge from everything else that was always whirling
about him at the racetrack. Once he pulled it on, it
meant it was time to go racing, and it effectively
locked out everything else but the car and the track
and the competition. Now, it felt as if the strap were
choking him, the mask suffocating him, and he
couldn't wait to get it off his head to feel cool wind
on his face.

Finally, he worked the strap loose and yanked the
thing off his head, trying to inhale sweet, fresh air.
He coughed and hacked though, his lungs still filled
with all the smoke he had inhaled in the fiery cockpit,
his mouth and tongue and throat still coated with oily
residue.

The safety crewmen set Rob down on the pavement
while they went to help grab the gurney from the
ambulance. He waved off the rescuers and got busy
checking himself all over to try to ascertain where all
the pain was coming from, making certain each ex-

tremity was still there and still where it was supposed to be.

He'd sit there a minute, he thought, maybe get an aspirin or two for the sudden massive headache that crept up on him. Then he'd wave to the crowd to let them know he was okay. And after he caught his breath, he'd jog on over to the pits and apologize to Will and the boys for wrecking their wonderful, winning racecar.

But some inner sense of ultimate logic told him he wouldn't be doing any jogging anytime soon. He seemed to ache mightily all over, but the worst of it, the awful, pounding worst of it, radiated from his left ankle as if somebody were rudely pounding on it repeatedly with a ball peen hammer. He yelped when his fingertips brushed the ankle, and then, when he looked at it, something immediately seemed odd about it. He gingerly tried to move it but a sharp pain shot up his leg.

Suddenly he felt the darkness returning, a quick, deep wave of nausea swept up from just below his diaphragm, and before he could help it, he heaved over and over. This time, he allowed the safety crewmen to lift him onto the stretcher and haul him to the ambulance before any more of his fans could see him lying there, retching like a common gutter drunk.

The fire crews made quick work of extinguishing the fire while the medical staff climbed into the back of the ambulance and began checking Rob over. The television announcers relayed their relief as they played and replayed the tape of Rob's cannonball exit from the blazing racecar. The camera followed him as he tried to hobble away before falling down, then stayed on him as he tore off his helmet and fought to breathe. Then, it zoomed in to catch the pain on his face but, thankfully, cut away before he began gagging. When the coverage resumed after commercials, they showed tape of the gurney going into the ambulance, of Rob's feeble wave to the crowd, and then of them slowly pulling away, headed for the infield care center.

The television announcers repeated their assessment for the viewing audience.

"Great to see the youngster climb out of that car," the announcer said.

"As hard as he hit that wall, let's just hope he's okay," the veteran driver doing the commentary added. The concern in his voice was obvious. He, of all people, knew a smack as hard as the kid had just taken could do lasting damage, causing all sorts of injuries that might not be obvious immediately.

The crowd was on its feet, giving the young driver a roaring cheer as the ambulance rolled away. But then, their attention as well as the focus of the television cameras, switched to the other cars. They were already in the midst of their yellow-flag pit stops and the television people sought out the new leader to watch his stop. They would switch back to catch the awesome pictures of the scorched and mangled "52" Ensoft Ford as it rested, dead, on the bed of the wrecker that was hauling it back to the garage. And they would cut later to one of the pit reporters as he talked with one of the care center physicians about Rob's condition. But the race would soon be going back to green. There was once again plenty of competition as the cars all made a mad dash for the win that had been, up until a few minutes before, apparently out of reach for them.

Will Hughes came around to where Michelle Fagan stood, crying softly as she watched the television monitor, her hands together at her chin as if she might still be praying.

"Michelle, come on. We need to get over to the care center," he told her quietly.

"Did you see him?" she said, pointing to the screen as if the camera might still be on him, lying there in pain on the asphalt. "Did you see his face? He was hurting so bad, Will. I couldn't stand it."

"He looks okay," Will said, but with little conviction. He too knew a collision with an immovable object at that speed could scramble a man's insides. But he also knew they needed to go and he didn't want to leave Michelle alone. "They'll probably take him on to the hospital as a precaution and we should ride with him."

"Hospital?"

Tears streamed down her face.

"Precaution. They always do that."

On some level, she knew that was true. She had seen enough drivers carted away on an ambulance only to show up in time for the media interviews after the race. But on another level, she could read the worry on Will's face.

"Sorry," she said weakly and used the back of her hand to try to wipe away the tears, a gesture that made her look like a vulnerable little girl. Just then, someone handed her a clean shop rag. Donnie Kline, his bald head shining with sweat and his face streaked with grease and perspiration, grinned feebly. "Thanks, Donnie."

"Now blow your nose and go on," the big man said. "Robbie is gonna need you."

He pushed her gently toward Will.

Will opened his mouth to say something to Donnie but realized he didn't have to utter a word. The crew was already at work, gathering everything up and getting ready to pull out for home, even as the engines roared out on the track at the restart of the race.

Will took Michelle's arm, hurrying her along as they made their way over to the entrance to the medical center. They half walked, half jogged down past the rows of pits, merely shrugging when crews all along the way looked at them with the same question on their faces.

They had no idea how badly their young driver might be hurt.

"Do they have good doctors here?" Michelle yelled in Will's ear to be heard over the cars.

"Supposed to be the best of any track in the world. He'll be fine, Chelle. He's just a little banged up, that's all." Will hoped he sounded convincing. He needed Michelle to stay together. But he too had been stunned with the ferocity of the wreck when he watched the replay. Watched it once. That's all he could manage. He had been around racing long enough to know the cars were built to take a lick much harder than what the Ford had taken. But not the human body. All the protection in the world couldn't keep a man completely safe in such a sudden-stop crash. "Just banged up," he repeated for emphasis.

"I hope so. That car . . . it just stopped when it hit the wall. Didn't bounce at all. I thought he was . . . uh . . . dead for sure."

Michelle stopped to wipe away a fresh round of tears from her face, no longer caring that she was smearing her mascara all over.

"Don't ever think like that!" Will said, stopping with her. "We build the best cars there are. Good and safe. Besides, Robbie's got a guardian angel that rides with him looking after him all the time."

"Aw, Will," she said, squinting at him through a new round of tears. "I know I'm acting like a silly woman but you don't have to patronize me. I've heard all the ghost stories for two years now. Sometimes I think you all actually have Rob believing them."

Will put his arms around her and hugged her close for a moment, then took her hand again and hurried her along to the care center. They flashed their credentials at the gate and were waved in by the security guard.

The ambulance's rear doors were just being opened as they ran up. Michelle swiped at her eyes again with the shop rag, trying to not let Rob know how worried and upset she was, how weak she felt.

She could be strong for him. She *would* be strong for him. Especially now.

The gurney was carefully rolled out the back of the vehicle and one of the emergency workers dropped down its wheels, locking them in place. They quickly swung it around, heading toward the open door of the small hospital.

Will and Michelle tried to get a glimpse of him as they rolled him past. His hands were sooty from all the smoke. The bright red driving uniform he was wearing, the one that had looked so natty earlier that morning, was now singed and blackened and ripped open in places where the crew had cut it away to look for contusions and broken bones and to attach monitoring equipment.

But it was his face that Will and Michelle both saw at the same instant. His face. His youthful, handsome face. His features were twisted with pain, his cheeks smudged, his eyes wild and wide in obvious agony.

Michelle gasped when she saw him. Will squeezed her arm gently and then stepped along to keep up with the gurney.

"Robbie, you okay?"

Lying there on the stretcher, Rob had trouble locating the familiar voice, the one calling him an even more familiar name. But who was this "Robbie"?

Though it hurt to move, he looked to his left, tried to focus his eyes, and saw Will and Michelle standing there. He wasn't sure who those people were, but somehow, it was good to see them. Even if they had the oddest looks on their faces.

He tried to smile.

"I'm okay," he heard someone say. Then, with the raw pain in his throat and the raspy voice inside his own ears, he realized it had been he who had spoken.

He grimaced but felt the need to add, "I'm just a little banged up, that's all."

The two familiar people seemed happy to hear him say those few words, but before he could ask who they were, he was wheeled inside the care center.

Will and Michelle had no choice but to wait outside until the doctors would let them come in to see him.

"You really think he's all right?" Michelle asked nervously, her expression revealing her own opinion.

"Hard to tell, honey. At best he's gonna be pretty badly beaten up. He'll think a bunch of mob guys have been doing a number on him in some back alley when he wakes up in the morning."

"Did you see any burns?" She could still see the creeping swirl of flames engulfing the driver's side window.

"I don't think he got burned. The suit protects him pretty good. I just hope he didn't break anything. Or get his brains scrambled."

The busted racecar they could fix. If their driver had broken something vital or had a serious head injury, the whole team could be in sad shape. Even though he was worried about Rob, he was already thinking of the contingencies. What if Rob wasn't able to drive the next week at Watkins Glen in New York State? It was a twisting, winding road course. And it was a tough, physical raceway, requiring constant steering, clutching, shifting, and braking. It was hard on a perfectly healthy driver, impossible for someone who might be nursing an injury.

Will smiled. Rob had been pointing toward the road course all year.

"It's just like those old roads up Brendlee Mountain me and my buddies used to race around on," he had boasted. "Turn me loose on that old winding track. Just turn me and that Ford loose!"

Michelle paced back and forth in front of the door into which Rob had disappeared. At least she had seen him, had seen him try to smile and to tell them he was okay. That was good. Especially since she had been convinced only a few minutes before that he might be dead.

They both jumped when the doctor finally opened the door and stepped outside.

"How is he?" Will asked, cutting to the chase.

"Well, we're going to transport him to the hospital. They're getting an ambulance lined up now to take him." Michelle gasped again. The doctor went on. "I don't think there's anything to worry about. We just need some more X rays and to keep him under observation, just in case." The doctor rubbed his eyes tiredly. "I'll tell you one thing. That's one lucky young man."

"You said X rays?"

"Yep. He's for sure got a fracture of his left ankle. They'll have to tend to that at the hospital. He inhaled a lot of smoke, as well, so they'll need to give him some breathing treatments. And they'll do some more X rays on his chest and shoulders. We need to see if he broke any ribs or a collarbone where the shoulder belts caught him. Crashes like that, as hard as the one he took, can do some considerable damage."

"Anything else?" Will asked. He looked anxiously at the doctor, afraid there might be more to come.

"Well, he's going to be one sore young man for the next several weeks. I don't see any sign of head injury and we always worry about that in a sudden-stop wreck. He has a few slight burns around his hands and face. Nothing serious but they'll be painful for several days. He's going to need bed rest for a week."

"But we have a race next Sunday—" Will started, but the doctor stopped him with a raised hand.

"I can't tell you what to do. But I don't think he'll feel like turning over in bed for a week or two, much less driving a racecar. You'll need to have him checked out by a doctor when you get him back home. Even when the soreness and stiffness go away, you're still going to have to deal with that ankle. He's not going to be able to drive for several weeks, I'd guess."

The doctor couldn't help but see the panicked look on Will's face.

That was not totally the report he had hoped for. And he already dreaded giving Rob the news, too. They were locked in a tight battle for "Rookie of the Year." Missing races this late in the season would most certainly destroy any chance for Rob to take the honor. The rest of their season flashed before his eyes as he stood there, half listening to the rest of what the doctor was saying.

"Can we see him?" Michelle asked.

"Oh, sure. A familiar face might cheer him up. He's in there now trying to talk us into letting him go back out and drive some more today. Remember, he's in a lot of pain and just a little bit disoriented."

"Can I ride to the hospital with him?"

"Sure," the doctor said and pointed the way to where Rob was still being checked over by some of the staff. "Now one of you better go tell the media how lucky that young man is."

But Michelle had already gone, headed back to where a pale Rob lay on a cot on the far side of the room. She stifled another gasp as she saw him lying there, lines and wires hooked up to him everywhere, breathing oxygen through a mask as the doctors continued to poke and prod him. He gave a slight wave at the sight of her, then another to Will as he pulled the mask from his mouth and nose.

"Hey, guys!" He grimaced as if the mere act of talking made his chest hurt. He was just happy that he could now remember who Will and Michelle were. "I guess I tore up a pretty decent racecar, didn't I?"

"We can build you another one. We're just glad

you're okay, Cowboy," Will said as he watched the doctors begin to place a temporary splint on the broken ankle for the trip to the hospital.

"Beaten but not broken. I'll be good as new in a couple of days," Rob said with a fairly respectable grin.

He didn't wince when the splint went on. Will decided that the painkillers must have kicked in. But they wouldn't even touch the pain Rob was about to feel when he learned the truth about his injuries.

"We got plenty of time to get you healed up. Just make sure you listen to what the docs here are telling you. Don't be your usual hardheaded self, okay?"

"I don't think there's a square inch of me that isn't throbbing right now. But don't you two worry about me. I'll behave. I need to help get the car ready for Watkins Glen. And I need to be in shape, too. That's a tough old course and I've got to be ready for her."

Will almost told him then, but, just in time, the ambulance crew came in to haul him to the hospital. There would be time later. Plenty of time.

The men gently loaded him back onto the stretcher and moved him outside to the ambulance. Michelle followed and then climbed in the back for the short ride over to the hospital. Will stood there watching them until they pulled away and then turned and trotted back to the garage to see how the load-up was going and to make sure everything was being taken care of. He would drive Michelle's rental car over to the hospital after the crew had pulled out and headed for Tennessee.

There was another reason he had not gone to the hospital with Michelle and Rob. The crew chief in him wanted to find out for sure what had happened, what had made a perfectly good racecar take a sudden turn to the wall. He suspected a blown tire, likely cut down by the fender that got bent with the contact earlier in the run. But he had to be absolutely certain it wasn't something over which he had control. He also was extremely curious to see how all the roll bars and safety equipment functioned in the car. From the quick replay he saw, the horrific impact was the best test of the car they had built that he would ever see. At least, he hoped so.

The truth was, though, that the fact that his driver was even slightly hurt only made Will more determined to confirm that they had done everything humanly possible to make the car safe. All teams did the same after their cars were involved in a bad accident. But Will Hughes went way beyond the norm on safety. He could thank Bubba Baxter for that trait. Years before, when Will worked at Lee Racing, Baxter constantly drilled the young mechanic on the importance of a truly safe racecar. Bubba swore that he would never build a car that could get a driver killed, and even after forty years in the sport, he had managed to keep his pledge.

Satisfied everything was being taken care of, Will finally stepped to where the wrecked car waited beneath a tarp in the garage stall. They would need the help of a wrecker to even get the mangled carcass up onto the hauler.

When Will flipped back the cover, his heart fell.

Jesus!

How in the world had the kid survived in this thing?

Suddenly, Will Hughes felt sick, light-headed, and almost lost his balance. He leaned back against a toolbox and tried to shake the dizziness from his head.

Lord, how in the world?

5

The King Air plane banked hard, angling for its final approach into the small airport. Just beyond the runway was Kingsport, Tennessee, and down the way, toward the dark smudge of mountains, lay the tiny town of Chandler Cove. The Sunday morning sun shone brightly as the brilliant green vegetation rushed by below the plane and its passengers.

Rob Wilder wasn't enjoying the scenery, though. He lounged back in one of the plane's seats, his left leg propped up in front of him, hoping that elevating it would belay some of the incessant throbbing pain. He had been mostly still the last half hour, having long since given up on trying to wriggle into some kind of position that didn't cause him to ache all over. The temporary cast on his ankle fit tightly, causing some discomfort, but it didn't hold a candle to all the other twinges and out-and-out agonizing pain that seemed to have sprung up all over his entire body.

The doc back at Indy had not lied. Rob was definitely one sore young racecar driver today!

The trip to the hospital and the ensuing overnight stay had brought at least one bit of good news. Despite the pain and swelling, the ankle fracture was not as bad as they had first feared. All Rob had to do was stay off the thing and it should heal up in four or five weeks without surgery, they said. "Staying off it" definitely meant not pushing a racecar clutch pedal or anything close to it, though. The orthopedic doctor had made that clear.

"Aggravate that thing or make it worse and you'll wear a screw in there for the rest of your days," he had warned.

Rob listened glumly to the prognosis but agreed it made sense. He promised he would do as he had been ordered to do by everybody from the hard-nosed hospital nurse to Billy Winton to Michelle Fagan. He would get plenty of rest and let a doctor back in Chandler Cove look him over in a few days after the swelling went down and some of the bruising went away. Best case, he might be able to drive after a couple of weeks if all went well. And if he was a good patient.

But Rob was not even back home yet and he was already having a problem with the instructions. He would have no problem staying off his feet, taking it easy. Sure, it would be hard not to go out to the garage and help the boys get the car ready. Considering the situation, he could manage that.

But he had no intention of staying out of the racecar. Heck, he might have a sore ankle, but there was nothing wrong with his accelerator foot or his grip on the wheel or the gearshift lever. He would be at Watkins Glen when the track opened. And he had every intention of driving the racecar every time the green flag flew. It would take something much worse than a slightly injured ankle to keep him out of the car on Sunday. The only thing that could get him through all the aches and discomfort he was feeling was the knowledge that he would be right back on the horse that had thrown him, driving the car toward the checkers.

Billy Winton was waiting for them when the plane taxied up to the general aviation hut. It had been a rare weekend for him, one in which he had not actually been at the track where his team was running. He had been laid low with a bad case of the flu and decided he would be more of a hindrance than a help at the racetrack. He was watching the Indy race on television while recuperating and, when he saw the wreck replayed over and over, he felt absolutely miserable. Even worse than he already felt with his alternating fever and chills.

But even before the crash, and for the first time since he had fired up this race team, Billy had actually been mentally questioning his wisdom in doing so after so many years of retirement. Now that he was involved full bore in this wild and woolly sport once again, he was reminded almost daily how expensive the game had become. It was even much more excessive than it had been when he was with Jodell Lee's team only a few short years before.

Ensoft was a great sponsor. They paid him plenty of money for the deal and had never balked at adding more if Billy requested it. But the cold, hard fact was that the seemingly unlimited dollars the multicar teams could rely on nowadays made it almost impossible for the single-car teams to compete. The old adage that money buys speed still applied, and was maybe even more applicable now than it had been back in the early days of racing. But Billy Winton refused to do anything halfway, and that often led to his spending more of his own money than he had planned to do when he started the venture.

Despite his fever and stuffed-up head and money

worries, Billy was suddenly feeling much better when the cameras showed his car take the lead at Indy. But then, he watched in horror as the bright red racecar took a sudden turn up the track and slammed hard into the wall. Not only was he sick as a dog, not only was his team mired in a financial quagmire, but he may have just witnessed his charismatic young driver getting himself killed right there in living color on national television. It was an absolutely horrific crash, one of the hardest stops Billy had ever seen.

He could only pace around the room while the television coverage showed the wreck over and over, then the cleanup, and his driver being hauled away in an ambulance. He coughed, paced some more, sneezed, and finally flopped back onto his sofa in utter relief when the track doctor reported on the tube that the kid would be okay. Never mind that his expensive racecar looked as though it had been crushed in a compactor. The kid was all right.

Now it was Sunday, the day after the crash. With his flu finally getting better, he had called a hasty meeting for later in the day with his accountant and attorney to go over the team's budget. They needed to try to find another revenue stream they could exploit, another angle they could take to maintain their momentum.

That was the ironic thing. The Ensoft team was running very well at this point in the season, the previous day's catastrophe notwithstanding. They were a good threat to actually win a race any week now, as the showing at Indy proved. Their driver was a marketing dream with his easy manner, movie-star features, and uncanny driving ability, and he was a good bet for "Rookie of the Year." Billy certainly didn't want a lack of resources or empty coffers to hold the team back now that they were finally peaking.

Of course, there was another fly in the ointment now. He had himself a hurting driver. How would that affect their efforts? That was a question Billy and everyone else connected with the Ensoft team would have to answer, and answer very quickly. And how he found the dispositions of his driver and crew chief when they climbed out of the King Air plane would be the first indication of what that answer might be.

The plane eased to a halt and the turboprop engines were shut off. The pilot waved at Billy through the cockpit window and then began looking over his final checklist. The fuselage door opened and the copilot dropped down the set of narrow aluminum steps. Michelle was first to appear in the doorway, waving to Billy before moving onto the steps so she could help Rob down. Billy rushed over to lend a hand, too. The last thing they needed now was for their driver to break his neck trying to hobble down the airplane stairs!

"Hey, kid!" Billy shouted hoarsely as Rob hobbled up to stand unsteadily in the narrow doorway. "How ya feelin'?"

"Like I been riding around inside a cement mixer. But I'll be fine, Billy. I'll be fine in a day or so."

The youngster's face was pale and there was an obvious wince of pain as he hunched over to move through the door. It was the kind of response Billy expected. The kid was hurting but he wasn't going to readily admit it.

That reminded Billy of another hardheaded young driver he had once known. Jodell Bob Lee was just as tough and just as likely to keep the pain to himself. Lee had hit the wall at Talladega during practice the year the giant track opened and that was the only crash Billy could remember that slowed him down at all. Rob Wilder's wreck the day before had been eerily similar. And from what Will had told him over the phone, the young driver's injuries were similar to what Jodell had suffered in that crash over thirty years before.

"Here, let us help you. We don't want you falling down and breaking that other leg."

For once Rob didn't argue. He steadied himself with an arm on Michelle's shoulder while Billy helped him down the narrow stairs. Once they reached the bottom, Rob rested, allowing Billy to support his weight while Michelle climbed back up into the plane to retrieve his crutches.

"Sore?"

"Pretty much. I don't think there's much of me that won't be part of a giant bruise. I didn't think you could hit a wall that hard."

"It looked pretty bad on TV."

"*You* thought it looked bad. You should have seen it from where I was watching! We were running along so good and then, the next thing I know, the car just stopped. It felt like those belts must have stretched half a foot or more."

"You're lucky, kid. Real lucky. I was afraid you were gonna burn up in that thing. It seemed like it took you forever to get out."

"I hit so hard it knocked me silly. All I wanted to do was just sit there and let the darkness suck me in." Rob looked up to make sure Michelle was still out of earshot. "Billy, I heard that voice again. Right before the tire cut down, it told me to hang on, like it knew something bad was about to happen. Then, while I was taking my little nap, it screamed at me to get out of the car. If I had been another fifteen or twenty seconds gathering my thoughts, you'd be looking at one deep-fried racecar driver."

"You and those ghost voices," Billy said, shaking his head. "Sometimes all that ghost talk you and Jodell carry on goes a little too far. You hear me?"

"I hear you, Billy. But it's not me. Sometimes I hear that Virginia drawl when I'd just as soon not be bothered."

Michelle bounded down the plane's steps then,

anxious to get Rob back on his crutches.

"Well, Michelle, what do you say we get old Hop-along moving so we can get him somewhere to rest and start growing back together?"

As they headed for Billy's big town car, Rob was already requesting that they stop at Latham's Barbe-cue when they got to Chandler Cove. That was a good sign. He was craving an inside-sliced pork sandwich and was certain that was the very medicine his sore and bruised body needed.

The next day, Rob lay sprawled on the couch in his apartment, futilely trying to dial in something decent to watch on the television. The shows all seemed to be folks screaming at each other or silly celebrities talking about themselves and how great they were. Even the race the sports channel was rerunning was one he had watched a dozen times from Billy Winton's extensive tape collection.

But it wasn't the television that had him so out of sorts. He actually hurt worse today than he had at any time since the Indy crash. The day before, he vowed to Billy and Michelle as he finished up the barbecue sandwich that he fully intended to show up at the shop this day. But when he tried to crawl out of bed that morning, the couch was about as far as he could make it.

It hurt to stand up. It hurt to try to pull the crutches under his arms. It hurt to hobble across the room to the sofa. It hurt to simply lie there and punch the remote control. Shoot, it hurt to blink his eyes!

Michelle had come by to check on him earlier, then she took off for the shop so she could try and get a little work done from there. She was not a bad mother hen, but Rob was actually glad to have her out of his hair for a while. Lately, she was spending more and more of her time on the East Coast, and a good por-tion of it right there in Chandler Cove. She finally decided to relinquish some of her other marketing duties at Ensoft so she could concentrate on the company's major push into motor sports marketing. Ensoft was more than pleased with their first foray into racing and they were looking for more ways to capitalize on the added exposure they were getting, both on and off the track.

Rob normally appreciated Michelle's friendship, her company, her obvious affection for him, and even her tendency to mother him. It went a long way toward filling a major void in his life. Rob Wilder had been mostly self-sufficient since his early teens, necessarily caring for himself, alone except for the friends who helped him crew his old junker racecar. The nice little things Michelle was always doing for him actually touched him deeply. He'd never had anyone do something for him simply to be nice, or because they truly wanted to. Though he couldn't understand why, it was obvious that Michelle cared for him as far more than the driver of the racecar her company happened to bankroll.

And sometimes, she seemed to care for him as something more than simply her sister's boyfriend, too.

Still, after putting up with her well-intentioned nursemaiding since Saturday's wreck, Rob was ready for a couple of hours' respite. He was bright enough to know that he had scared her deeply, that she was still not over the fright she had suffered when he had plowed into the wall. But whatever her kind intentions, she had more than worn out her welcome at the hospital in Indy and on the plane coming home. She had treated him like an invalid, a helpless soul on his last legs. She wouldn't allow him to do anything on his own, even when he told her he wanted to move around to keep from stiffening up.

He aimlessly flipped through the channels, jumping quickly from one inane show to another, trying to find something besides talk shows and soap operas. His stomach grumbled and he thought about trying to climb up on the crutches, angling over to the telephone on the far wall, and ordering himself a pizza. But before he could begin the move, there was a knock at the apartment's front door.

"Dang it, Michelle!" he snorted, using about the strongest language he ever employed.

He didn't remember her locking the door when she left that morning. She would have left it unlocked so she could pop back in and check on him without him having to let her in. Rob fumbled with the metal crutches and slowly pulled himself up off the couch. He hopped on his good leg until he could pull the crutches beneath his arms and cross toward the door. He'd have to lose these things soon. They were more trouble than they were worth.

Then, there was the light knock at the door again.

"Coming, Michelle! Just give me a minute," he yelled, hopefully loud enough that she could hear.

Once at the door, he fumbled with the latch before he realized the door was, in fact, unlocked. Why didn't she just come on in? He swung the door open, ready to give Michelle a good broadside for making him get up and let her in.

"I can't believe . . ." he started, but it was not Michelle standing there, after all.

There was a slight, older, light-haired woman, a gentle smile on her lips. She held in her hand a basket covered with a kitchen towel.

Catherine Lee. Catherine, of course, was Jodell's wife. She was another one who had taken it upon herself to keep an eye on young Rob Wilder since the first day Billy had brought him to East Tennessee. He was a frequent dinner guest at the Lee household whenever his schedule would allow. The grandkids, Jodell's daughter's kids, loved Rob, too, and the way he played and wrestled all over the house with them, Catherine and Jodell sometimes wondered if Rob might still be more comfortable acting their age instead of his.

Jodell enjoyed Rob's visits because he saw so much of himself in the young man, not only in the way he drove a racecar, but in his demeanor, his dedication, his desire to always win at anything he tried to do. For his part, Rob never missed an opportunity for a home-cooked meal and rarely left when he didn't tote a care package of leftovers home with him for the next day's supper. But he also loved the company. Not just Jodell's racing stories and advice, but the feeling of sitting around a table with a real family, a group of folks who truly enjoyed being with each other. It was something Rob Wilder had never experienced before and it was a most pleasant thing to experience whenever he could.

"Mrs. Lee? Well, what a surprise! How are you, ma'am?"

"I'm fine, thank you. I thought you might be hungry and in the mood for something besides a sandwich so I fixed you a good, hot lunch."

"That is so kind of you. Where's my manners? Come on in."

He twisted around on his crutches, trying to hold the door open for her. In the process, he almost lost his balance, forcing him to drop a crutch and grab the door facing to keep from falling out into the hallway and flat onto his face.

Catherine helped him steady himself then stepped back.

"You just go on over there and sit back down. You need to be getting plenty of rest anyway. I'll take this in the kitchen and warm it up and put it on a plate for you."

"I appreciate it. Michelle, bless her heart, tries, but cooking real food isn't necessarily one of her many talents."

"Now, honey, she means well. And she's been worried to death about you. You're all she could talk about last night when she got in. We must have stayed up at least an hour or more past our bedtime. She wanted to talk it out, I guess. And it seemed to help her to have someone to talk with about the wreck."

Lately, Michelle Fagan had been staying in one of the guest rooms at Jodell Lee's place when she was in Chandler Cove. They had taken her in as if she were merely one more grandkid or race crewmember. And she had quickly adopted Jodell and Catherine as her East Coast set of parents.

"I know, Mrs. Lee. I realize she means well, but you know she . . ." Rob began but then thought better of what he was about to say.

Catherine Lee looked around the corner at him.

"That girl really cares about you, Robbie. If you weren't dating her sister, I'd say it would be a match made in heaven, you two."

"But Mrs. Lee—"

"How many times am I going to have to tell you it's 'Catherine,' not 'Mrs. Lee,' " she called as she slid one of the dishes she had bought into the oven.

"Okay . . . Catherine. I'm appreciative of what she's doing, but I've got a race to run this weekend. All her 'mother hen' stuff is keeping me from getting any rest at all. If I don't get healed up real quick then I'll never be able to run the car this weekend. Billy and Will and the boys on the team are counting on me and I can't let them down again."

She glanced around the corner again and grinned at him but let the last of the remark pass. Jodell always blamed himself too when the car got into a crash, whether it was his fault or not. "I was drivin' the fool thing when it hit, wadn't I?" he'd usually grouse.

"You just need to sit back and relax a bit," Catherine advised. "You let Michelle do her thing and you just take it easy. It'll all work out." She sang softly to herself as she adjusted the control on the stove. "And about racing. You drive that car when you're ready and not before. The boys in the shop know you're banged up. You can't do the team any good if you go out and try to drive when you can't. If you're ready this weekend, then fine. If you're not, the bravest thing you can do is to tell them so or you'll really let them down. Remember, I've lived a lot of years with an ornery old racecar driver myself."

"I guess you're right, Mrs. . . . uh . . . Catherine. I just don't want to consider the possibility of me not racing this weekend."

"Well, just remember what I told you, and it's based on a lot of years of doing this. I'm going up to Watkins Glen this weekend myself. It's such a beautiful, peaceful place between races, not what you expect when you think of New York at all. So I'm giving you fair warning that I intend to keep a close eye on you, young man." She seemed to suddenly think of something and stepped into the living room, still wiping her hands with a dishtowel. "Oh, yes. I meant to tell you. Bob junior is coming over from the city to spend the weekend with us at the track. He hasn't done that in at least four or five years. Come to one of the tracks, that is."

Rob perked up. Bob junior was Jodell and Catherine's son. Rob thought it odd that he had never met the man, not at the Lee house nor at any of the tracks. They always spoke of him fondly, proudly, and there didn't seem to be any typical family problems going on, but Bob never seemed to come for a visit with his folks. The kid couldn't imagine such a thing. If he had parents like Jodell and Catherine Lee, he wouldn't let them out of his sight.

Rob knew Bob junior was an investment banker on Wall Street or something like that, but he still remained something of a mysterious figure. Jodell and Catherine sometimes talked about him as if he were their only child, much to the dismay of their daughter, Glynn, the mother of their grandchildren. And sometimes it seemed as if he were almost mythical, bigger than life.

"You mean I'm finally going to get to meet him?"

"You get rested up good and we'll see how it goes at the Glen. I'm going to put Jodell on you when he gets back from his trip. Promise me this. If you're not ready to drive when we get to New York, you'll tell Will and Billy and stay out of the car. I don't want you to hurt yourself any worse."

"I will, Catherine. I promise. But this is what I do. I don't know what I would do if I couldn't race."

They talked then while Jodell ate the delicious lunch she had brought him. Rob subtly probed her to tell him more about Bob junior, but Catherine seemed to dance around his questions. Finally, worn out from the pain, Rob stopped pushing and enjoyed the food and Catherine Lee's company.

The phone rang after a while. Catherine waved him off and picked it up for him, answering cheerfully.

"Hello? Oh, he's doing fine since he got some of my fried chicken and biscuits in him. I keep trying to get him to take a nap but all he wants to do is talk. Imagine that."

Rob wondered who it could be.

"It's for you," Catherine finally said and passed the phone over to him, winking at him.

"Hello?" he answered cautiously, then smiled broadly. "Christy! I thought you were working all day or I would've called. I was going to wait until tonight."

Catherine made sure he saw her retreat to the kitchen to clean up and afford him some privacy. But as she cleared away the dishes and put them into the dishwasher, she fished her cell phone out of her purse and dialed a long-distance number.

"Robert Lee," barked the impatient voice on the other end of the line.

"You're still Bob junior to me," Catherine said. "And you always will be."

She could picture him, sitting there in his high-rise office. He would be decked out in his tailored suit, wide suspenders, the shirt still buttoned at the collar and the tie still knotted perfectly. He would be talking to her from behind his massive desk that looked to be the size of her whole kitchen back home, his perch overlooking the canyons of Wall Street through his full-glass office wall. That's where she had seen him, almost a year before, the last time they had visited.

"Mom! What's up?"

"Not much, honey. I won't keep you but a minute. I'm fixing lunch for Rob Wilder and thought I would call and check on what time you were planning on meeting us Friday?"

There was that pause that she had come to know so well. Plans had changed. Something had come up. Her stomach fell.

"Aw, Mom, change of plans. I've got a late meeting Friday afternoon I can't blow off so I thought I would wait and drive up Saturday morning. I should be there around lunchtime."

"I was hoping you could make it up Friday so we could all go out to dinner together. But that's okay. Your dad will be so excited to see you. It's all he's talked about for the last week or so. He misses you, you know."

"Well, Mom, don't forget he's the one who wouldn't let me anywhere near racing in the first place. Wouldn't even hear of me coming to the garage or hanging around the track for fear I'd climb in a car and get hooked like I'd taken a drug or something. A master's degree in finance doesn't do much good if you're planning on working in a race shop or driving a car."

"You know your father only wanted you to have your own career. He always felt like he would be forcing you to race if you stayed too close to it. He'd love to have you around the shop sometimes now, I bet."

There was another short pause on the phone then.

"Sometimes, Mom, when I'm dealing with some of the things I have to deal with here, I wish I were back at the shop, helping Uncle Joe and Bubba get a car ready to race. New York's okay but it's not the mountains back home." Catherine could clearly hear his sigh. "Are Bubba and Uncle Joe coming, too?"

"Yes. I don't think Joe is going to come in until Saturday but Bubba's riding up with the hauler. They both can't wait to see you. Neither can I. Well, honey, I need to put what's left of Rob's lunch in the fridge and be on my way."

"How is Rob? I saw the crash on television. It looked like he took an awful lick."

"He's pretty sore. Broke his ankle, but they say he'll be fine. And he swears he'll drive Sunday, broken ankle and all."

"Sounds just like another hardheaded racecar driver that we both know and love dearly."

"Yes. Yes, it does. I'll see you Saturday. Love you."

"Bye, Mom! Miss you."

Far from Chandler Cove, Tennessee, in an office suite on the thirtieth floor of a high-rise building on the lower tip of Manhattan, Bob Lee Jr. dropped the telephone handset into the cradle next to the other three phones on his desk. He leaned back in his plush chair and rocked for a moment as he watched a jetliner angle in toward LaGuardia out there beyond the East River.

He had just come as close to lying to his mother as he ever had in his life.

But then, before he even had a chance to think about it, the buzzer on his desk intercom shrieked at him, two lights on one of his telephones blinked demandingly, and the beeper on his belt began screeching at him, all simultaneously. He shook his head and tried to grin.

Was this really the way he wanted to spend the rest of his life? He knew his father would never understand how desperately he wanted to return to his roots. But Bob Lee Jr. also knew that now was finally the time. The time to see if he really had what it took to make that fateful step.

Without hesitation, he ignored the flashing lights, the piercing buzzer, the insistent beeper. Rocking forward in the big chair, he reached, picked up one of the telephones that wasn't pealing, and punched in a number.

6

Joe Banker sat at the console to the engine dynamometer, lost in deep concentration. He was ready to test the engine that his assistant had just finished setting up on the stand on the other side of the heavy glass wall in front of him. Banker's dark hair and trim physique belied his age. It would be hard to convince a visitor to Banker's engine shop that this man was on the right side of sixty, that he had been around serious racing for better than forty years, that he had been building high-performance racing engines for three decades' worth of stock car champions.

Now, as he pored over the checklist in front of him to set up the parameters he wanted to measure in the computer, there was one telltale sign of his age, of his longtime proximity to grumbling, ear-piercing racing engines. When the telephone hanging on the wall not five feet from where he sat suddenly jingled, he had to stop, cock his head sideways for a moment, and listen carefully before he could tell for certain that it was ringing.

"What now?" he said in frustration as he got up to answer the blamed thing.

Seemed to him as if the device had been ringing all dang morning and it was usually bad news. Parts supplier couldn't get the engine blocks he needed to him by the time he needed them. One of the marginal race teams he worked with had blown up through sheer carelessness one of the best engines he had ever built and now they wanted to blame him for it. Now, he was behind on this project and wanted to get the first run of this particular engine before he broke for lunch. Another dadgum telephone call with some other tangled-up problem to have to deal with that was not exactly on his schedule right now.

Everyone else had already gone off to lunch. It could be some business or better news on those engine blocks. Joe Banker had to answer the fool thing. All the boys in the shop knew not to bother him when he was in the dyno room. And, in a second, so would the poor feller on the other end of the telephone line!

He yanked the headset off the hook, more than ready to give a piece of his mind to whoever it was that dared to disturb him.

"Hello!" he spat into the phone, the patented scowl on his face matching his mood perfectly, as if the caller could see through the phone how irritated Joe was at the interruption.

But when he heard the voice on the other end of the line, he lost the frown immediately and replaced it with some semblance of a smile. Joe tapped the wall with his pencil as he first exchanged pleasantries with the caller. Then, as he listened, he broke into a full grin.

"Yeah, I suppose I could come up a day early if you need me to." He said the words almost in a growl but he still listened some more. And the smile never left his face. "Naw, you know I won't tell your daddy nothing. But I'll say this. I'll be glad to help you out all I can however I can with whatever it is, but I ain't wadin' into the middle of no fight between you and Jodell now. That's your battle, young'un."

Then, as the voice on the phone went on, Joe Banker leaned back against the wall and wondered how he could manage the logistics of what he had just promised to do. He would work it out, though. Except for the part where he knew he would be going behind the back of his cousin, Jodell Lee. He had no idea what was so mysterious about what he was being asked to help out with, but he didn't want to be seen as guilty of aiding and abetting when whatever it was blew up some way.

And blow up it would. Blow up as sure as if somebody tossed a handful of grit into the craw of a perfectly humming engine. It was one tough assignment to try to do something behind Jodell Lee's back, no matter who the instigator was or the nature of the thing.

But if he were needed, he would go. Especially for the person who was asking him to.

"Let me make some arrangements," he said. "I'll let you know when I can get in there. Why don't you give me a call tomorrow and I'll let you know what I can work out?"

When Joe softly replaced the telephone on its hook, he could only stand there for a moment and look at it, shaking his head, a wry grin on his face. Finally, he settled back into the chair at the dyno console. But before he went back to work, he quickly scribbled some notes to himself on a pad. Then he sat there a bit longer, idly tapping the top of the console with his pencil, thinking.

He couldn't help but wonder what Jodell would think about what he was about to do. But he had a pretty decent idea.

It didn't matter, though. The boy had come right out and requested his assistance on something that was bothering him. That had to be a difficult thing for the young man to do after all this time. It had taken some nerve on his part to ask Joe Banker for help. But why had he come to him instead of his daddy?

Suddenly, Joe shook his head, stood back up, went over to the phone, and punched a well-used button on the speed dial. Sally Gossom answered on the first ring.

"Honey, how you doin'?" he asked at the cheery sound of her voice.

Sally was their travel secretary. She made all the team's arrangements when they were on the road.

"I'm just gettin' over that same flu Billy Winton's got. I don't know who gave it to who."

"That's what you get for smoochin' with that old redheaded son of a—"

"You hush, Joe Banker, before I come over there and take a tire tool to your knotty old head."

"Sally, I hate to bother you but I need you to change my tickets for this weekend. I need to leave Friday morning instead of Saturday. And I need a flight into New York City instead. I got something I got to do in the city Friday and I'll meet up with the others at the track Saturday like I planned in the first place."

"You'll need a rental car, then," she offered.

"Naw. Naw, I got a ride over to the track. And one last thing. Don't mention this little change of plans to anybody else. 'Specially Jodell. If anybody asks, just tell 'em you don't know when I'm going up. Okay?"

"No problem, Joe. You know I can keep a secret."

Sally was more than accustomed to Joe Banker's unusual travel habits so his request for secrecy wasn't at all a surprise. Besides, there had always seemed to be a sort of running skirmish going on between Joe and Jodell as long as she had known them, and that stretched for most of thirty years. She knew better than to even try to speculate on what might be going on this time.

Joe hung up the phone and settled back into the seat at the dyno one more time. He flipped a couple of switches and fired up the engine, then watched through the glass as the big, powerful motor hummed along. He advanced the throttle while he watched the power curve on the computer monitor next to him. All the while he was studying how the engine responded as he gave it a little more throttle, pushed it a bit harder, until he was forcing all the horsepower out of it that he could.

Still, it sang beautifully, running big and strong, just the way it was born to do. That's what Joe loved so much about building these brawny engines. He loved seeing them do what they were born to do once he was finished with them.

But now, as he worked, Joe tried to shove the phone call out of his mind, to pay attention to the engine and how it performed. But he couldn't help it. He was about to put one big strain on sixty years' worth of a kinship that went far beyond blood.

But he knew too that he had absolutely no choice in the thing at all. He had to do it and let the chips fall where they may.

7

Rob Wilder limped across the tarmac, still struggling with using his crutches as he slowly made his way to the waiting King Air. Michelle trailed alongside him, carrying their bags, talking all the way. The plane sat there waiting patiently for them outside the flight service at the airport, still in practically the same place where they had left it the previous Sunday. The narrow steps were already folded down invitingly, ready for boarding, ready for the trip to New York. The pilots were finishing up their preflight checks as they waited for all three of the passengers to board. Rob and Michelle were the first two to show up.

Rob still hobbled along on crutches but he felt infinitely better, even more than he had a mere two days before. The extra day between the Saturday run at Indy and the coming Sunday race at Watkins Glen could not have come at a better time for the Ensoft team. Its driver had spent the previous afternoon at the doctor's office, getting fitted for a more mobile cast. The doctor had reluctantly cleared him to race this weekend, but the okay came with a stern warning. Rob was pushing his recovery and it could hurt him down the road.

The old doctor knew only too well what he was dealing with, though. Having treated Jodell Lee and his various racing scrapes and breaks down through the years, he was used to racecar drivers and their peculiarities, familiar with how stubborn this breed of man could be. Thankfully, the kid was in exceptional shape, even for someone his age. The bumps and bruises would still be around for a few more days, just enough to keep the youngster aggravated and frustrated. The fracture, while painful, was still manageable if he watched what he did. The primary risk was in his taking another hard lick in an accident at Watkins Glen.

Rob had already been worrying about how he was going to work the clutch as he navigated the twisting, winding road course. It would be necessary to shift from gear to gear several times every time he went around. Part of the problem was solved with the Jerrico transmission. It could usually be up- and down-shifted without clutching. The difficulty came in using the clutch to start and stop the car when coming into the pits. The hectic seconds could be agonizing ones for the young driver when he was forced to use the foot with the fractured ankle.

Rob and Will spent a long evening in the shop one night rearranging the clutch and brake pedals to make sure there would be room to depress the clutch without the bulk of the cast on his left ankle getting in the way. That would allow him to work the pedal without actually putting pressure on the ankle itself. Will lay on the floorboard of the racecar just before it was loaded on the hauler for the long trip to New York. He fiddled with the placement of the clutch pedal, then climbed out and had Rob try it. Then he would adjust it a half-inch more and see how that worked. After an hour of trying, Will was finally satisfied with the pedal placement, long after Rob tried to tell him that it was plenty good enough.

The boys in the crew stood around, patiently waiting for Will's pronouncement that the car was ready. Then they could get it loaded up onto the truck and get started on their long trip. Rob stood there, leaning on his crutch, as the car was pushed onto the ramp and hoisted carefully up into its spot in the top of the trailer. Will tried to shoo him home while the crew finished up but Rob wanted to stay around to see the truck and hauler on its way.

Will only shook his head. He needed a rested, comfortable driver for Sunday's race.

Rob was indeed rested but not necessarily comfortable as he settled into a seat on the plane next to Michelle. He continued to ache from all the bruises and contusions he still wore like battle wounds. A week of lying around his apartment after the frantic pace of the last year had been welcome at first, but it had become downright maddening by the last couple of days.

Rob Wilder was ready to go to a racetrack. Michelle immediately noticed the upswing in his disposition when she stopped by early that morning to pick him up for breakfast and the trip to the airport. All he could talk about was getting back into the racecar.

"I'm ready to climb back up on that bronco and I'll hold on better this time," he declared with a crooked grin once they were settled on the plane.

"Yeah, but how are you feeling?"

His skin color looked better, his eyes were no longer dull with pain, but he still sat sideways in the seat and seemed to be having trouble getting the ankle situated in a comfortable position.

"Pretty good, I guess. I think I'm about as sore

from sitting on my butt all week as I am from running into that old wall."

"You sure you're ready to do this?"

"More than ready. I can't tolerate being laid up. I've got to be doing something. I'd take a dozen aspirins and have Will and them strap me in the car in a hospital bed if that's what it took to run Sunday."

"I think that's what Billy is afraid of."

"Y'all worry too much, Michelle. I'm fine. This leg is the only thing slowing me down. Once I get in the car, I'll be okay what with the way Will rearranged the pedals for me."

He could see the questioning concern in her eyes. He knew she still had no concept of what drove men like him to race a car right out there on the ragged edge, to do whatever it took to win no matter how bad the hurt might be. And he also knew he didn't have the words to explain it to her. Maybe she'd get the message someday.

"I still don't see why you don't give it one more week and let Billy get a relief driver this week," she said, her eyes narrowed for emphasis.

"If I didn't think I could drive the car well enough to win then I would never try. I'll be fine come Sunday. You'll see."

Will had climbed into the plane by then and was up front, talking with the pilots. Rob hoped he couldn't hear his and Michelle's conversation. He didn't want him to get any ideas about a replacement driver.

"I don't believe you," she stated matter-of-factly, suddenly turning serious. "You just said you'd race from a hospital bed if Will would bolt it in the car for you."

"You know I wouldn't drive if I thought I couldn't safely operate the thing," he told her.

He appreciated her concern. He really did. And he knew it came from the heart, from her affection for him. A sponsor representative would typically be the last person to try to talk a young, star driver out of his car for a big race. But Michelle was speaking her mind out of friendship and sincere worry.

"Prove it to me."

She looked him straight in the eyes. Her own blue eyes were wide, deep, and dead serious.

"Look, Michelle, I will make you a promise. When we get there and get the car off the hauler, I'll go out and take a few laps." His eyes never left hers. "If I can't drive the thing like I need to, if I don't think I have a legitimate chance at winning, I'll climb out of that old Ford and tell Will to find somebody else to drive it on Sunday. I promise on a stack of Catherine Lee's flapjacks."

Michelle still looked skeptical, though, likely assuming he was only trying to humor her. He had lowered his voice on the last part so Will wouldn't hear him. She knew him well enough to know he would drive as long as he had a breath left. She studied his face intently and he finally shifted uncomfortably under her gaze.

"Do you promise me?"

"Yes, I promise you. If I can't drive, I won't."

The pilot fired up one of the engines then and that drowned out any further conversation for the moment. Rob was thankful for the respite.

He glanced out the plane's window, toward where the brilliant sun was trying to pull its lazy self up above the mountains that piled up to their east like quilts on a bed. But when he turned back toward her, Michelle was still studying him intensely.

What made this bright, handsome young man do what he did? she wondered. And do it so intensely, even when he was so obviously hurting? Lord knows it wasn't the money. Half the time he didn't even cash Billy Winton's checks until Billy fussed at him for messing up his bookkeeping. He still drove the rusted-out, battered old pickup truck he had nursed all the way over from Hazel Green the day he joined Billy's team for good. The only new clothes he wore were the ones she had pressured him to buy, or picked up for him herself, so he would have something presentable to wear for appearances and to dinner with clients.

He seemed to enjoy his celebrity so far. That was obvious. But that wasn't why he risked his life to try to lead the field to the checkered flag week in and week out. There had to be more than that that drove him so relentlessly to excel.

He was still such a little boy in so many ways. She studied him even now as he watched wide-eyed the plane ahead of them on the taxiway as it revved its engines and rolled away to its takeoff. He never watched with such fascination the horde of young women who now seemed to always be following him around. He could take or leave the autograph seekers, the media people, or the dignitaries and stars that now sought him out.

The car, the track, the garage. That's all that seemed to capture his attention. That and winning. Always the quest for the victory.

Would he keep his promise to her? Yes, she suspected he would. But she also knew it would not be easy for him if he had to admit he was not fit to drive the car.

She vowed then to say something to both Billy and Jodell when they followed later in the day on Jodell's plane. Jodell Lee seemed to be the only person who could get through to Rob sometimes.

Him and those stupid ghosts of his.

She smiled as she watched Rob close his eyes tightly as they took off, his knuckles white as he gripped the armrests hard and gritted his teeth. He always got nervous flying. This fearless man who casually took a car through a racetrack corner at close to two hundred miles per hour was still skittish about traveling in an airplane.

What in the world am I doing here? she suddenly thought with a shake of her long blond hair. Who would ever have believed that I'd have to compete with all these oddball distractions just for the attention of a man?

A bright red car?

A sixty-year-old racecar jockey?

A sack full of Southern-fried ghosts?

It was enough to give a girl a complex!

8

Will Hughes stood there, rocking from one foot to the other, watching the team's truck driver carefully maneuver the hauler trailer into its spot next to the garage area. He was on edge, nervous almost to the point of nausea as he impatiently waited. He was past ready to get started with the preparations on the car for the first tech inspection. The road courses were always tricky to set the car up for. Now, he not only had that to worry about, but he also had a busted-up driver to get set up, as well.

There had been no courses back in engineering school for that part of the job.

Will still harbored serious doubts as to whether Rob would be up to the task, physically or mentally. Not only would the kid have to maneuver a heavy, powerful machine over a strenuous course all afternoon, but he would also have to bounce back from his first serious injury, his first really close call. Nobody, not even Will and the others who had lived with this young man for the better part of two years now, could be sure how he would respond once he was strapped back onto that bucking bull and set loose out there in that high-octane rodeo.

Billy Winton had been adamant in his refusal to even discuss having a relief driver standing by. And not just for the race on Sunday. Not for practice and qualifying, either.

"Billy, I've had three good drivers approach me and volunteer. It won't cost us anything to have one of them be ready and suited up."

"Listen to your driver, Will. He'll tell you if he can't go. Then we'll get somebody if we absolutely have to."

"What would it hurt to just be ready? Like a spare ignition or an extra set of tires?"

"We got to trust our driver, Will. If we got a spare driver hanging around the garage, he's gonna know we don't trust him to tell us the truth." Billy grinned then. "And besides, I got a feeling he's going to be able to go Sunday. I just have a strong feeling it's gonna take more than a bum ankle and a little collision with a wall to keep that kid down."

And Will Hughes knew, deep inside, that Billy was right. Still, he was the crew chief and he could worry about it if he wanted to.

Billy reminded him many times that Rob Wilder was of a different breed than many of the new, young drivers who were trying to break into the circuit. This slim, blond-haired youngster seemed to be more a throwback, a leftover from the old school, from the rough-and-tumble fifties and sixties. He lived to race a car and that was it. The money, the women, the fame that seemed to draw the others into the sport appeared to mean little or nothing to Wilder. It seemed even his girlfriend was an afterthought when it was time to crawl into that car. When it came time to concentrate on racing, that's precisely what he did. Glory, money, fame, Christy Fagan way out there in California . . . they all faded away when it came time to think of shocks, sway bars, and tire pressures, of braking points and inside passes.

A little old fractured ankle or frightening memories of the car suddenly deserting him in a split-second crash wouldn't deter this kid from running a race.

Michelle swung the rental car up to the hotel entrance, hopped out and ran around to open the passenger-side door. Rob fought with the revolving doorway to the lobby that kept trying to knock the crutches away from him, to capture him and drag him around and around. When he finally got out of its clutches, he hobbled clumsily over to where she waited. He still had trouble maneuvering about on the crutches and then, even as he tried as hard as he could to be smooth and nonchalant for her, he missed a step with one of the cussed things, almost falling head-foremost into the open car door.

Michelle grabbed him, steadied him, then took the crutches from him and gave him a hand settling awkwardly into the seat.

"Look at you. You can't even get into a regular car without almost breaking your fool neck. Tell me. How do you think you're ever going to be able to climb in and drive that racecar?"

"I was doing just fine until you tried to trip me, thank you," he snapped.

"Fine at almost breaking your neck."

"I am trying to *not* break my neck," he growled, his irritation growing. He truly hoped he would not have to spend the entire weekend up until the green flag fighting with her.

"I'm just pointing out the obvious, that's all. You'd be in a world of hurt if you didn't have me along to nursemaid you."

"Nursemaid that's constantly . . ." he started, but

then stopped before he mentioned "nagging" and "doting" and "annoying the slobber out of me." "I can get along fine by myself, thank you very much."

"Just say the word and I'll leave you alone." Her blue eyes flashed angrily when she looked over at him. "I have plenty of work that I've been neglecting this week while I was looking after you, trying to make you as comfortable as I could."

He dropped his head.

"Aw, Michelle. I . . . uh . . . that's not what I mean. I'm sorry. I'm trying to focus on this race, on driving the car. You know how I am. I don't want to keep getting reminded that I might not be able to race."

"I know. It's like I've tried to tell you before. There are more things than driving a racecar on any particular Sunday. Sometimes you need to at least take a glance at the roses you pass along the way. Even if you don't actually take the time to stop and smell them."

"Okay, okay. I hear you." He was rubbing his rib cage on the left side where the bruises were still black and ugly and constantly aching. He hated it when Michelle or Christy talked common sense to him. Life was much simpler when he could dwell on the car and the track and beating everybody else to the checkers and forget every other little thing. "Now let's just get on over to the racetrack. I bet Will and them are wondering where we're at."

"They're probably wondering why you aren't home in bed where the doctor told you that you ought to be."

Rob bit his tongue before he said something else. He realized he was losing this battle and losing it badly. Anything he said would only keep her going on the subject and he didn't have the strength or desire to keep exchanging potshots with her just now.

Rob was glad to see the entrance to the speedway appear in the windshield then. It was easily the best sight he'd seen in almost a week. He felt a surge of adrenaline as he anticipated finally strapping himself back into the racecar and taking to the serpentine track. And it would also get him out of earshot of Michelle's nagging and out of sight of Will Hughes and his hand-wringing. Now, he was moments from their garage stall, from the sights and smells and noise there that were like an elixir to him. He would even welcome seeing Donnie and Paul and the rest of the guys and being the brunt of their good-natured ribbing.

The number of people, fans, officials, and other folks made the long trip on crutches from the parking area to the garage even longer. So did the members of the other teams who stopped him to ask how he was, to wish him luck. It was a surprise to Rob. He figured no one would have even noticed a gimpy rookie whose claim to fame was tearing up a good racecar the week before. But all of them seemed sincerely glad to see he was up and around and back at the track. Few of them seemed surprised to find out that he planned on driving.

Then Rob spied Stacy Locklear off to one side, talking to a group of people. The sun picked that precise moment to duck behind a passing cloud. Rob steeled himself for the taunts he knew were coming if Locklear saw him. It seemed guys like him never missed the chance to kick a man, and especially when that man was down or weakened in some way.

Rob ducked his head and tried to hop on past unseen. No such luck. Locklear spotted him and rudely broke away from his group to trot over and catch up to him.

Uh-oh, Rob thought. No escape here. He simply was not nimble enough on the crutches to run away.

"Hmmm, what's this?" Locklear sneered, looking sideways at the crutches and the ankle cast. "Has

Pretty Boy done went and growed hisself an extra set of legs here or what?"

Rob could only stand there, waiting for the abuse to truly begin. How far would Locklear push him?

One thing was certain, though. Rob was not about to be intimidated by Stacy Locklear or anybody like him. Crutches or not, he could hold his own with the likes of him. Exactly how, he wasn't sure at that very moment, but he could and he would.

"Yeah, I had myself a hard collision with the wall, Stacy."

Locklear stood back and shook his head. Rob braced himself for the next shot.

"Yeah, it sure looked like it. You really had me worried when I went by and saw the fire."

Now what was this fool up to? He had actually uttered a couple of civil sentences, one right after the other. Rob squinted warily, then pulled his baseball cap down, as if the sun that had just peeked back out from behind the cloud might be in his eyes.

"It wasn't any fun to be in it, I can tell you."

"I bet. I smashed a car up real bad at Dover one time. Backed it into the wall hard as I've ever hit anything. Busted the gas tank and the blamed thing caught fire. Closest I ever come to gettin' scared in a racecar."

Rob cocked his head sideways, still on guard for something vile to suddenly spew forth from this guy.

"I know what you mean. I thought for a minute that I wasn't going to get out myself."

"Well, I'm truly glad to see you're okay, kid. I don't like to see nobody get hurt in a racecar. Even somebody who gets in my way most of the time like you always seem to do."

Even the jab at the end was good-natured, typical race driver talk and delivered with a sincere smile. Rob couldn't believe he was hearing Locklear right. Could he actually have a human side, or was he just setting him up, about to kick a crutch out from under him when he least expected it?

"Uh . . . thanks, Stacy. I think I'm gonna be okay. It makes me feel better just to be back at the racetrack."

Stacy reached over and patted him on the shoulder then. Rob fought the impulse to flinch.

"You take it easy on that leg now. Oh, and stay out of my way out there on the track. I don't wanna have to be pushing no cripple out of my way when you block up the track."

Again, the dig had been lighthearted, totally out of character. Locklear nodded and stepped aside, allowing Rob to continue on his way.

Michelle was just catching up with him. She had stopped to talk to another sponsor rep back by the gate, but she came running when she spotted Stacy Locklear temporarily blocking Rob's path.

"What was that all about?" she asked breathlessly, nodding toward Locklear's back as he swaggered off to greet a clump of fans.

"You wouldn't believe it if I told you," Rob grinned.

"Try me. I can't believe that creep would try to pick a fight with you in the condition you're in."

"Not at all. He just wanted to tell me that he was glad I was okay. He said when he came by the crash Sunday and saw the fire that he was worried about me."

"You're kidding, aren't you?"

"No, really. That's what he said."

"You were right the first time. I don't believe it. Neither would anybody else in this garage. Wait'll Will hears about that."

"Aw, Michelle, maybe he's not the bad guy we've thought he is?"

"I want to hear you say that the next time he runs

over you out there or puts you into the fence. See if you want to join his fan club then!"

More people stopped them as they walked on, including the champion driver from the previous season. It was clear to him why racing was considered to be a family sport. These drivers and their teams might bump each other and fight and argue among themselves, but none of the competitors wanted to see one of their own hurt. And the reception he was getting made Rob feel all the better. Their concern and good wishes gave him a sense of belonging, a feeling that maybe he actually was being accepted into the racing fraternity.

As he hopped away from the latest bunch of well-wishers, Rob thought to himself that this must be what having a real family would be like. And it was a wonderful feeling, too.

Then, finally, they stepped around the corner and into their garage stall. Will, Donnie, and the boys had their bodies sticking out of the racecar at various angles, each man working on something vital. The car itself was sitting there in a shaft of early morning sunlight, its brilliant red paint job gleaming.

And Rob Wilder knew then that the worst week so far in his young racing career was now officially over. Beginning right this minute, he could forget the pain and worry and finally point toward the victory that he would capture on Sunday.

9

Donnie Kline helped Rob work his lanky frame into the open window of the Ford and settle into the seat. The start of the first practice session was only minutes away.

Rob eased down and sat there for a moment. The cockpit felt amazingly comfortable after his careful slide down into the seat, being extra careful not to bump the busted ankle on something and get it to throbbing. He shifted around, working to get himself situated in the padding of the formfitting seat. Gingerly, he stretched out his left leg to test its stiffness. The mobile cast rode along the outside of his leg, outside his driving suit, holding the ankle practically immobile.

Donnie stuck his head through the window.

"How she feel?" he asked.

"Good, so far."

Rob cautiously moved his foot over to the clutch pedal. Donnie watched, studying the clearance between the ankle brace on the cast and the brake pedal.

"You got enough room there?"

"Yeah, I can get to it pretty easy."

"You're not gonna catch the brake by accident, are you?"

"No, I don't think so. The biggest thing is remembering to not try and brake with my left foot. If I can do that then I should be fine."

"Put the steering wheel on and see how you fit in there, then."

Rob pulled the padded wheel down off the dash and slid it onto the metal bar that formed the steering column. He had to twist it over once to untangle the radio cord before he finally slid it home. He snapped the ring clip on to secure it in place. The wheel sat about a foot from his chest then. He reached up to grip it tightly, in the same position he would assume once he was out on the track and running at speed. He moved his foot to the clutch pedal in the same motion he had made a million times, bending his knee, finding the pedal without looking, giving it a shove with his foot. Somehow, though, it felt as if he were performing some odd and unfamiliar exercise.

Donnie studied his every move.

"That looks good. You comfortable?"

"As much as I can be. We'll know more after I throw this thing through a few corners."

"Do me one favor?"

"What, Donnie?"

"Listen to me and Will for once and take it easy on the first couple of laps so we can get things sorted out. I know you're God's gift to racecars and all but please don't go out there and charge off into one of those corners until we're sure everything is set like it needs to be. Okay, sweetheart?"

Rob looked up sheepishly at Donnie. He knew exactly what the big, slick-headed man was actually saying. Donnie wasn't talking about getting the handling setup in the car right. He was talking about making sure the car's driver was set up and comfortable in the seat and able to make the most basic of his driving moves.

"This time you'll get no fight from me."

"Good. Glad to hear you're listening for once. We don't have that much practice before qualifying and we need to get you situated in a hurry so we can start working on getting the setup under the car."

Fifteen minutes later, Rob steered his Ford out onto the twisting, winding road course for the first time. He eased slowly off the pit road, then gunned his car. He raced off down the hill toward the sharp right-hand turn that lay in wait at the bottom. The car built speed dramatically as he flew down the grade. He eased off the gas and moved his right foot over to hit the brake as he did a quick downshift, changing gears smoothly. Then he jerked the wheel sharply, sending the car screeching through the corner.

The angle of the turn shoved Rob hard over in the seat. He set his sights on the next set of turns already but, as he straightened out the wheel, he felt the pain for the first time. A sharp stab of hurt ran up the left side of his chest as the g-forces rudely slung him sideways in the seat.

He gasped, winced, took a deep breath, but never took his eyes off the approaching corner. And he didn't slow the car down a bit, either.

He flung the wheel again, throwing the Ford briskly into the turn. Again the pain stabbed him hard, but this time it was on the other side of his body. No matter how hard he had tried to will his battered and bruised body to heal itself, the process was going to take more time than he had. The two days until Sunday were certainly not going to be enough.

By the time he finished his first trip around the circuit, it actually occurred to him that maybe Michelle was right after all. Maybe it would be better to put someone else in the car for the weekend.

Rob fought off the thought as quickly as it popped up and vowed again to try to keep an open mind until after he had made a few more laps. He refocused on ignoring the pain, on shoving it out of his mind like any other negative thought. It would take more than a little twinge to keep him out of the racecar, to bump him from this race.

A couple of hours later, Rob pulled the car in for the last time that day. The red flag had flown over the racetrack, ending the opening practice session. He cut the engine and brought the car to a halt in the garage area. Donnie immediately shoved the jack up under the car, hoisting up her right side. Paul and one of the other crewmembers produced a pair of jack stands and carefully placed them under the right side of the car. Will barked out orders to the crew all around, making clear the changes he wanted to make to have the car ready for the upcoming qualifying session.

Once he had driven the car to a stop, Rob sat there in the car for a long moment before he started to slowly unbuckle the helmet. His arms were stiff and his entire midsection pulsed with a dull, throbbing pain with each beat of his heart. But that was not the worst of it. His entire left leg pulsated with continuous spasms. The brace worked fine on the ankle. What he had not anticipated was the intense vibration from the car as it circled the track. It seemed the oscillations radiated directly up his foot and to the point of the bone break. He was already wondering how he would ever make the ninety laps around the two-point-four-five-mile track. While it wasn't a long distance at all compared to the usual five hundred miles they drove most Sundays, all the twisting and shifting and braking still added up to a long day, however it was measured.

He was still fiddling with his helmet when Michelle stuck a clean towel and a cold drink for him through the window. She knew he was hurting. She could read his face, his eyes. But she didn't say anything. They had covered that ground already. He was still in the car. He had not told anyone anything different. That told her that he planned on driving, no matter what. After he had made his decision, there was no point in her trying to talk him out of it. It would be like arguing with the sun or trying to convince the moon not to rise tonight. While she might not be happy with his stubbornness, she knew he was a big boy. He was more than capable of making his own decisions. Once he had, she had decided she would do nothing but support him.

He took the offered towel from her and wiped the sweat from his face.

"Thanks, Chelle."

"You okay?"

She asked the question in a tone that clearly showed she was concerned, not that she might be picking another fight.

"I hurt all over. I'll admit it. But I can drive this thing. Will's got a good setup under her and she'll fly out there."

He finished unbuckling and began to try to climb out of the car. Then, he quickly realized he simply didn't have the energy. Michelle motioned for Donnie to come over and help him and mouthed the words, "Be careful," so Rob wouldn't hear her.

Donnie suspected that Rob was still hurting, too. But the kid had not once exited the car during the hour-and-a-half session. Nor had he uttered one word of complaint on the radio.

Rob reached up and grabbed the roof rail while Donnie gently reached beneath his arms and helped him out. Will stepped around the car to check on him.

"You look terrible, Cowboy."

"Thanks for those kind words, Boss. But I'm fine. I just got bounced around a little more in the car than

I was expecting. I guess I had better take Jodell up on his offer of that flak jacket of his. I thought I was wedged in the seat pretty tight but there was just enough wiggle room to put a lot of pressure on my ribs. That's what was wearing me out. The ankle I can stand."

"Well, you don't look too good," Will said bluntly, as usual, as he surveyed him with a critical eye.

"You want me to go get the flak jacket?" Michelle asked. She suspected Rob and Will needed some time to talk things over without her standing there listening.

Rob nodded. She pursed her lips and almost said something before she decided to just go on. She headed off toward where the Lee Racing truck was parked.

Rob hobbled over to one of the toolboxes, easing down on the top of it as if he might crack into a thousand pieces if he sat down too hard. Will sat down next to him and studied a grease spot on the floor for a while.

"So how do you really feel?" he finally asked.

"I hurt everywhere," Rob admitted with a slight grin. "Another day or two without getting banged up too bad and I bet most of that will go away. The vibrations on my ankle are the worst."

"Is it going to affect your driving?" Will asked, homing right in on the point of the matter.

"No, I don't think so."

"Tell me the truth, Robbie. I need to know if you can go the distance on Sunday. We're locked in a tight battle for the rookie points. If you can't go, then I need to get somebody lined up to take over after you start the car. We have to have you healthy for this next stretch of races coming up and this one is not worth the risk if it's gonna put you out of commission."

"I hear you, Will. I can go the distance."

"Remember, we have Bristol coming up in a couple of weeks. The night race there is as tough as they come. Then we got to go to Darlington, Dover, and Martinsville. All of those are going to be tough, physical races. We need you one hundred percent when we get to those places."

"Will, I'll be all right by Sunday. I can drive this car. Don't you worry." The kid turned up and drained most of the bottle of water Michelle had given him. When he was able to catch his breath after the cold drink, he went on. "Jodell's always telling me about the times he drove five hundred miles when he was busted up a lot worse than I am. And that was back when the cars weren't nearly as good as they are now. If he could do it then, then I think I can do it now."

"You're our driver. Tell me what I can do to make you more comfortable in the car," Will said.

There was no mistaking the determined look in Rob Wilder's eyes. It was the look that any crew chief yearned to see, the hungry, resolute look of a driver who was determined to race, driven to win regardless of the cost.

And it was reassuring for him to see it now. Will crewed for drivers before Rob came on board who seemed reluctant to go out there, even when they felt fine. Others bounced back slowly after a crash, even when they had not been hurt at all. Some lost their edge when the car broke or racing luck inevitably went against them. They typically didn't make this level, though. And if they did, they were only around for a cup of coffee, and then back running Saturday-night features at local bullrings for not much more than gasoline money.

Will Hughes carried no desire to work with any of those kinds of drivers again. He signed on with Billy Winton's team to be a winner and nothing else. He needed a driver to feel the same way.

Now, this was his first chance to see how this

skinny youngster would react to true adversity. The look in the kid's eyes had just confirmed for him the moxie that he had fully expected to see there.

"Naw, Will. Just make sure this thing flies so we can take the pole here in a few minutes."

Will slapped Rob on the shoulder, then he immediately felt bad when the kid winced.

"Oops, sorry. All right, then," the crew chief said. "Here's what I think we'll do with the setup. We'll take the tire stagger . . ."

10

Jodell Bob Lee walked quickly across his racing shop and headed out the back door toward the engine shop. The building was just across the narrow alley from the other shop. He was due to leave for the airport in a little over half an hour then fly up to Watkins Glen. But first, before he picked up Catherine and headed out, he wanted to look up his cousin Joe Banker and ask him a bothersome question.

He stepped into the spacious building that housed one of the top engine programs in the game. In addition to building racing engines for the Jodell Lee team, they also developed powerful engines for several of the other teams, not only in Cup but in other racing divisions, as well. That allowed them to spread all the research and development costs across a much larger base and, incidentally, provided a good living for Joe Banker.

As Jodell stepped into the shop, he could hear an engine being put through its paces by one of Joe's assistants. But he didn't see Banker anywhere. He stuck his head into one doorway after another in search of his cousin.

Finally, he found him in one of the assembly rooms, bent over a half-finished motor. Joe was not beyond still assembling engines himself, even though he had a squad of assistants at his disposal. For certain races, Joe liked to personally put together the engines to be used for either qualifying or racing. When Jodell found him, he was elbow deep in one of his prize creations. He waited to speak until Joe had finished measuring whatever it was he had the calipers to and had stepped back to admire his work.

"Hey, cuz! What you working on there?"

Joe hesitated a brief moment before he answered.

"Building a real good engine for your protégé, Mr. Rocket Rob Wilder." He stepped back even farther, bowed and waved at the motor with a flourish. "This here is a special motor for them to run at Bristol in two weeks. This one is going to be bulletproof."

Joe leaned back against a worktable that was scattered with tools and parts and various instruments.

"Reckon what Rex would think about that?"

Rex Lawford drove Jodell Lee's Ford. He would be competing against Rob Wilder and his Joe Banker engine at Bristol. With the kind of season Rex was having, Jodell likely figured he needed the bulletproof Bristol engine worse than Rob Wilder and Billy Winton could.

"Aw, Joe Dee, you know me. You listen to your ghost voices. I have spirits telling me which engines I need to build and for who. The kid is hot on the trail of winning that first race and I wanna make sure he's got all the motor he needs to get it done. That little accident of his last week is gonna slow him down, but he's got a win coming, and it's likely coming soon."

Jodell knew what Joe was talking about. About

sensing which engine belonged to which driver before they were even built. And about Rob Wilder and his impending breakthrough win. The accident could either hinder or help the young man's chances. If the kid kept the hunger he'd demonstrated through June and July, and if he didn't allow the little mishap at Indy to take his focus away, then the win could come sooner rather than later. And it wouldn't be the only win of his career, either.

"So what I came to ask you is why you aren't heading up to Watkins Glen with us this morning like we planned?"

The question caught Joe Banker off guard.

"I was going to but . . . uh . . . I got behind on a few things here at the shop. I'm flying commercial to Newark later this afternoon. I'll be at the track some time tomorrow. I want to finish this engine up, then make a stop in New York City for the night to get myself a big-city fix. I thought I'd just rent a car and drive over to the Glen first thing in the morning."

"Can't this engine wait? Billy's flying up with us and Joyce is coming with Catherine. Bob junior is coming up Saturday, too, and you know how rare it is for him to want to come to a racetrack. I thought it would be like old times, all of us together."

Jodell had fond, wistful memories of the old days when they all traveled together to races, like some Gypsy caravan. Even Bob junior and Glynn, his daughter, who had been named after legendary driver Glen "Fireball" Roberts. He was always trying to get all the principals together so they could relive the period when they had first been building their race team. Joe often reminded him that sleeping under the car in roadside parks and living off Vienna sausages and soda crackers weren't quite so glamorous when they actually had to do it to keep racing.

"I planned on it, but I got behind this week working on that motor for Waltrip. I'll catch up with y'all tomorrow and we can all sit around and tell lies about 1960." Joe winked. "Hey, to tell you the truth, I'm looking forward to getting to the track. I ain't been to a race in a while and, from what I see on the TV, the girls that come to the tracks are even prettier than they used to be."

Joe hoped Jodell would cease the questioning. He didn't want to have to explain any more. And he certainly couldn't tell Lee about Bob junior and the phone call. The boy had asked him not to and he would honor that request.

"All right, all right. Suit yourself, then. We'll see you at the track tomorrow, I guess. Call us if you get lost."

Jodell was only half joking. He wouldn't be one bit surprised if Joe got distracted somewhere between Chandler Cove, New York City, and the track. Joe might be happily married and settled down now but that didn't mean he couldn't occasionally still get caught up in a good time if one happened along and reached out and grabbed him.

Jodell hustled on out to pick up Catherine without another thought about the reason for Joe's sudden decision to not fly up with them. He was just glad his cousin was coming at all. He had a hard time getting him to the tracks anymore. He preferred watching his handiwork on the television broadcasts, if he even caught the races at all.

That afternoon, Jodell and Catherine Lee, Bubba and Joyce Baxter, and Billy Winton all stood together atop the Lee Racing truck, watching the start of the qualifying session. Billy was especially nervous after getting the update on the morning's practice from Will. Luckily, he had not seen Rob being helped out of the car after the first practice or he would have been even more fidgety.

By the time they arrived at the track, Rob had had time to catch his breath, swallow a handful of aspirin, and recover somewhat. He was reclined on the sofa in the Winton Racing truck's lounge when Billy stuck his head in the door and offered his greetings.

Now, as the group atop the truck watched, the first cars began to roll out, making their qualifying runs one by one. Luckily for Rob, he had drawn a late number. That allowed him an extra hour of recuperation before he had to join the car on the line. For once, he stayed inside the air-conditioned truck, listening to the description of the qualifying session over the radio. Michelle was there, too, riding herd over him at Will's behest. Rob was not to leave the truck, or, for that matter, get off the sofa, until they called for him over the radio.

He was beginning to get restless when the call finally came for him to head to the car. Somehow, Michelle managed to shanghai a golf cart to haul him over to where the car waited in line on pit road. Rob climbed out of the cart and straight into the car since it would take several extra minutes to get him situated and buckled in. He tried to ignore the several television cameras that chronicled his arrival and efforts to get into the Ford. As he worked, the cars ahead of him rolled away one by one and took to the track.

Finally he was strapped and buckled in place. Rob stared straight out the windshield of the Ensoft Ford, watching the others roll out, ready to be waved out onto the track.

Oh, man, was he ready! Somehow, getting out there with a real goal ahead of him, the effort to win the pole position, seemed as if it would cause the aches and pains to finally subside.

The car that was already out on the track making its run shot by their position then, dashing off toward the finish line. Rob was checking the tightness of his belts one final time when the official finally waved him out onto the track. He couldn't afford any looseness because if his body could move around in the cockpit at all he knew he would be in trouble, even in a single qualifying lap.

He reached over and hit the starter switch and felt the usual surge of exhilaration when he heard the answering rumble of the engine out there beneath the hood in front of him. He shifted the car up into gear then gingerly released the clutch with his left foot. He was conscious of the cast, of a twinge of pain when he bent the knee, but only for a quick moment. After that, his only focus was on the winding strip of asphalt that played out ahead of him like a gray ribbon. There was no more fractured ankle, no bruised ribs, no pounding headache. There was only a bucking, primed racecar around him and it was his job to push it as hard as he could for the next few minutes. He'd have plenty of time to hurt and nurse his wounds after the lap was done.

He quickly built speed in the car as he ran up through the gears, sending the red rocket off toward the first turn. He stood on the throttle as he lunged down the hill and made the hard turn to the right. It was either his own intense power of concentration or Jodell Lee's flak jacket, but he hardly noticed any hurt at all as the g-forces shoved him hard against the padding of the wraparound seat. He guided the car up the hill, trying to get his rhythm down before he finished the course and came back around to catch the green flag from the starter for the money lap.

Rhythm. Concentrate on the rhythm.

The misery of the last week had already disappeared in the series of right-hand turns around the sprawling speedway. It felt good.

No, it felt wonderful!

Rob dove deep into the last corner attempting to get a good run up toward the waving green flag. The back end of the Ford wanted to kick out away from him as he exited the corner. He fought the wheel and managed to keep the surging car under control by mostly brute force. But somehow he managed to hold her straight as he shot beneath the flag stand and drove off in the direction of the first turn again.

High up on the top of the hauler truck, Billy Winton and Jodell Lee both clicked the stopwatches that hung from their necks. But they kept their eyes on the car as it sailed off in a scarlet blur down toward the sharp right-hander at the bottom of the hill. Rob disappeared from their sight then, lost in the rolling terrain of the speedway as he pushed the car hard through the twisting, winding course, aiming for the tight chicane at the end of the long straightaway. In what seemed like no time, they picked up sight of him in the distance again, charging into the final turn once more as he hustled toward the waving checkered flag.

Both had seen the car's slight wobble the last time the kid had powered out of the last turn and headed for the flag stand. Neither man breathed this time until he made it through.

The flagman waved the end of the run as the Ensoft Ford barreled by underneath him. Rob immediately got out of the gas as soon as the car flashed across the start/finish line. He allowed normal friction to slow the car down, staying off the brakes and allowing it to roll easily around the track as the next driver to qualify passed him, building up speed for his own run.

Rob exhaled in a big sigh of relief. He waited for Will's call over the radio, reporting his time. He was already approaching the final turn on the cool-down lap when the word came.

"Twelfth fastest so far," Will said, calmly, coolly.

With three-quarters of the cars already qualified, worst case they would still have a top-twenty starting spot. Considering how far they had come since the start of the week, a top twenty didn't look so bad. Even Rob, who rarely felt good about anything that wasn't the pole, admitted to himself that he was satisfied with this particular run. He had just given all that he had today and he knew it. There was nothing more he could have done.

Rob coasted the car down onto the pit lane and took the hard turn into the garage, for once glad that the day was done. He brought her to a stop in their stall in the garage where Donnie and Paul stood waiting. Will was still down in the pit area timing the rest of the cars that were still making their runs. Rob had seen Michelle jogging his way from where she had been watching the run alongside Will.

Rob reached to get the window net but he had trouble raising his arm. It was still wedged tightly in the seat. No doubt about it now. The borrowed flak jacket provided his sore rib cage with the support that was missing in the morning practice session. It had been a lifesaver. He flipped the buckle on the harness that held the safety belts, unsnapped the helmet, and hung it on the small clip on the roll bar. He tossed the steering wheel up on the dash then followed it with the driving gloves.

Donnie and Paul were already unsnapping the hood pins and raising it up, hooking the blower over the radiator. They would need the wind to cool the qualifying engine down so they could set about pulling it and putting the race motor in the car.

As Michelle trotted up to the driver's side of the car, she noticed the net was still up on the window. When she leaned down to check on him, Rob motioned for her to pull the net down for him. She reached up, unsnapped it, and dropped it down against the side of the door.

"That was a great run!"

"Yeah, that was about all me and the car had today. But we made the field."

Rob seemed determined to let her see him climb out of the car under his own power. He gritted his teeth then reached up to grab the ridge railing that ran along the roof of the car. He gave a pull, sliding up to the edge of the window, but he had to sit there for a moment to let the pain subside.

"You okay?" she asked. She had seen the grimace on his sweating face as he pulled himself up out of the seat.

"I'm fine now. I think I'll go on back to the hotel and lay down, though. I'll be a lot more fun to be around tomorrow. Could you hand an old crippled man his crutches?"

She picked them up from where they leaned against the large rolling toolbox.

"Here you go. You need some help?"

"Naw, I got it," Rob answered, delicately swinging the busted ankle out of the car's window. He got his good leg firmly planted on the floor before hoisting himself up onto first one crutch then the other.

He grinned and then winked at her but neither the smile nor the wink carried its usual flair.

"Could you grab me a cold drink?" he asked her as he limped over to one of the equipment boxes so he could sit down.

"You want water or a soda?"

"Soda."

"That was a great run . . . for somebody on his last leg!" Donnie Kline crowed. The big man was obviously still pumped from how well the run went. He knew how tough this qualifying session was on the young driver. It was important for the kid as well as for this fledgling team for them to have done so well with their driver hurting. No one had said a word, but if Rob had not been able to bounce back and qualify on the first day after such a hard crash, it would have had a disastrous effect on them.

"Thanks, Donnie. You guys made this car run perfect."

"Aw, kid, we just build 'em. You're the one what's

gotta go out there and make the old buggy run real fast."

Rob managed a weak grin. It was about the first time that he had ever heard Donnie be so complimentary without inserting a dig or two somewhere along the way.

"I just wish I felt up to driving this car as fast as you all built it to go."

"Robbie, you looked like you were going pretty fast out there to me. There are going to be some good cars going home 'cause their healthy drivers weren't fast enough to make the field."

Donnie took the can of soda from Michelle and relayed it over to Rob.

"Thanks," Rob said. He took the can and fumbled with the pull top.

"Here, let me get that," Donnie said, snatching the can back. "I don't want you straining one of your little bitty old dainty fingers to go along with that little bump on your leg."

Rob showed him the meanest look he could manage, even jutting out his jaw and balling up a fist as if he might actually take a swing at him. But he couldn't hold it long. He burst into laughter and flipped a little of the condensation from the soda can off his fingers in Donnie's direction.

It was wonderful to laugh out loud again, even if it did hurt his chest and ribs when he did. And it was good to finally leave Indianapolis and its solid outside wall behind, once and for all.

11

Joe Banker asked the kid who ran parts for them to give him a lift up to the Tri-Cities airport. It had only been a half hour since Jodell Lee's visit to the dyno room and he wanted to be sure not to run into his cousin at the airport. Jodell should be headed directly for the general aviation building, though, while Joe was going commercial from the main terminal.

Joe couldn't help but wonder what his little side trip to New York City might bring. The phone call the other day had definitely piqued his curiosity and the possibilities of where it could lead were intriguing, to say the least.

That was still very much on Joe's mind as the 737 angled into the airport at Newark, gliding in from the south over rows and rows of houses, sending up a slight puff of tire smoke when the wheels touched down. Still deep in thought, Joe sat quietly in his seat while the rest of the passengers jumped up and stood in the aisles, waiting for the door to finally open and let them escape to the jetway. Finally, he grabbed the small overnight bag from the overhead compartment, winked at and waved good-bye to the cute stewardess who'd been so friendly to him during the flight, and followed the tail end of the line out of the plane.

The heels of his scuffed cowboy boots clicked softly on the smooth, polished tile in the gate area. But when he was out of the chute in the open area beyond the gate, he stopped and stood there for a moment, getting his bearings. Several of the other passengers stared at his Lee Racing button-down shirt and tried to read his name that had been stitched carefully over the breast pocket. But Joe ignored them. He was looking for someone.

And then he spotted the tall, slender, well-dressed young man standing only a few feet away, smiling at him. He was handsome, his hair was carefully styled, and the suit he wore was obviously expensive, custom-tailored.

"Bob junior? That you?"

Joe did a double take. Jodell Bob Lee Jr. had only been a gangly kid the last few times he had seen him, walking up to get his bachelor's degree at that fancy school he had gone to in Boston, the family trips to New York for holiday visits. But the startling thing was how much this young man, now in his early thirties, looked like his daddy at that same age.

"Uncle Joe? I'm so glad you came!" Bob junior called as he ran to meet him, to give him a sincere hug. Joe wasn't really his uncle, he was his daddy's first cousin, but that's what Bob and his sister, Glynn, had always called him. When they finally broke the embrace, it was Bob who said what was on both men's minds. "We haven't seen nearly enough of each other over the last ten years, Uncle Joe. Maybe that's about to change."

Joe nodded but he wasn't sure exactly what had changed.

"Maybe so, young'un. Maybe so."

They talked easily then as they walked side by side down the terminal's long concourse, exchanging the usual reports on other kinfolk as any relatives might have after being apart for such a long time. They exited the front of the terminal and joined the long line of people, mostly businessmen, waiting for a cab.

Joe was powerfully curious. He wanted desperately to find out more about what might have triggered the out-of-the-blue telephone call from Bob junior. But he avoided asking those questions. He was actually looking forward to rekindling what had once been a great relationship with his cousin's only boy.

Bob junior had loved to hang out at the racing shop when he was a kid, from the time he was five or six years old. Some complained that he got in their way but Joe had taken him under his wing, let him help with chores and menial jobs, until, by the time he turned thirteen, the boy had become a fairly decent wrench and far more of a help than a hindrance.

But, as the boy worked, all he wanted to talk about was driving a racecar. About how he couldn't wait until his daddy would let him in one of his cars so he could start gaining experience. About when he would eventually proudly tote the Lee banner around all those tracks his dad had run, carrying on the family's winning tradition.

During the cab ride to the train station, the conversation was mostly about how various family members were getting along, who had gotten married, who was sickly. But gradually, it turned to racing. Bob was eager to get the latest news on his father's race team. Joe was glad to fill him in because he never tired of the subject, even though he didn't make nearly as many of the races anymore as he once had. Finally married and settled down, Joe now preferred staying back home at the shop, working with his precious engines, using the extra time to build special motors for certain events and favored drivers, like Rob Wilder. He had long since grown tired of the road, of airplanes, hotels, rental cars, and greasy restaurant meals. But he still loved the sport and was pleased with Bob's interest.

Now, as they talked racing, as Bob gently reminded him that he preferred leaving the junior off his name, Joe Banker studied the young man's face, his demeanor. Jodell's boy was tall and athletic and obviously worked out to stay in such good shape. But something was out of whack, though. Something about his hands he couldn't quite get a grip on. They seemed rough and callused, more like a mechanic's than a moneyman's. The boy still had more than a trace of his Southern accent left but there was also a hint of the brittle Northern lilt crowding into his speech. He was polished, articulate, and smooth, but direct and no-nonsense, too. There was an intelligence there that was obvious to anyone, not just to a proud, doting "uncle." No wonder he was such a success among all those sharks he swam among over yonder on Wall Street!

Still, as they talked, he noticed how well informed the young man was about racing and what was going on with the sport. He couldn't help but wonder now how it would have turned out if Bob junior—sorry, Bob—had followed his heart and climbed into one of those racecars instead of finishing second in his class at college and getting his MBA and diving directly into a pressure-cooker job with a Wall Street banking firm in New York City. Joe was already looking forward to spending the evening with this young man, regardless of the real reasons he had invited him up here. It would be like old times, the kid hanging around, believing his uncle Joe's lies. Maybe in some cockeyed way, Joe thought, he might actually recapture a bit of his own youth hanging around this kid who had, at times, seemed like his son.

In several ways, Bob's personality was actually more like that of Joe Banker than it was his dad's. Both men were known for having a good time. Although, in Bob's defense, he had never taken his frolicking to the extremes that Joe once did. Banker's early exploits around the circuit were still the stuff of legend.

The cab ride from the terminal to the train station was over in no time at all, and, when they climbed out, Joe slapped the driver on the back and told him he could have a job with a race team if he ever wanted one. Anybody who could put a car through some of the holes he just had and in as big a hurry as he had managed could drive a racecar for him anytime! Bob didn't tell Joe until later that the man had not understood a thing he had said, that he hardly spoke any English at all, much less Joe's flavor of East Tennessee English.

Soon they were on the train, headed out to one of the mostly green suburban Jersey towns that rested away from the city but still within sight of Manhattan when the smoke allowed. Bob's house was a couple of blocks' walk from the station. It was a relatively modest house on a quiet block of newer homes, and had what looked like an oversized garage in back.

"You want to take a look?" Bob asked, nodding toward the garage.

"Sure!" Joe answered, not at all sure what it was that he was supposed to be taking a look at.

"Follow me," Bob said, ignoring the flower-lined walkway to the front door and leading him up a short driveway and to the garage behind the house. "She's in here."

She? Joe kept quiet as he followed along. Bob unhinged a big padlock on the door with a key from his pocket, stepped inside, and flipped the switch on a bank of bright overhead shop lights. He motioned for Joe to step inside.

"What do you think?"

With a flourish, Bob guided Joe's gaze toward the car that rested there in the center of a surprisingly spacious work area.

"Nice. Real nice," Joe said, clearly meaning it.

It was a beautiful, gleaming racecar, the sheen of its dark blue paint job glimmering gloriously in the bright fluorescent light. It could have been lifted from a batch of very similar racecars, all wearing the distinctive dark blue Lee Racing paint job and sitting at that very moment in Jodell Lee's race shop down in Chandler Cove, Tennessee. Or the twin of the one that was likely, at that very moment, being wiped down in the Lee garage area over at Watkins Glen.

Joe stepped closer and gently ran his hand along the smooth surface of the car's carefully sculpted left front fender.

"Ain't she beautiful?" Bob asked, likely saying "ain't" for the first time in ten years.

"Where'd you get this beautiful baby?"

"Me and a couple of my buddies built her in our spare time. We run it when we can at a couple of the local speedways."

"Your daddy never mentioned this to me. How long has this been going on?" Joe asked as he lifted the hood, not even bothering to ask permission. His practiced eye scanned the car, her sleek lines, the motor beneath the hood.

"I don't guess . . . uh . . . that he knows about it. I've only been fooling around with it for the last several years. Starting out, I drove cars that belonged to some of the other guys for a while. But heck, I figured that I could build better cars than those old jalopies, so we started building this one."

"You *built* this?"

Joe didn't even try to keep the doubt out of his voice.

"Yeah, I built it with the help of a couple of guys I know from some of the tracks around here. There's a lot of racing that goes on here in Jersey, out on the Island, up in Connecticut, believe it or not."

Joe studied the detailing on the car. It was obviously a solid, well-built racecar, something that, with a little work, many of the teams at the Busch and Cup level would be proud to race.

Then, Joe Banker suddenly had a big question. How in the world could Jodell Lee not have known his boy wanted to race?

"Where did you learn how to do all this?" Joe asked, still wide-eyed and marveling at the workmanship in the car.

"What do you mean, Uncle Joe? I learned everything from you and Bubba. Do you know how many times I've dreamed about chucking it all here and coming back to work in the shop with y'all?" The young man slipped out of his jacket and tie and hung them on a hook next to the door. Even Joe saw shedding the coat and tie as an almost symbolic gesture. Bob hopped up to take a seat on the workbench and began talking, his voice low and deliberate, using his hands for emphasis at key points. "I spend all day every day trapped in that high-rise office building downtown, playing with Monopoly money, arguing with professional arguers, looking at spreadsheets, business plans, and stock quotes until my eyes cross and my butt hurts and my head feels like it's about to blow a gasket. And Uncle Joe, you know what I really want to do all the time I'm playing with other people's money? What I was born to do. Build championship racecars. Drive them at Talladega and Darlington and Daytona. Compete with Jarrett and Gordon and Earnhardt. That's what I really want to do. What I was put on this planet to do. And it's really all I want to do for the rest of my life."

Bob dropped his head then, obviously having just said out loud something he had been wanting to say for a long, long time.

Then it all suddenly came clear to Joe Banker, and he felt like a fool for not recognizing it before. There had never been any obvious good reason for Bob not showing up at the tracks where his daddy raced. No good excuse for him never coming home to Chandler Cove where the race shop was right next to his daddy's house. No rhyme or reason for why any visitation had always been in New York or at some neutral, patently nonracing location.

Joe had always assumed it was because Jodell had done such a good job of discouraging his boy from racing that he had turned the kid against anything and everything to do with the sport. He figured the boy simply wanted nothing to do with grease, rubber, gas fumes, or crumpled sheet metal. It made sense that Bob junior was so wrapped up in his career in high finance that he had no desire anymore to drive an old racecar round and round in circles real fast.

Now the boy had told him just the opposite.

All a fellow had to do was take a look at the long bloodlines that ran through the different families involved in stock car racing. It was clear there was something genetic going on, a multigenerational strand that ran long and deep. Now it appeared that Joe Banker was about to find out if the Lee family tree might match up after all with the Allisons, the Pettys, the Jarretts, and all the others who passed down the racing gene from generation to generation.

"Your daddy doesn't know anything about this, does he?"

"No, Uncle Joe. That's why I called you to come up here and asked you not to mention it to him. I need your help with the car. It's good but still not good enough to win every time I go out there. That's what I want to do. Win every race I enter. And I need you to help me find what's missing."

Joe was quiet for a moment, mulling it all over. Bob's request on the telephone had been mysterious. He had asked Joe to come up to New York on his way to Watkins Glen and help him with something he knew would likely make his daddy furious if he knew about it. Something Joe could not mention to his father. At least not yet. Joe had figured the boy was in some kind of trouble. Maybe broke or in trouble with the law or having woman troubles. But he had agreed to come on, no matter how much it might get him in Dutch with his cousin. There still was a special place in his heart for Jodell's boy and he was, quite frankly, proud he had asked him for help.

He just never dreamed the help he needed was in preparing a racecar.

"I can probably help you pick up a few things. When you gonna race it next?"

"Tonight. The boys should be here within the hour. The track is about a half hour away. That's one of the reasons I live out here now even though it's a long train ride into the city. It's close to this and a couple of other good tracks. I've been racing at this one about every week for the last few months. They got a couple of cats that run out there that seem to have unlimited budgets. I've got a bunch of seconds and thirds, but I'm missing something. Something that's keeping me out of victory lane. And it's about to kill me. You hear me?" The man had a look in his eyes that sent a shiver down Joe Banker's spine. That was a thirty-year-old Jodell Lee sitting there on that workbench, sure as the world. Oh, Jodell would never be wearing an Italian suit like that or have his hair cut and slicked back that way. But those eyes? Those were Jodell Lee's eyes. And the hungry look on that face? Joe Banker had seen it a thousand times before.

"I was hoping you could look the car over and see if you can get a handle on it for me. I plan on winning the feature tonight. I need to find a little more in the car to do it."

"Well, I could take a look at it, I suppose. I might find something."

"Look, I'm going to run inside and change." He hopped down off the workbench and dusted off the seat of his neatly pressed slacks. "Feel free to look her over. Need anything to eat or drink?"

"Nah. I had delicious airplane food. I'll take a look at her."

He was already bent over, his head beneath the hood, examining the A-frames and the rest of the front suspension.

It didn't take him long to confirm his initial impression that this was a good, solid, well-built racecar. The kid had clearly learned his craft well. There were a few things that caught his eye, a couple of things that he might suggest, but it looked to Joe as if the car mostly only needed a tweak here and a slight change there. He was even prouder now that he got the call to come give Bob some help. And he couldn't wait to see Jodell's boy drive. If he had inherited as much of his old man's talent as he did his desire, he would be exciting to watch.

Joe rolled up his sleeves and dug deeper into the car. The first thing he noticed was the relative lack of body repair that had been done on her. Bob was clearly not one of the push-'em-out-of-the-way type drivers or the car would have more evidence of slamming and banging. He was likely more of a steady, finesse driver, similar to his father.

Joe climbed inside the cockpit to examine the seat and safety belts. Everything looked impressive, much more sophisticated than what one would expect to find in a "Friday night" racer.

A few hours later they were at the small half-mile

speedway carved out of the New Jersey countryside. Two of Bob's friends, Sammy and Wayne, had joined them to help crew and work on the racecar. They had been in awe when they met Joe Banker and saw him in his official Lee Racing Team shirt. Somehow, Bob had never gotten around to mentioning to them who his famous father was, and they had never associated their investment banker friend who just happened to be named Lee with one of stock car racing's living legends. He explained to them that he had made up his mind once he decided to start racing that he wanted to make it in the sport on his own talent, not on his father's reputation. Or not embarrass his famous father if he failed.

Riding the smaller tracks in the area had allowed him to learn and hone his skills anonymously. But now, he was convinced that he could take his desire for racing to a higher level. His "uncle" and the friends who had helped him so far were the first to know.

Joe was under the car's hood as soon as they rolled it off the trailer at the track. He wanted to spend some time with the tune of the motor. While the actual power of the engine was limited by the carburetor rules for this particular track, Joe had already found several things he could do with the jetting and the timing to add a little power. Just being able to perfectly jet the carburetor for the weather on this night should make a big difference in the strength of the motor.

While he worked under the hood, he barked instructions for some of the other little adjustments they needed to make to the suspension to fine-tune the car for this particular track's layout. Bob Lee smiled as he worked, impressed with all the seemingly minor things Joe found with little more than a cursory once-over of the racecar. And Sammy and Wayne were thrilled to have someone of Joe Banker's caliber giv-

ing them direction. If Joe had told them to pull off
the tires and race on the rims, they would have gone
to work removing the lugs with no questions asked.

Bob was covered in grease and dirt when he slid
out from under the car. He walked over to the toolbox
to grab a wrench. Seeing Joe working under the hood
of his racecar did bring one twinge of regret. Asking
Joe to come up and help him with the car was something that was long overdue. He wished now that he
had done it sooner. And that he had invited his father,
as well.

What was he afraid of? Why was it so difficult for
him, a thirty-year-old man, to bring himself to confess
to his father that he had taken up racing? Surely, of
all people, Jodell Bob Lee would understand the craving he had for competition. If he were going to realize
his dream of one day driving seriously, then he would
eventually have to come clean with him. With the
plans he had, it would be hard to keep it a secret from
him much longer, and especially now that he had let
Uncle Joe into his confidence.

As he worked on the car, Joe Banker was wrestling
with very similar questions. The continual pressures
of big-time racing finally wiped out most of the fun
of the sport for Joe. He still loved it, enjoyed race
days as much as ever. But the hectic schedule for
everything else between Sundays finally wore him
down after almost forty years. He still had the competitive fires burning inside him as brightly as ever,
but he stoked those blazes by building his motors and
watching on television to see how they did. And he
could do that from home.

Tonight, as he worked under the hood, he watched
the eager but relatively inexperienced crew crawling
around underneath the car. It reminded him of all the
things he missed from the old days, from when he,
Jodell, and Bubba Baxter barnstormed all over, living
to race, sometimes winning enough to eat and put gas

in the tow truck, sometimes not. These guys could just as easily be his old bunch, scrambling to get their car ready to run on this little speedway in the middle of nowhere, intent on taking home the winner's trophy and a few dollars' prize money. Never mind one of them was a well-paid investment banker, and of the other two men, one was a stockbroker and the other a book editor. And those lights off in the distance beyond turn three? They weren't stars in the Carolina sky. They were the towering skyscrapers of Manhattan.

Joe finally stood and stepped back from the car, wiping the sweat from his face with a greasy rag. He could see the other crews frantically working on their cars, the spectators slowly filing into the grandstands. And he could smell hot dogs and popcorn as he listened to the distorted music that was blaring from the track PA system. It all served to transport him back to a time he thought for sure that he had left behind forever. If only Bubba Baxter were to come loping around the corner, stuffing hot dogs into his mouth. Or if Jodell were standing there in jeans and a T-shirt, that determined look on his face, pulling on his helmet as he got ready to climb into the racecar and take her out for a spin.

He was filled with a powerful feeling then. They should be here for this. Bubba and Jodell both. And the boy's mamma, too. He wondered if Catherine knew. He suspected that if she did, she would be here for certain. He shook his head with regret, then went back to work on the engine.

Joe was a tangle of nerves by the time of the feature race. They might just as well be getting ready to run Rockingham or Charlotte. Bob qualified second for his event but the field was inverted back to tenth place. That meant Bob would start ninth instead of second. The promoters often inverted the fields to enhance the competition, forcing the faster cars to have to work their way up through the field. That usually made for a better show for the fans watching. Still, for the higher qualifiers, when the green flag fell on the forty-lap event, they had to scramble to get to the front.

Joe was surprised to see that there would be several very fast cars out there running. Once the race started, he watched the action for a few laps, trying to figure out which of the fast cars had good drivers and which were just well-funded teams. Money could buy speed for sure, but it would take a good driver to win the race ahead of the twenty-five-car field.

Joe watched with pride as Bob showed plenty of patience, working his way up, picking off one spot after another. The car with the fastest qualifying time was quick once the race started, too. But its driver was what Bubba Baxter would call a "BCS," a "bull in a china shop."

With eight laps to go, Bob was running in fourth place but right on the back bumper of the third-place car. There had been one close call a while back, a wild pileup on the backstretch. But with a remarkable bit of driving, Bob had survived it without getting a scratch on the car. Somehow he threaded the needle through the mess of spinning cars, missing several of them by inches.

Joe proudly watched the young driver make the move, elated that he was apparently showing some of his family roots. But now he would find out for sure if that had been luck or skill. Stuck in fourth place, hounding the third-place driver, the young man now had a chance to show what he was made of.

Bob looked high as they entered into the shallow banking of the first turn. There was just not enough room there for him to get by. He shot down the short backstretch, inches off the rear of the red car that was sponsored by Wiley's Body Shop, according to its gaudy paint job. Bob looked down to the inside as they raced into turn three, then he got a nose alongside as he tried to push out ahead. He held the car down tightly on the inside, giving the red car plenty of room to race. Then a slower car ahead of them drifted up into the high line, forcing the car on the outside to crack the throttle.

That was all Bob needed. He smoothly completed the pass, seemingly with little effort.

Joe Banker knew differently. It had been a big-time pass.

Next he set his sights on the two lead cars. They were tangled in their own tight battle up there, having swapped the lead back and forth several times over the last half-dozen laps or so. Bob desperately wanted to join the skirmish. He worked his car smoothly, reveling in the extra power Joe had coaxed from the engine with his prerace adjustments. Bob could easily feel the difference over the previous week when they had raced this same track and finished fourth to the same batch of cars.

Bringing Uncle Joe in for advice had been a good idea.

The extra power helped, but he still needed to be careful not to spin the rear tires coming off the corners. That's exactly what he'd done the first couple of laps after the green flag fell. It took him eight to ten laps to get used to the extra oomph the car had every time he jumped on the gas as he exited the turns. Now, in the waning laps of the feature, Bob used the newfound juice to his advantage. He charged after the two leaders, quickly closing the half-dozen or so car lengths that separated him from their back bumpers.

Joe watched carefully, studying every move the young man made out there. The more he saw the wider his smile became. Regardless of how this race played out, Joe Banker had learned one thing here tonight. There was plenty of Jodell Lee in Bob junior.

He could drive a racecar. Joe couldn't help but wonder what might have been if Jodell had allowed his son to pursue his dreams from the start.

As a father himself, he understood the pushes and pulls of parenting, of wanting to provide the very best for his children while also giving them the right to pursue their dreams and make their own mistakes if that's what made them truly happy. As he watched Bob working on the car before the start of the race, and now, as he watched him drive around out there, Joe learned all he needed to know. And he made a decision. If this was Bob Lee's dream, then he would do everything in his power to help him realize it. He would also keep this secret from Jodell until the time was right, until Bob wanted to tell him.

Meanwhile, all those thoughts were far from Bob's mind at the moment. He concentrated on nothing but the two cars running out there in front of him as they all three raced off into the corner. The laps were running out and he knew he had the fastest car on the track, plenty enough muscle to take the other cars. The question was, did he have the driving ability to get around them? He would know over the next couple of laps. Time and again, victory had eluded him. Would tonight be another disappointment? Would he embarrass himself in front of Uncle Joe? Would he find it wasn't the car after all that had kept him out of victory lane?

Bob hammered the throttle as the car came out of turn two, trying to jump low and underneath the second-place car. The only problem was the second-place car had the same idea at the exact same instant as Bob did. Both racecars shot for the same spot on the track, coming together briefly, before Bob backed out of the gas for half a second. If he had stubbornly stayed in the gas, both cars would have been pushed into the outside wall. Neither of them would win the race.

Joe felt his heart stop as the two cars bumped together. This was small-track racing at its best. He instinctively pumped his fist in the air as he watched Bob recover brilliantly, not missing a beat, still hanging with the leaders.

Bob was already back in the throttle, determined to make the pass for the victory. The second-place car held his ground on the low side, though, sailing into the lead. Bob tried to follow him but was blocked by a slower car down on the inside as they drove into the next corner.

Then the leaders bumped together, sliding slightly wide as they raced hard into the turn.

Bob never hesitated. He saw the oh-so-brief opportunity that was being offered him and held the car down to the inside, trying to take advantage of the narrow opening presented by the two leaders getting together. With only three laps to go, Bob pressed his advantage. He felt the rear tires break loose again as he got back in the throttle out of the corner. As fast as the gap opened up beneath the two spinning cars, it would certainly close again even more tightly. This could well be his only chance.

But an instant was all it took. Bob held the car steady and shot through the narrow opening.

The lead was his!

It happened so fast that he didn't even have time for it to register. Bob just kept pushing the car as hard as he dared. He plunged into the next corner, concentrating on being as smooth as possible. He was aiming to put a few car lengths on the other two racecars while they were still locked in their own battle behind him. But he knew that all it would take was for him to drive a little too hard into the next corner, for him to push up on the track into the rougher outside line. Then the two cars behind him would be likely to pull the same move on him that he just used on them.

Joe watched Wayne and Sammy as they jumped up and down when Bob assumed the lead. There was nothing like a frustrated team's excitement when their driver finally took the lead late in a race. The young pit crew's excitement was infectious and Joe forgot his usual reserve and whooped and cheered right along with them.

Bob flashed by the finish line to take the white flag. Shooting under the flagman, he finally realized that there was a white flag being shown to the field, and the starter was waving it specifically at him, the leader. He unconsciously squeezed the wheel a little tighter, as if the better grip might help him keep the car under control on this last lap. Try as he might, he had been unable to shake the two cars behind him. Racing for the first turn for the final time, he found them still disturbingly close to his back bumper, menacing as they filled his rearview mirror.

The car trailing him actually tapped Bob junior's rear bumper and that caused the rear end of his dark blue car to wiggle a bit. He felt his instincts take over as he held on to the steering wheel, doing what came naturally to try to keep the car headed straight and not backing out of the throttle at all. That's what the guy behind him expected: if he bumped Bob, he'd surely blink, lift out of the gas, and the lead would be his again.

Looking back in the mirror, Bob could see the determined face of the other driver, dead set on rooting him out of the way in his quest to secure the victory. Bob gritted his teeth, equally as determined to hold on to his position and notch his first win ever at this track.

Bob got another good jump off the second corner, leading the three cars down the short back straightaway. The extra power from Joe's prerace tuning let him build a three-car-length lead going into turn three. Bob dove into the corner for the last time, using all the strength he could muster to hold the car down low on the track, trying to protect the inside line.

The driver behind him was not giving up. He charged in hard, running up close once again after running deep into the last turn. Then, he drew back and popped Bob hard in the rear end. The impact raised the back end of Bob's car high as the nose of the trailing car pushed him through the center of the corner.

The contact kicked the rear wheels loose, sending the car skating through the corner while Bob twisted back and forth on the wheel, trying to keep the car underneath him, trying to maintain the lead. Then as all three cars came off the corner in one frantic last dash for the checkered flag, Bob boldly stood on the throttle because that seemed like the thing to do.

And it worked. The pull straightened the car right out and left the challenger safely behind as he rocketed toward the finish line.

Bob could see the checkered banner in the flagman's hand as he aimed the nose of the car that way. Then it was clear that the car behind him simply didn't have enough horses under the hood to pull past Bob as they came off the final corner.

The dark blue car flashed under the checkered flag, taking the win by two car lengths.

Sammy and Wayne hugged each other, hugged Joe, hugged people they didn't even know who just happened to be standing nearby. Joe Banker stepped back and smiled broadly, crossing his arms across his chest, completely satisfied, sublimely happy.

This was the way it had been thirty or forty years before, when they all raced as much for the thrill, the satisfaction, the glory, as for the money. For a moment, Joe Banker was standing there in the middle of 1963.

And for a moment he felt every bit of twenty-five years old.

12

The celebration only intensified when Bob rolled his late-model stock car to a stop in the cramped little victory circle near the pits. Despite his age, Joe Banker led the other two crewmembers in a mad dash over to meet him. Bob was already starting to climb out of the car as they arrived. There were whoops and hollers and high fives all around. Even the spectators in the stands had stayed around to enjoy the emotional jubilation of the first-time victor and his excited friends.

Bob climbed up on the roof of his car, mimicking the move of winning drivers he had seen on television, waving at the cheering crowd, pointing to Sammy and Wayne. And, of course, to his "Uncle Joe." Someone produced a large plastic bottle of soda. Bob Lee was only too happy to take it, shake it vigorously, uncap it, and spray it all over everybody within thirty feet of the car.

Joe Banker backed away to avoid the shower of

soda. He stood to the side, again satisfied with watching the scene around him. It reminded him so much of their first win, his and Bubba's and Jodell's, back forty years before at the rough old track at Meyers' farm. Rough or not, that track had given them a victory as sweet and memorable as any they had managed since.

And once again, he was taken by how much Bob resembled a young Jodell Lee as he danced atop the racecar. Seeing the exuberance of any young racer upon winning his first contest would have given Joe a warm feeling. But the fact that it was Bob junior who was up there, finally realizing a closely guarded dream, made it oh so sweet.

One thing was missing, though. One person who would have made it all perfect if he could only have been here to see the kind of race the young man had just run to win the thing. Joe shook his head. Jodell should be here to see this, he thought, but it was his cousin's own stubborn fault that he had never seen or accepted his boy's vision. But somehow Joe knew that time would come. And he vowed right then and there that he would do everything within his power to see that the rest of the kid's dreams were fulfilled, that his daddy would eventually see and appreciate his own boy's talents.

This was one special victory and Joe Banker sensed that the celebration was in no danger of winding down anytime soon. He realized too that he was in the perfect mood to continue the party as long as it lasted.

They finally got the car loaded back up on the trailer, but not until after the last of the photos were taken, the final congratulations accepted, and even a few autographs scrawled on the backs of the evening's program. Apparently several of the fans thought they might hear more from this Bob Lee somewhere down the road and they could brag they saw him win his first, right there in Jersey on a wild night of racing.

Bob and his buddies also picked up a sizable band of friends who were more than willing to follow them home. A regular procession of cars pulled in behind them and trailed them out of the racetrack and onto the highway. Once back to Bob's home, they backed the trailer and racecar into the driveway while all the followers disassembled their parade and parked along the street and in the front yard.

Several of them unloaded coolers that clearly contained beverages of various types and lugged them up the driveway and into the door of Bob's shop where the lights already shone in welcome. Phase two of the celebration would soon be officially under way.

Joe Banker grabbed himself something cold to drink from a passing cooler and claimed a seat on the workbench. He had forgotten how thirsty a fellow could get when he was helping somebody named Lee win a stock car race. Now that word had spread through the crowd about who this older man was, he was only too willing to hold court and share with anyone who would listen his stories about the "good old days."

Once again, Joe might just as well have stepped into a time machine that transported him back thirty years or so. The garage was full of people, maybe twenty-five or thirty folks, mostly young, some of them attractive females, and all of them already excited by the night's action. And, in addition to listening to Joe's tall tales, they were dancing to the music of a radio someone had found, talking, drinking, laughing, and generally having themselves a good time.

Joe paused long enough in his yarn-spinning to think of how much this little get-together reminded him of the legendary parties once thrown almost every week by a couple of drivers and true characters named Curtis Turner and Little Joe Weatherley. All they needed was a pig on a spit somewhere, Turner's entourage of lovely women, and the broad Virginia drawl of Weatherley holding his flower vase filled with who knows what kind of liquor concoction urging everybody to go ahead and have themselves a good time.

The party went on long into the night. Finally, Joe decided he needed a break, excused himself, and made a quick trip into the house. A few minutes later he stepped back out onto the stoop at the rear of the house and watched for a moment the happy crowd celebrating the big victory.

The moon was low, the crickets already silent for the evening, the night almost done, and, at some level, Joe Banker knew he should be in bed by now, that he and Bob had a long day coming up. But he grinned when he heard the happy laughter spilling out from inside the shop.

Sure, some of the folks in there probably didn't fully appreciate the magnitude of Bob's victory. For them, it was mostly an excuse to have a party. But to a few of them, this win was as big as any at Daytona or Talladega, the culmination of many hours of hard work. That's what they were really celebrating.

Joe couldn't help it. He wondered if there would be more victory celebrations in this young man's future. And even if there were, would they only be for wins at crumbling little out-of-the-way tracks? Or would they be kicked off with the wind filled with brightly colored confetti as they celebrated in the victory lanes of places like Atlanta and Charlotte?

Someone turned up the song that was playing on the radio and one of the pretty young women's laughter could be heard over the rest of the happy noise of the party. There was also the unmistakable clinking together of bottles, signifying still more toasts dedicated to the night's winner.

Joe Banker stepped down off the stoop and hurried back, eager to rejoin the celebration.

13

I t was mid-morning when Bob junior and Joe
pulled onto the grounds of the speedway at Watkins Glen. Bob was freshly shaven, hair perfect,
dressed in casual slacks and a fashionable pullover
sweater. When he hopped out of his car, he had a
noticeable bounce in his step.

Joe Banker, on the other hand, was still sound
asleep in the passenger seat of the car when they
pulled to a stop. Bob gave him a shake when he finally had the car parked and his passenger showed no
signs of coming to life. When Joe did open his eyes,
they were bloodshot, red-rimmed. His hair was askew
and he quickly covered it with a baseball cap, but that
did nothing to hide the stubble of a beard that he
hadn't gotten around to whacking away before they
left that morning.

He was a little slow in following Bob but fifteen
minutes later they strolled up to the Lee Racing truck
in the garage area. They found Bubba Baxter, Jodell

Lee, and Billy Winton standing there together in a close knot, talking animatedly among themselves, each offering his opinion on various race setups. The two new arrivals stood there next to them for a moment before anyone seemed to notice them. Jodell spotted his cousin finally and shot him a piercing, disapproving glance, as he took in Joe's unshaven face, his wrinkled clothes, his wild tangle of hair, and his tired, red eyes.

"You look like you might've slept under a car somewhere last night," he said without any other greeting. His words were light and joking, but there was still a hard look on his face.

"What happened to 'Hey, Joe?' 'Glad you could come up here to help me with the motor, Joe?' 'How's the wife and kids, Joe?' "

Part of Joe Banker paid little attention to his straight-arrow cousin and his judgmental bent. But part of him had always coveted Jodell Lee's approval, too. He just wished sometimes that the son of a gun would lighten up!

"I just wanna make certain you ain't swimmy-headed before you take a wrench to that motor we plan on qualifying with directly."

"Why, Jodell Lee, I could be drunker than a bicycle and still be the best engine man in all of racing," Joe countered with a broad grin.

The others laughed uncomfortably and looked at the ground. None of them wanted to be in the middle of a fight between the two cousins. But Joe seemed to be taking Jodell's words in stride. He winked at Bubba and Billy as he shook their hands.

"Now Daddy, quit picking on Uncle Joe."

Jodell spotted his boy then, half-hidden by the mass of Bubba Baxter.

"Well, look what the cat dragged in! Bobby!"

Jodell lit up as if someone had thrown a switch.

He stepped over to grab his boy in a tight bear hug while Joe and the others watched.

On the ride over, Bob made Joe promise not to tell his father about the race the night before, to not say a word about his victory. Bob wanted to have that honor eventually. Joe had his doubts. He wasn't positive that Bob could work up the nerve to tell his dad such a thing, to let him know that he was actually thinking of giving up the world of high finance for a hot, noisy racecar cockpit.

Still, Joe had his own reasons for obeying the young man's wishes. The previous night, he had seen a man who appeared to have an almost unnatural desire to compete in a racecar. It was a hunger that would not be sated until Bob ultimately gave it a real shot, until he could find out for himself if he really craved such a radical change in careers. As he watched the two men embrace, Joe realized that he already knew the answer, though. There was too much of his father in the boy.

He had watched how the younger Lee drove the racecar the night before and it just as easily could have been Jodell Lee behind the wheel of that racer. The talent was there. No doubt about that. It appeared the desire was, too. But did Bob junior have the winning instinct, the almost fanatical need to always finish first in any race he ran? He had hinted at it the night before. But would it still be there when it was hot and miserable inside that car? When the racing gods frowned on him and left him sitting idle in a broken, busted racecar? Joe figured that was ultimately the only thing that might separate the young man from becoming a good racecar driver.

Joe renewed his determination right then and there to do all he could to help his cousin's boy give it a good shot, find out if he had a chance to become as much a winner as his dad always had been.

"Let me have a look at you," Jodell was saying to

Bob. He held him at arm's length and looked him up and down. "You could still put on a few pounds, but I guess you'll do."

"It's that Yankee food," Joe offered before Bob could defend himself. "Bagels and raw fish. Boy needs some biscuits and gravy."

Jodell shot Joe a sideways glance, a quizzical look on his face. Something had just dawned on him.

"Y'all come over from the city together?" he asked Bob.

"Yessir. Uncle Joe stopped by for a visit yesterday and we rode up this morning."

Jodell looked from Joe to Bob and back to Joe again.

"What did this old fool do?" he asked his son. "Keep you out at some juke joint all night?"

"Aw, Dad, Uncle Joe came up to visit and I took him out last night and showed him around the city a little bit. That's all."

"I've seen him looking like this plenty of times before," Jodell said as he gave Joe another disapproving once-over.

Bubba and Billy remained silent. They too had seen Joe the morning after parties plenty of times before. There was no doubt he had enjoyed himself the previous evening, too. The signs were all there. They simply couldn't imagine such a thing with such a levelheaded escort as Bob junior, and with old Joe so far away from his usual haunts and partying buddies. But the man always did have a knack for making a party, even when one didn't exist before he showed up.

Joe Banker slid his cap back on his head and half watched out of the corner of his eye as a pair of fetching young race fans in cutoffs and tank tops walked past.

"Boys, I believe I'll go in and take myself a shower," he announced. "Then we might see if y'all have messed up my engine so bad even I can't get it back in tune again."

Jodell scowled but Bubba and Billy laughed as Joe disappeared into the back of the truck.

"I swear, one of these days that crazy—"

"Don't worry, Dad. We stayed relatively sane last night," Bob said. "It was good to get to visit with him. Seems like Uncle Joe and I haven't had much time to talk the last few years."

"I know. I know. I just never understood why he cared so much about all that foolishness when we had so much serious work to do." Jodell shook his head, seemingly baffled by anyone who would prefer having a good time when there was backbreaking work to be done to get ready to run some races. He gave his boy another hug. "Hey, Bobby, I know you don't want to be spending all your time hanging around these dirty old grease monkeys. Anyway, your momma's dying to see you. She's over yonder in the motor home with Joyce."

Bob exchanged greetings with Bubba and Billy before he headed off to the RV where his mother and Bubba Baxter's wife, Joyce, were relaxing. The men were back into their racecar setup discussion before he was out of earshot.

He grinned. He would actually have preferred staying there, listening, learning, maybe even contributing to the conversation. As he wandered off through the garage, Bob spoke to several of the old-timers who had known him since he was a boy, visiting his dad's garage stall at the tracks. But as he walked amid all the frenzied activity, as he surveyed all the cars getting primed for the first practice session, he felt his pulse quicken.

And he knew. He knew as certainly as he had ever known anything in his life. Wall Street could be exciting. It was definitely a good living. But this was what he was born to do.

It was time for him to come home.

Now, all he had to do was figure out exactly how he was going to make it happen.

14

When Rob woke up Saturday morning, he carefully rolled from one side to the other in the hotel-room bed, testing, experimenting. He was still sore but not nearly as stiff or tender as he had been the day before. He felt more than ready to get into the car and start helping Will and the boys zero in on the race setup. Rob also wanted to try to get in as many laps as he could stand during the couple of practice sessions that were left. He knew he was still lacking experience on the road course and could use all the lap time he could stand.

Donnie Kline helped ease Rob into the seat of the racecar.

"We don't want him to hurt him little ribs," the big man cooed in a hilarious attempt at mock baby talk.

Donnie had somehow produced and mounted some extra padding in the cockpit since the last practice the day before, all in an attempt to make Rob more comfortable in the racecar. Rob settled into the seat, shifting about while Donnie fiddled with the padding. Once he appeared set and cozy, Donnie left him to finish buckling up while he made some other last-minute checks for Will. Hughes was underneath the rear end of the car helping Paul move the rear sway bar over a notch.

Rob went through his normal preparations in the cockpit, determined to put the aches and pains out of his mind so he could concentrate on getting himself and the car ready to race. The ankle pain he was confident he could ignore. The ribs would be hardest. But it was time to go racing and there was no way he could win if he was worrying about a few twinges and smarts instead of concentrating on helping get the car right for the race tomorrow.

The first spins around the track felt good. The car was encouragingly fast with Rob's lap times putting him into the top twenty among all the cars that were practicing with him out on the track. While running off the practice laps, Rob worked on his powers of concentration even as he learned all he could about the track itself. He tried to hit each turn perfectly, catch every shift point, all while getting on the brakes at the perfect moment in every corner. The slightest slipup during the race could be disastrous. If the race ran true to form, most of the cars would finish on the lead lap. If he should get careless and slide through a corner, or if he suffered a mental lapse and spun out into the grass, then a top-ten car could easily finish twenty-fifth or thirtieth. The Glen course could be cruelly unforgiving.

Rob brought the car in after the first ten-lap run, satisfied with both the car and himself. Will studied his driver's face as he leaned in the window to show him the clipboard with the tire temperatures. The wide grin on Rob's face told him all he needed to know. The kid was ready. Lingering pains or not, he would be ready to start the race on Sunday. And with any luck, he might actually finish it, too. Still, any thoughts Will might still be harboring about having a relief driver standing by quickly vanished when he saw the kid's expression.

"Good run!" he hollered over the sound of the Ford's revving engine.

"It felt great!" Rob answered, his voice muffled by his helmet. "What are we gonna do on the next run?"

"I wanna make a couple of little changes that ought to help us going into turn one. It might let you pick something up when you go through that tight left-hander."

"How many laps?"

"Let's do four or five so we can get some comparisons on the stopwatch, then we'll see. If they look good, we may have you do a longer. If you feel up to it, that is."

Will had no doubt what Rob's reaction would be.

"Feel up to it? I feel great! Let's do a long run and really see what we got," Rob yelped excitedly. Even when there were no doubts about his physical condition, Rob was impatient with all the starts and stops of the practice rounds. He always wanted to get the car out on the track and run it as hard as it would go, just like in a race.

"Patience now. We got to get the car right first. Once we do, then we'll let you go out there and run till they make you stop."

"Patience, patience, patience. You sound like a broken record, Will."

"That's all you ever hear from me because that's one of the words you still haven't managed to learn yet. When you do, I'll teach you another word, like maybe 'winning.' How would you like that?"

Rob gave him a mean look and pretended to draw back to throw a punch. Will grinned and pulled back out of the racecar.

Then, they went back to work and there was noth-

ing glamorous about how they did it. They made a
few changes then headed back out and ran a few laps.
Once a base line was established, Rob would steer the
car back to the garage, more changes were made, then
he would head back out once again. This was repeated
several times for the remaining hour or so of practice.

Rob was still running laps when the red flag finally
came out, officially ending the session. He accelerated
off the corner onto the long straightaway leading
down to the chicane. Rob jumped hard on the brakes
and worked the steering wheel, strong-arming the car
into the tight turn. He grabbed a gear, downshifting
before shooting off toward the next corner. He only
eased off when the entrance to pit road came into
sight.

Finally, he cut the engine, coasted onto pit road,
and rolled easily back to the garage where Will and
the boys were waiting for him. He dropped the window net as he coasted smoothly to a stop, then unbuckled the safety belts, unsnapped the steering
wheel, and tossed it up onto the dash. Now it was
Donnie Kline's turn to help him out of the car.

Rob steadied himself on his crutches and looked
around for Michelle and the cold drink she would
usually have there waiting for him after a practice run.
He didn't see her, though. He hobbled over to the
doorway, looking around for her. Then, there she was,
halfway down the row of stalls, animatedly talking
with someone.

"Who's that over there with Michelle?" Rob asked,
somewhat suspiciously. He couldn't tell who the man
was that she was talking with, but he assumed from
the broad smile on her face and the way she tossed
her hair that he was flirting with her.

"Why do you wanna know?" Donnie asked. He
knew that Rob could be very protective of her. Or
jealous. The crew often accused him of being jealous

of others who showed her attention, despite his pro-
tests to the contrary.

"She looks awfully taken in, that's all."

"What's it matter to you, anyway? Maybe he wants
to ask her out."

"Who is it? Is he bothering her?"

"I don't think so." Donnie had walked out to stand
next to him, wiping his face and shaved head with a
shop rag. "From the looks of it, I'd say she's enjoying
herself."

"I don't know . . ."

Rob couldn't help it. He only wanted to shield
Michelle from the cocky hotshots who seemed to always be prowling through the garage like hungry li-
ons looking for prey. It was easy for them to mistake
Michelle's open, friendly manner for an invitation to
move in for the kill.

Rob, red-faced, leaned forward on his crutches,
ready to hike on over and save Michelle from this
character.

"Hold on, Lone Ranger," Donnie said with a laugh
and then grabbed Rob's shoulder. "That's Bob Lee
she's talking to. What's got into you, anyway? If I
didn't know you were so hung up on her sister, I'd
say you were pretty dang hung up on Miss Michelle."

"Oh," Rob exclaimed, stopping so fast he almost
did a face-first dive onto the asphalt.

Now he recognized Bob Lee for himself. He remembered him from pictures over at the Lees'. He
regained his footing and some of his composure before tottering over to where they stood.

Michelle happily introduced them to each other.
She didn't seem to notice the embarrassed look on
Rob's face. He still smarted from Donnie's insinua-
tion. Could it be true, though? Could he actually be
jealous of Bob Lee?

He tried not to think about it as he renewed his
acquaintance with Jodell's son. But still, when he saw

the way Michelle looked at Bob as he talked, when he heard her lyrical laugh at something funny he said that wasn't really all that funny, he couldn't help the odd feeling he had in the pit of his stomach.

He tried to ignore it, but it was there all the same.

15

Rob Wilder had found himself a cool, comfortable place on the back stoop of the truck and was hungrily inhaling a baloney, cheese, and hot sauce sandwich, washing it down with a root beer, and all the while talking with Bob Lee. For his own lunch, Bob had scouted about until he located a half-decent fast food salad.

"I guess I'll have a hard time getting used to racetrack food," Bob said, half under his breath, as he watched Rob chomp off another big bite of the sandwich.

Rob only half heard him and it never occurred to him to wonder why Bob might be spending more time at a racetrack. He was already thinking about the start of the final "happy hour" practice coming up in less than an hour. And, though he had not mentioned it to anyone, the aches and pains from the day before had grabbed hold of him again and were settling in. He kept his foot elevated, propped up on the hauler, trying to keep some of the pressure off his bad ankle. That seemed to help some, but the only way he could get his ribs to stop hurting was to cease breathing.

The two of them, Rob and Bob, now talked easily with each other. Rob was happy to learn how knowledgeable Jodell's son was about racing. He was, after all, the offspring of one of the sport's legends. But Rob had always heard that Bob junior lost all interest in the sport in his mid-teens and never looked back. For somebody who didn't follow the game, he sure was up-to-date on all that was going on.

Talking with Bob also gave Rob some relief from the steady parade of fans passing though the garage area and their constant barrage of questions about his condition for Sunday's race. If he heard "Who's gonna be standing by to be your relief driver on Sunday?" one more time, then he might well snap and start angrily tossing tools and parts at somebody.

Eventually, the conversation turned to the subject of investing, subtly steered that way by Rob Wilder. He was only too happy to pick his new friend's brain on the matter, and Rob still assumed Bob would rather talk about that sort of thing than tire stagger and carburetor jetting. Besides, the kid had grown tired of the well-intentioned but constant prodding from Billy Winton and Will Hughes, from his accountant, Randy Weems, and his attorney, Clifford Stanley. They seemed intent on pestering him totally to death about his money and how much he was losing on it by merely socking it away in a passbook savings account at the Chandler County Savings and Loan. If he could pick up a tip or two from a real pro over a sandwich and root beer and keep from boring Bob to tears with race talk, then all the better.

Still, Bob Lee seemed to not want to talk shop at all. He kept steering the conversation back to racing and racecars.

Meanwhile, Bubba Baxter cornered Joe Banker

coming out of the shower over in the Lee Racing hauler. Sometimes Baxter was as perceptive about people and their behavior as he was the peculiarity of cars and tracks. And he had smelled something odd the minute he saw Joe and Bob junior walk up that morning. He waited to pursue it, though, until Jodell had gone off somewhere.

"All right. What on earth did you get into last night?" Bubba asked. "Jodell is fit to be tied. He's been mutterin' and spittin' ever since you and the boy got here. He thinks you're about to corrupt his only son and lead him down a path of sin and transgression like you used to travel."

Joe ran his fingers through what had once been long, dark, and wavy hair, one of the features that had made him so popular with ladies at racetracks all over America. He had a sly grin on his face as he waited a long moment to answer, until Bubba's normally red face had turned an even brighter shade of crimson.

"Bubba, you wouldn't believe me if I told you. In fact, I'm still having a hard time believing it myself."

Then he paused again, deliberately pulling a comb from his pocket, finding himself in one of the hauler truck's side mirrors, and parting his still-wet hair.

"Okay. Okay. Try me. I'm listening."

Bubba was hopping impatiently from one foot to the other like a kid waiting for his buddy to share a secret. The two men had grown up together and spent the better part of the past forty years on the road together. Joe knew exactly how to get the giant man's goat.

"I mean, Bubba, you are really not going to believe this."

Still, he combed, parting the hair just right, then messed it all up with a shake of his head and started all over again.

"I swear, Joe Banker. If you don't—"

"All right. All right. Hold your water, Big'un. I'll

tell you what me and Bob junior done last night, but
you have got to promise me one thing."

"What's that?"

Now Bubba was truly perplexed. He had heard
every ridiculous excuse there was for Joe's behavior
down through the years, every meager explanation for
his misconduct. Some of them were downright crea-
tive, if totally impossible. But the truth was, he too,
just like Jodell, had quickly grown tired of Joe's continual lapses, his habitual oversleeping, his all-night
partying, his penchant to lose all concentration if an
attractive woman happened to stroll past, no matter
how crucial or urgent the current task might be. Such
carryings-on had actually hurt the team on occasion.
Maybe not enough to offset all the good he did with
his natural ability with racing engines, but racing and
winning were far too important to Jodell Lee and
Bubba Baxter for them to ever tolerate anything like
the stunts Joe pulled sometimes.

"What if I gave you three—"

"Tell me, Joe Banker, before I stuff you in that
parts box with all the rest of the lug nuts!"

"We went racin' last night."

Joe whispered the words so quietly that Bubba
wasn't sure he heard him right.

"What?"

"We went racin' last night. Racing. You know. Racin' like we used to do. Me and you and Joe-dee. Flat
out on some nameless track."

"You're kiddin' me, ain't you? Bob junior don't
care nothin' about racin'. And I think it's a crying
shame you're trying to use him as an excuse for your
going out and trying to paint the town—"

"Listen to me. I'm telling you the gospel truth."
Joe glanced around conspiratorially. He dropped back
into a whisper. "What I'm telling you is that me and
Bob junior went to the racetrack last night. And we
did some racing. It was so much like it used to be

when we started, Bub, out there on that little, bitty track. It made me realize something. I've done forgot why we got into all this in the first place. But after last night, it's all come back to me now. Man, Bub, it was one good feeling!"

Bubba was truly interested now. Racing? And did Joe say they "did some racing"?

"You gonna tell me or am I gonna have to turn you upside down and shake it out of you?"

Joe knew he might well do that very thing. He grabbed the collar of Bubba's Lee Racing shirt and pulled him even closer.

"Listen to me. Breathe a word of this to Jodell and we're both as good as dead. He'll skin both of us alive because he'll automatically figure me and you was behind it from the beginning, whether we was or not. You know Jodell."

"Joe!"

"I got this call last week from Bob junior. He told me he needed me to come by on my way to the Glen, that he needed my help on a little problem he had. That's all he told me. That and 'don't you dare tell my daddy.' I figured if it was important enough for him to call me and ask, then I ought to do it. And the part about not telling Jodell got me curiouser than an old cat. Anyways, I figured I'd get to spend a night in the big city doing the family-visiting thing since I ain't hardly seen the boy in the last five or ten years at all. I'd help Bobby with his problem, maybe party a bit if I could slip off or maybe get the boy to recommend some hot spot, and then I'd hop on over here today. No big deal."

Bubba eased back to sit down on the hauler ramp, his ear cocked.

"So what happened?"

"He meets me at the airport and we head out to his place. And he leads me around to the back of the house where he's got this big old two-car garage. He opens the door and I expect to see an antique car or maybe a hot rod or something. Instead, right there in the middle of a fairly decent shop sits a perfectly maintained, late-model stock car. Sharply painted and well built, I might add."

Bubba's eyes widened. All the pieces were starting to fall into place.

He listened intently as Joe told the story, of helping him work on the car, of the trip to the track in Jersey, of Bob junior driving a beautiful race to take the checkered flag. He didn't share quite as much of the detail about the after-race victory party, partly because he didn't want to dwell on that part of the night and partly because, frankly, he didn't remember a good part of it.

"So the boy wants to drive," Bubba said, shaking his head.

"That's what he says. And if he inherited that stubborn streak his daddy's got, he'll bust if he don't."

"You're right about one thing. Jodell will die when he finds out. But I thought the boy didn't care anything about racing."

"You know how Jodell discouraged him about it. How he preached about him going to school and getting a good education and a real job. I guess, at some point, the boy just decided he needed to follow his heart and not his old man's marching orders."

Bubba leaned back and thought for a moment. It was easy to tell when the big man was thinking. He developed an almost pained expression on his broad face.

"So Joe, tell me what you really think," he finally said. "What kind of driver is he? Can he really drive a racecar?"

For once, Joe Banker's countenance was serious.

"He's a blamed good one. A real good one. We'll be able to tell more when he gets in a good car on a big track but he impressed the dawg out of me last night. I got some ideas—"

Bubba stuck up a big hand and dodged as if Joe had thrown something hard and hot at him.

"Whoa! Wait a minute! What ideas? What you talkin' about?"

"Oh, nothing," Joe answered, taking a step back. He realized he had already said too much. "I was just thinking how nice it would be to watch the boy race again sometime, him driving so much like his daddy and all. That's all."

Bubba looked at him warily, not sure he was getting all the story yet.

"Yeah, I would love to have been there with you. That had to have been something, seeing Jodell's boy out there in a racecar," he said.

Joe put his fingers to his lips to remind Bubba how crucial it was that he keep quiet about what he had just told him.

"Look, Fat Boy, we got work to do," he announced loudly. "You been bellyachin' all morning about how sour Rex's motor is. You gonna sit here and gossip or you gonna come help me make it run like a sewing machine?"

With that, he sauntered on over to the racecar and poked his head underneath the hood. If there was something wrong with the motor, he would fix it, make it right.

Joe Banker figured if something was wrong, something was out of whack, he had the gift for making it right. Even the obligation to do so.

And that's exactly what he would do.

16

When the last round of practice was finally red-flagged, Rob Wilder was more than ready to immediately head back to the hotel. Michelle was standing right there waiting, as instructed, as soon as Rob exited the car. Will was satisfied with where the car was by the end of the last run. He quickly made plans to meet up with Rob later if they needed to discuss any changes once everybody had found dinner and were back at the hotel. Bob bummed a ride from Michelle, too. He had reservations at the same hotel as they did. Michelle was obviously excited to have him join them.

By now, Rob was too exhausted to care. He liked Bob, but something bothered him about the way he came riding onto the scene and swept Michelle off her feet with his dark good looks and his smooth, big-city charm.

Rob half reclined in the back seat and kept quiet as they made the short drive back to the hotel. It was hard, though. Bob had a naturally likable personality, a certain suaveness that Rob felt he himself had not yet developed since deserting his rural background. And he was more than a bit intimidated when Bob and Michelle talked easily of subjects he knew only little about and in a language that was totally foreign to him. He had come a long way in a short time. He had worked hard to learn about business and the economy and computers and the Ensoft software. But it turned out Bob had done a full analysis of Ensoft for his firm and knew more about the company and its products and the people who ran it than Rob could ever hope to learn.

He tried to close his eyes and rest as they inched along in the thick traffic, everyone trying to leave the speedway at once. But he could hear Bob's easy laugh and what he quickly recognized as Michelle's "happy" voice.

He gritted his teeth, closed his eyes tighter, and tried to stay hidden there behind his new aviator sunglasses. But the traffic was knotted hopelessly, their progress no more than a crawl. He sank lower in the seat and attempted to ignore the pulsating ache in his ankle, the dull throb from his rib cage with each beat of his heart, the chatter from the front seat.

But try as he might, he couldn't work up much resentment against Bob Lee. He certainly seemed to be a good guy, not a snobby New Yorker, convinced he was better than everybody else simply because he resided in the business and cultural center of the universe. Since he was Jodell Lee's boy, that shouldn't be surprising, Rob thought.

But then he noticed that the talk up front had turned from analyst ratings and stock issues to racing. And it was Bob who was asking all the questions. Just as he had with Rob earlier that afternoon, Bob seemed genuinely interested in the sport, his questions more than just the stuff of polite conversation. And he certainly seemed to have far more knowledge about it than one would expect from the typical Wall Street portfolio jockey. Maybe, being the son of a racing legend and all, he had simply picked it up by osmosis. But still, he seemed far more enthralled with the sport than everyone had indicated.

Once they finally got back to the hotel, Rob was about to tell Michelle good night and head for a hot shower and an early bed. But then, when Bob asked Michelle if she had dinner plans, he had a quick change of heart. He was so hungry his stomach thought his throat must have been cut. At least, that's what he told Bob and Michelle.

"I'll be glad to bring you something back," Michelle offered. "You look beat."

"Aw, I feel like a million dollars," he said, but then he caught a glimpse of himself in a mirror in the lobby. His hair was unkempt, his face pale, his eyes sunken and dark circled.

"Upstairs. Upstairs with you right this minute," Michelle ordered. Then she practically pushed him to the elevator, stepped on behind him and hit the button for his floor. "In case you've forgotten, you've got a big race to run tomorrow and your sponsor, for one, is counting heavily on you, Mr. Rob Wilder."

Was she sincere or was she trying to dump the odd man out? He had no choice. He obeyed her. And he didn't really think much about her and Bob, out enjoying dinner, talking all that talk. He almost fell asleep in the shower, the stinging hot water helping ease some of the aches and pains. Then, once he had sprawled across the bed, he was out, slumbering deeply, even before he could grab the remote control off the nightstand and switch the television from his usual favorite, the Cartoon Network, over to the financial channel.

It was close to nine o'clock when Michelle tapped lightly on Rob's door.

"Rob, you awake?" she whispered as she knocked again.

She held a Styrofoam box filled with the closest thing to Southern cooking she could find around Watkins Glen, New York. There was only silence from the other side of the door. Finally, she set the box of food down on the floor, fished in her purse until she found the second room key he had given her, and slid it into the lock until the tiny red light turned to green.

Rob was still sleeping soundly, his mouth open, snoring slightly, with his broken ankle elevated on a couple of extra pillows. On the television screen, the Tasmanian Devil was winding around in circles while Bugs Bunny watched nonchalantly.

She smiled as she set his dinner on the nightstand, then picked up the remote control and turned down the volume. She tried to pull the corner of the blanket from underneath him so she could spread it over him, but in the process she stirred him awake.

"How was dinner?" he asked, yawning sleepily.

"Wonderful. I wish you could have come along with us. Bob is so interested in racing. All he could talk about was you and how well you're doing so early in your career."

Me? I bet! He's at dinner with you and all he wants to talk about is me?

Rob only thought the words. Even as sleepy as he was, he knew better than to say them out loud.

"Yeah, I really wanted to go with y'all. But you were right, as usual. I needed the rest. What you got there?"

"Some steak and ribs with a potato and some coleslaw. I asked them if they had some catfish but they looked at me like I was crazy. It's all a heart attack waiting to happen to me. Now, a nice piece of grilled salmon, a salad with a light vinaigrette . . ."

Sometimes the Californian in her showed through. She could not fathom how special a batch of fried

catfish was to Southerners. She wasn't at all surprised
that such a delicacy was foreign here, too. There were
mountains that made the landscape look very similar
to East Tennessee and North Carolina, but they were
still in the Finger Lakes region of New York State.
The waitress's blank stare when she inquired about
catfish confirmed it.

Rob hungrily opened the container. He was worn
out from the day at the track but the shower and the
nap had revived him. Now, some wonderful red meat
would do some more rejuvenating.

"You wanna stay and watch some television with
me?" he asked hesitantly. He truly wanted her company.

"Well, I was planning on going back to the room.
I need to make some calls." She paused a moment,
thinking, deciding. "But they'll wait." She fell onto
the room's other bed, stacked up the pillows under
her head, and settled in. Then she looked over at him
as if she had just thought of something. "You want
me to get you some ice for that ankle first?"

"No, I'm okay. It feels a lot better. The cast is
working great. It's all the other little aches and pains
that are wearing me out. They didn't really bother me
today until we got stuck in all that traffic on the way
back over here. That's when those little gremlins went
to banging away on me with their tiny little ham-
mers."

"I thought you were feeling better today."

"I was when I got up this morning. I guess it was
getting bounced around in the car all day when I was
throwing her through the corners. It didn't hurt at the
time but then . . ."

"How about a back rub? Would that help?"

He thought for a minute, watching Bugs Bunny
pulling carrot after carrot out of sight into the ground
as a perplexed Elmer Fudd watched them disappear.

"Yeah. Yeah, maybe after a little while. Maybe after I finish eating and call Christy. She should be home by now."

They watched the television silently then while Rob worked on his dinner. He started once to get up to grab a soda out of the cooler, but then he fell back onto the bed when he missed the crutch he was reaching for. Michelle chuckled, shook her head, and rolled off the bed to get the drink for him.

Before she could lie back down there was another knock at the door. She opened it a crack, making certain it wasn't a racing fan who had somehow found Rob's room number. It happened.

Will Hughes stood there, his notebooks under his arm.

"Hey. How's the patient?"

"Come on in and see for yourself."

She swung the door open for him.

"I brought someone with me. I hope you don't mind." Bob Lee Jr. stood there in the hallway behind Will. "I caught him loitering in the lobby, waiting for his daddy and momma to get back from dinner."

"You better ask that ornery old race driver lying over there if he's up for any more company," Michelle answered.

She checked the expression on Rob's face. She knew him well enough by now to instantly pick up on his mood change whenever Bob Lee was around them. But now he actually brightened when he saw Will and Bob.

Sure enough, all the race talk caused Rob to cheer up considerably. He now ignored the animated figures cavorting around on the television screen and he completely forgot to call his girlfriend out in California. Will dove right in, going over different setups and shock combinations based on what he had learned during the two days of practice. The car was good and fast, but Will Hughes was always on a mission to make it even better and faster.

Meanwhile, Bob and Michelle sat on the room's couch and made small talk. But Michelle noticed something odd. As easy as Bob had been to talk with ever since she had met him, he now seemed distracted, only giving her half his attention. Then she realized he was trying to hear what Will and Rob were saying. He actually seemed more interested in their technical racing talk than he was in her evaluation of the business book she had recently read.

Suddenly, Will stopped and turned to Bob and Michelle. They had apparently just run out of conversation.

"Hey, Bob. How'd it feel winning that race last night?"

Bob's eyes grew wide. Michelle's mouth dropped open. Rob looked sharply at Will as if he had just spoken French.

During the day, Bob had shared his story with Will. With his mother, too. She would have guessed something was up anyway so he had to. And, of course, Uncle Joe knew. But that was it. And he didn't really want this secret to be any more widespread just yet, either.

"Aw, don't worry about Rob and Michelle. They aren't about to tell Jodell. Your little secret is safe with them."

But both Rob and Michelle were staring at Bob Lee as if he had just sprouted a second head. Bob was driving a racecar last night? Driving and winning, apparently.

All either of them had ever heard from Jodell was that his boy had no interest in racing, that he avoided the tracks most of the time because of the noise and grit, that he even stayed away from Chandler Cove because the race shop was right there. He preferred having them up to New York City for his mom's birthdays or to spend Christmas on a cruise ship in the Caribbean.

So, what was this all about?

Will winked at Bob, then went back to his notes. There was nothing for him to do then but tell his story. Rob was off the bed, hopping over to join them.

Bob had been the good son. He had accepted his father's wishes that he not pursue racing, even though the desire continued to smolder somewhere deep inside him all along. He got his degree, went on for his MBA, landed the job with a major firm on Wall Street and had moved on up the ladder as if it all had been preordained. But somehow, all along, he had wondered what it would have been like to lead a pack of snarling, growling racecars off turn four and take the checkered flag at one of the legendary tracks.

Once he put an old car together and did a few spins at some of the tiny tracks not far from Manhattan, he knew his fate was sealed. He would drive if he had the talent. If not, he'd still have to be involved some way in the game in which he had been raised.

"Folks, I've got 10-W-30 in my veins, I think," he told them. "This is what I was born to do. And I've got to do it."

Any opinions Rob had held earlier in the day were now overshadowed by one obvious thought. He could identify completely with Bob Lee's dream. His had been the same since before he could remember. When Bob talked about racing his tricycle around his front yard in Chandler Cove, Rob remembered doing the same thing. They had both simulated racing on their bikes, too. Then there were go-carts both Rob and Bob put together themselves. It was Rob's mother who had discouraged him, telling him to quit wasting his time with thoughts of such a dangerous and foolish thing as racecar driving. For Bob, it had been Jodell Lee.

"When I came off that corner for the final time, I couldn't believe it when I saw that checkered flag waving," Bob was saying with a sparkle in his dark eyes. "It was hard to imagine that it was waving for me, that I finally had my first win in the Late Model Division."

"I haven't ever forgotten my first checkered flag, either," Rob offered, fondly remembering the night of his first win at the old track outside Huntsville, Alabama. He had only been seventeen.

"You should have seen Uncle Joe," Bob said with a grin. "I have never seen him so excited in my whole life."

"I bet he was! Too bad your daddy didn't get to come with him." Rob paused for a second then went ahead with the question he had wanted to ask for the last twenty minutes. "Why was he so dead set against you racing?"

"I don't know. He never really said I couldn't. He never actually came out and forbade me to race. He just never seemed to give me any encouragement to do it. And it was almost a foregone conclusion that I would have nothing to do with racing at all."

"Did you ever ask him?" Rob asked.

"I didn't have to. He made it clear right from the start that I was to go to school and then work somewhere outside of racing."

Rob thought about it quietly for a bit but somehow he couldn't square that with the Jodell that he knew. After all, it had been Jodell Lee himself who had taken him under his wing and treated him like his own son, giving him all the advice and help anyone could ever ask for to get going in the sport. And he continued to do it to this very day. He had even taken time that afternoon before practice to give him a hint or two for negotiating the tricky road course.

Now he was hearing that Jodell had not only not encouraged his own son's love for racing, but he had actually very deliberately quashed it.

There was something going on here that Rob

couldn't quite put his finger on. But what in the world was it? He decided he would make it his business to find out as soon as he didn't have a twisting, turning, breakneck race to worry about.

17

There was no mistaking the look on Rob Wilder's face as he sat there in his racecar on the starting line, patiently awaiting the command to fire the engines. He was concentrating hard on the task at hand, ignoring all the color and noise that swirled around him.

A truly festive atmosphere prevailed around the road course track that wound through the gently rolling hills of southwestern New York State. Unlike an oval track, with its long rows of grandstands fronting broad straightaways, the fans here were spread out all along the sweeping course in little pockets. It was impossible for anyone to actually see the entire track from any one position. But still, judging from the size of the crowd and the noise they were already making, they were primed for the reverberating thunder from the forty-three powerful racing machines that were about to contest for their favor.

Rob was doing exactly what he always did in those

last tense minutes before the field rolled away to start a race. He was mentally running that first lap around the track, imagining each foot of it. Here, though, it was quite a mental exercise. There were more than the usual four turns and the occasional trioval to ponder.

Then, totally uninvited, thoughts of Bob Lee's revelation the night before intruded into his routine. He could still see the excitement in Bob's eyes as he described his win at the little New Jersey speedway on Friday night. Rob could identify. He still woke up many nights, his heart pounding excitedly from dreaming of his first win at that dusty, ragged little track not far from home. It had not even made the local papers but it still shone brightly on his own mental highlight reel. So did his first win in a feature at the area's biggest track, and, of course, that initial Grand National victory at Nashville the previous year.

Now, he was wondering, would today be another dream day?

He was confident he had the car beneath him to get that first big-time win. But what about its driver? Was he up to it? Without the accident the week before at Indy, many of those in attendance here would have certainly considered him to be one of the favorites. No doubt he would have been the favored rookie in the field. But there were several well-known names lining up with him who had been racing for years but had never found victory lane in a Cup event. What made him, a raw rookie with a bum leg and wounded ribs, think he could manage something they had not?

And was he physically able? Was he mentally up to the task today?

He shook his head vigorously to clear the negative thoughts. Rob certainly felt better today than he had at any time since the Indy crash. Not quite his old self, but much closer. It seemed all the work he did in the practice sessions the day before had actually helped to drive some of the stiffness out of his sore muscles. That didn't apply, though, to the ankle. It ached dully and had since he had crawled from the bed early that morning. The blamed thing seemed determined to continually remind him that he was back in a racecar only a bit over a week after almost getting himself killed in one, as if the throbbing ankle were determined to keep him humble and off balance.

Still, Rob was confident that once they got moving, once the adrenaline was pumping and his ears were numbed by the howl of his own engine along with that of his competitors, the ache would be chased away. He had told Will Hughes as much after he climbed into the car and his crew chief nodded his agreement. It was no longer a concern of his.

Now Will kneeled down next to the car and smiled. The national anthem had been sung, the final announcements made, and the dignitary who was going to give the "start engines" command was being introduced on the public address system.

"You ready to go, Cowboy?"

There was not a second's hesitation and the words were sure.

"I'm ready."

"How're those pedals feeling?"

"Perfect. I can get to the clutch okay without getting tangled up in the brake."

"Good. Remember now that you got a busted-up ankle when you go jamming in that clutch. You don't have to kick it to the pavement, you know."

"Don't worry about me doing that. This thing has a way of reminding me that's hard to miss."

Rob nodded toward the floorboard and grinned.

"Right. Remember to keep an eye on the temperatures today. It's a little warmer out here today than we were planning on." It was good advice, right off the checklist on his clipboard, but Will also knew it would serve to take Rob's mind off the nagging pain from the ankle. He needed his driver thinking of the steps necessary to win this race, not on his aches and pains. "We'll pull some tape off the front grille on the first stop if we need to."

Then, right on time, came the command to start the engines. Rob flipped the starter switch and felt more than heard the engine rumble to life at his command. Then he reached up and flipped down the visor on his helmet, looking for all the world like a knight of old about to go off to battle.

The kid was tired of all the attention and concern over his injury. It was time to do what he came up here to do. Race! Race and win! Indianapolis and his crunching collision with the wall were now behind him. No more members of the media could ask him about the leg, about who would be subbing for him. They could now sit up there and see for themselves that he was ready to run. He gingerly held the sole of his plastic cast on the clutch pedal, waiting for the signal from the official at the head of the line to roll the car off and toward the track.

Seven laps into the race, Rob was more than holding his own. The car was working well as he boldly tossed it back and forth through the course's quick, tight corners. He had already picked up a few spots and felt good. His mind was focused, fully concentrating on what he was doing, all reminders of his injuries blissfully forgotten.

Then, as he steered out of one of the turns, the car behind him drove up onto his bumper, pressing him hard, trying to take away the spot. He actually tapped Rob in the rear several times as they fought for the preferred line through each corner, but the kid was determined to hold on to the hard-won position.

If the guy was better or his car faster, let him make the pass. If not, stay back there and follow on to the front!

Rob dove into the next sharp right-hander, yanking

the shifter out of third gear and shoving it down into second as the car slowed for the turn. Then, quickly, decisively, he jumped back hard in the gas as he held the car's left-side tires right out on the edge of the grass, using both hands to hold the wheel steady as he accelerated boldly off the corner. Then, with his right hand, he grabbed the shifter again, ready to slam the car back up into third gear while the RPMs in the engine built higher and higher as he fed it the gasoline.

Rob hit his shift point and burped the throttle while he pushed the shifter toward where third gear waited to mesh. But then, he took a sudden sharp jolt in the bumper from the car running behind him. Instinctively he hammered the throttle hard to try to pull away.

The shot in the back broke Rob's concentration for only a fraction of a second, but that was all it took to make him miss the shift. His foot was already shoving the accelerator hard to the floor. The powerful engine revved furiously, immediately hitting the rev limiter, a device specifically designed to protect the motor in just such a case. Still Rob could hear the straining engine screaming as if in pain before the limiter cut in and he jerked his foot off the gas and worked to gather the fishtailing car back up.

The driver behind him shot right on past while Rob fought to get the car back into gear. He finally slipped the shifter back into second, pulled on away, and found third with no trouble, thankful that no one else behind him had plowed into him and shoved him off the course.

But almost immediately he felt the engine pause noticeably, sputter again, and start to miss badly. He didn't hesitate. He reached over and flipped the switch on the ignition box to the other set.

Please, he thought. Let it be the ignition. Not the motor.

But switching to the backup ignition did nothing to solve his problem. The car was missing all the way down the long straightaway and a terrible knocking sound was beginning under the hood.

As much as he hated to, Rob hit the radio microphone button with his thumb.

"Will, I overrevved her back there when I got kicked in the back end. She's picked up a bad miss. I'm afraid she's sucked up a valve."

Fans on their scanners could doubtless hear the dejection in the kid's voice. So could Will Hughes.

"Did you switch the ignition box?"

"Yeah, it's not the ignition. She's knocking like a carpenter in a nailing contest."

"Stay out of everybody's way and try to ride it out," Will ordered, but he knew it was likely curtains. "She gets worse, then bring her on in and we'll have to take a look at her."

Hardly forty-five minutes later, Michelle Fagan was wheeling the rental car out of the track toward the airport. Rob Wilder changed to street clothes as soon as he parked the car. He had no need of a shower. He had not even had time to conjure up a sweat out there on the track before his day ended.

The race continued, but it was not even at the halfway point when the King Air lifted off the ground, a subdued Michelle and Rob aboard, heading sadly back to Chandler Cove.

Rob managed a sickly grin while the Shenandoah Valley slipped by beneath them.

"I felt good, Chelle. I could have won today. I know it."

She smiled back and put a hand on his shoulder.

"I know. It'll come. You're going to get your win this year. I just know it."

"From your lips to God's ears," he said.

She gave him a quick sisterly kiss on the cheek and slid an arm around his shoulder. They rode that way most of the way back to East Tennessee.

Back at the Glen, Will Hughes and Billy Winton were overseeing the crew as they put the last of their equipment onto the hauler.

"Tough day for the Ensoft team," Billy said, doing his best imitation of a race commentator.

"We'll have better ones," Will added. A covey of racecars buzzed past them then, racing for position, and Billy waited for them to pass before he spoke again.

"Can't say it's all bad, though."

"What you mean, Billy? We busted a motor not even ten laps in. Hard to find any silver lining in that mean old cloud."

Will nodded toward the cars on the course still running, still racing for the win, while theirs was inside the hauler, dead.

"We came in with a beat-up driver and we're going home to race again. He's no worse off than when we got here." Billy ran his hands through his trademark long red hair. A broad grin split his face. "I reckon they'll run some more of these danged-fool races before the year is over. And I suspect we might just win ourselves some of them, too."

Will matched his boss's smile and slapped the older man on the back. He ignored the odd looks from the news photographers and television cameramen who were hovering nearby, looking for anguish and despair, not grins, on the faces of the owner and crew chief of this early-retiring racecar.

"I'm with you, Billy Winton. I suspect we might just do that very thing."

18

I t was hot as a racecar's manifold after five hundred laps. Even deep in the usually cooler hollows and coves where the mountains normally maintained their own natural air-conditioning system, most everyone had scampered inside for precious artificial cool. The tourists had apparently gone to ground, waiting for the evening to seek souvenirs while on their way to and from the Smokies. Even the farmers had prolonged lunch, leaving hay to cure another few hours, joining their cattle in finding a cooler spot in the shade to while away the hottest part of the day.

At Jodell Lee's racing shop it was cool enough inside the big building, but the activity was frantic and feverish. Several cars rested there, scattered around the vast shop floor in various states of preparation, awaiting their next shot at coming to life on a racetrack somewhere.

There had been a time when Bubba Baxter would have been right out there among the racecars. Not

anymore. He was in his cramped office, his face il-
luminated by the computer screen, sorting through the
flurry of notes for the race at Michigan. He was busily
trying to plan the setup that needed to go into the car
they were going to use next before they finally loaded
it onto the truck. It would be hard to do anything to
it once they began the long drive north.

Joe Banker stuck his head in the door.

"What you working on, chief?"

"Just trying to get the setup nailed down for Michigan."

"I thought you had the setup burned into your
brain, as many times as we've been up there all these
years."

Bubba just snorted.

"You'd think so. We ran like junk the last time we
were there. I promised Rex that I'd have him a better
car this time around and I intend to do that very
thing."

"I've been trying to forget about that race," Joe
agreed. "We were pretty pathetic, weren't we?"

"We ought to have brought the fool thing back
home after the first practice. We were bad and just
got worse. And to think that Jodell dominated that
place for years."

"You'll get it right, big'un. I'll see you later . . ."
Joe said with a wave and backed out the door.

"Hey, I could use some help here. The boys down
in the engine shop said you were caught up. Mind
giving me a hand? You might see something I've
been missing."

Bubba waved toward the piles of paper, most of it
covered with his peculiar style of chicken scratching,
and at the lines and symbols on the computer screen.

"I'd like to, but I think I'm gonna take the afternoon off. I promised somebody I'd help them out this
afternoon. The boys have got everything under con-

trol back in the shop, and you'll get this thing whipped."

Bubba stood, his face already getting red.

"Joe, dadgummit! When are you gonna quit fixing people's cars on the side? We're trying to run a race shop here, not a garage."

"Here, here!" Joe interrupted. "Unlike you and Joe Dee, I remember where we came from. And I ain't afraid to get my hands dirty and get under a hood to help somebody out that needs it, just like we done back then."

"Them days are long gone, you old fool. We got our own cars to look out after. The way they been running lately, we may all have to get a job fixin' other folks' vehicles when the sponsors get tired of us losing. You know old Rex is gettin' mighty antsy these days, too, with other teams coming at him left and right, telling him the Lee team ain't got the magic no more."

"Relax, Bub. You'll get a handle on it. I got you a good motor and you'll hit the setup okay when you get up there and run around some. Look, this is something I promised somebody I would do and I hate to go back on my word. Heck, sometimes you ought to take an afternoon off yourself. It'd do you some good. We pay all these other cats to do all the heavy lifting these days and they'd prob'ly appreciate not having to look at your ugly mug for a few minutes. Why don't you come join me? Be just like the old days."

For the shortest moment, it almost looked as if Bubba Baxter were about to actually agree with Joe. But then he shook his head and bent back over the papers he was writing on.

"Naw, I got way too much work to do to waste the afternoon changing the spark plugs in some old grandmomma's '56 Buick."

Bubba was always chastising Joe for allowing some of the old ladies at the church to play him for a sucker, getting their mechanic work done in exchange for coconut cakes and chicken dumplings.

"Suit yourself," Joe said, shrugging his shoulders and letting loose with the wicked little laugh he had perfected over the years specifically to aggravate Bubba. It always worked and this time was no exception. "But it might do you some good to get back to your roots sometime."

Bubba waved him out the door with an angry grunt. Joe and his carefree attitude had always irritated him, even from the very start of their racing. Now, here they were, four days before a big contest on a tough track, their team struggling mightily from race to race, and their engine builder was off on some lark as if they might have just won the last six races in a row.

The longer he sat there and sweated over the frustrating paperwork the more he fumed over Joe's nonchalance. And what was that stuff about "getting back to your roots"? He had plenty of racing to watch over, and that seemed far truer to their "roots" than getting his knuckles skinned up putting brake pads on the deacon's wife's minivan!

Joe Banker was still shaking his head as he stepped out of the shop and into the bright sunshine. The intense heat hit him as soon as he opened the outside door. As he climbed into his pickup and drove the short distance down the road to his own farm, he wondered how Bubba and Jodell could ever have gotten so far from the down-and-dirty aspects of the sport. It seemed Jodell spent all his time nowadays courting some sponsor or playing footsy with the media. And Bubba was more likely to be pecking away in front of a computer monitor or scribbling on a clipboard than he was to be under the car wielding a wrench.

Didn't either one of them ever wonder what they were missing? Ever think back to how it had been not that long ago when they were so much closer to their machines?

Once in his driveway, he pulled right on past the house where he had been born and raised, heading for the old barn down by the stock pond in the back. He parked the truck under a big oak tree that was kicking off a nice circle of shade in front of the barn.

He hopped out of the truck, stepped high through the weeds that had grown up around the ancient barn, and finally approached the wide double doors on the front of the dilapidated building. It took him a minute to work the rusty latch until he could get it opened. With a loud creak, the first door swung open, then the other, and Joe propped them back with a couple of rocks.

Somehow, as the light spilled into the dusty interior of the barn, it seemed almost like he was opening the doors to an ancient crypt. It would not have been surprising at all to see mummies inside, or the treasures of an ancient king's burial tomb. Even the air smelled dry and musty, as if the old barn might have been sealed tightly for centuries.

Joe Banker stood there, outlined in the doorway by the bright light behind him, and studied the inside of the place. It did seem almost mystical inside there. He wouldn't have been one bit surprised to see a ghost or two flit by.

But instead, what he saw as his eyes grew accustomed to the darkness were the skeletons of several long-dead racecars. Faded numbers and sponsor logos on their sides told as much about them as the chiseled inscription on a grave marker might have done.

There was a dark blue '64 Ford Galaxie that had been shoved off into a back corner. A '69 Torino had found its final resting place in another. Off to one side, like an unmarked grave, were the remains of a car that was unidentifiable at first glance. The fins on the back hinted of a late-fifties vintage, though the numbers and logo had faded away long ago.

But there was another car there, too. She was resting in the very center of the barn's rough packed-dirt floor. Despite all the dust and cobwebs that had claimed her, though, there was something about her that seemed to shout that she was not yet ready for the bone pile. She was obviously from a far more recent era than the others, too.

Joe stepped to each of the old machines in turn, touching each one reverently, recalling special memories each one seemed to contain. It was sweltering inside the barn, its tin roof cracking continuously in the heat, but he hardly seemed to notice. His were the only handprints in the dust on the cars. It was obvious nothing had been touched inside this barn for a long, long time.

Joe Banker smiled as he finally reached out to caress the newer car in the center of the place. Today, that was about to change. This last ghost car was his reason for coming back to this place.

A drop of sweat fell off the end of his nose and reminded him how stifling it was inside the barn. He stepped quickly to the back of the barn and, with quite a bit of effort, managed to swing open the matching rear doors, hoping to create some kind of cross breeze through the place. Next, he grabbed a handful of old rags from the corner and began wiping the accumulated dust and grime off the newer car. He sneezed and coughed and swabbed sweat off his forehead with his sleeves but gradually made progress.

Slowly, a sleek '92-model Thunderbird began to emerge from beneath all the dirt and grime.

Three of the tires were flat and the fourth was likely dry-rotted. He slid an old jack under the car and cranked it up. Soon, the faded beauty sat on a set of jack stands and, with the bad tires and their dusty wheels gone, she looked much more like she might, at one time, have been something special.

Joe only admired her for a moment. He quickly went back to work in a methodical fashion, as if following a mental checklist he had long been planning. He checked her over thoroughly, looking for cracks in the metal, for any blemish, but all the time he could still almost feel the power that was inherent in her, sense the kinetic power she still possessed. He stepped back out to his truck and began several trips to bring in extra tools he would need in addition to those that were scattered around the place, then began to strip the T-bird down to only her frame and body.

Several hours later, he was up to his elbows in springs and shocks when his wife, Sammie, quietly set down a plate of food and a big glass of iced tea next to him. She only grinned and accepted his wink as thanks for supper. She almost asked him what in the dickens he was doing out there in that old barn among all those old racing hulks, but she knew him well enough not to even bother. She'd been around the whole clan of racers long enough to know that when the time came, he would tell her.

Finally darkness descended over the hollow and the oppressive heat of the day slowly gave way to the cool of the evening. Now, the tin roof overhead cracked and popped as it cooled with the first dew. A brilliant white light spilled out through the open doors of the barn while a growing pile of discarded parts grew to fill one of the corners.

Joe sang loudly to the country music from the radio he had plugged into the electrical outlet next to the one the work light was using. Covered in sweat, up to his elbows in dirt, he worked away. With his concentration centered firmly on stripping down the car without doing any damage, and with his attempt at singing so painfully loud that it had even kept the crickets quiet, he never noticed a set of headlights as they rolled past his house and swung down the old rutted road toward the barn.

The pickup truck pulled to a halt in front of where the bright light shone out the open doors. A giant figure of a man climbed from the truck, stopping first to hitch up his pants and shake his head at the loud singing that came from inside the barn. Finally, he stepped inside.

Bubba Baxter stopped in amazement. It had been years since he had been down here, since he had been anywhere past Joe Banker's house and Sammie Banker's kitchen table. He supposed he had known some of their old racecars had ended up down here but now, seeing them, even covered with dust and spiderwebs, they sent a flood of memories rushing through him. It was like they had been frozen in time. Even the work space and the giant old tool cabinet, circa 1970, added to the feeling that he had somehow stepped into a time warp.

Joe finally looked up from where he was removing one of the right front springs, but he finished the line he was singing before he acknowledged Bubba's presence with a wink and a nod.

"I had a hunch I'd find you here," Bubba finally said, still surveying the scene wide-eyed. "Why didn't you tell me you were coming down here?"

"I asked you to come, if you'll remember, but you didn't want to work on some old car," Joe retorted. He deliberately leaned back against the side of the T-bird, wiped the sweat from his brow with an oily shop rag, then downed what was left of his iced tea from supper. "This is something I have to do. If you wanna help, pick up a wrench and pitch in. We got a ton of work to do."

Without even thinking, Bubba began rambling through the big toolbox. He stopped suddenly.

"Wait a second. What are we doing, anyway?"

"We are going to rebuild us a racecar. I got a plan for Bob junior and we need a racecar for him."

Bubba wrinkled up his brow.

"Why not just get one from the shop? We probably got a couple that we need to weed out, anyway."

Joe looked at Bubba as if he had just uttered the silliest statement ever.

"First of all, we take one from the shop and Jodell will surely find out. He may be my first cousin, but so far as I know, I'll still be just as dead when he kills me. Secondly, I want a car that I know is capable of winning. In case you ain't noticed, we haven't been running real good lately."

"But why this car? Where on earth did you get it, anyway? It looks like it ought to be in Jodell's museum instead of on a racetrack."

"Remember when Jodell went through that spell right after he retired? How he wanted to get rid of all the old cars and replace them with brand, spanking new ones?" Joe asked.

"Yeah, I remember. We sold off some mighty fine racecars, now that you mention it. Some of 'em came back and bit us on the track, too, as I recall."

"That's right, but we couldn't talk a lick of sense into that stubborn so-and-so. All new cars or bust. 'Well,' I said to myself, 'why scrap every single one of them great cars?' So I had the boys bring this one over here. I just hated to see it go, for some reason."

Joe patted the car on the fender affectionately.

"But why this car?" Bubba asked. She still looked a little ragged but there was something so familiar about her.

"You don't recognize her, do you? This is Misty," Joe said and then watched as the light came on in the big man's eyes.

Jodell Lee had always given his racecars a woman's name, but only for one race at a time. It would be a totally different one the next time he ran. It had been a deep-seated superstition for Jodell to never use the same woman's name for more than a single race.

But this particular car had been christened Misty and the name had stuck. Everyone knew that for Jodell Lee to break a superstition and name a car permanently, it had to be a special ride. A very special ride.

"Misty!" Bubba let the word form slowly on his lips. "I remember her now!"

"Best car Jodell had in those last couple of years while he was still driving. Won his last race in her, matter of fact."

"But ain't she a little old and tired?"

"Old? Yep. But when we get through with her, she'll be ready to go to victory lane again."

"Okay, but speaking of victory lane, where are we planning on racing her?"

"Talladega!" Joe barked, then he studied Bubba's broad face as he watched the reaction to what he had just said spread across his countenance like a slow-moving cloud.

"Talladega," Bubba repeated back to him.

"Yes, Talladega. What better place to let Bob junior get his first taste of big-time racing? We'll do the Automobile Club race on Saturday before the '500.'"

"But Joe, we'll have to update everything on this car. New sheet metal, new suspension, new wiring, new everything."

"That's right, but then she'll be good as new. She'll make a good enough car for us to see if Bob's got what I think he has. The trick will be keeping Jodell from finding out and putting a stop to it."

"Don't worry about me. I won't breathe a word to a soul," Bubba said and the look on his face confirmed it. Then, without further hesitation, he stepped over to the relic of a toolbox and grabbed a handful of wrenches.

He quickly dove under the left front and went to work with a vigor Joe had not witnessed in years. There was a steady clink of metal on metal and the occasional ringing of a tool dropped on the concrete floor.

It was long past midnight when they finally reached a good stopping point. Before Bubba headed for home, he and Joe compiled a list of parts they would need to borrow from the Lee Racing stockroom the next day.

As he stepped out into the cool night air, Bubba paused before stepping up into the truck, looked up at the half-moon, then back inside the dusty barn. It had been good, actually digging into the innards of a racecar again alongside Joe. Though his muscles hurt and he had grease all over him and his hands were scratched and skinned and it was well past his usual bedtime and he knew he should be concentrating on getting his own racecar ready for Sunday, it still felt wonderful to him. To actually be building a car from scratch with his own hands, swapping good-natured jibes with his friend as they worked late into the night, just like old times.

Joe had been right. It was good to get back to their roots.

Now, as he looked back into the yellow light inside the barn, he could see a heartwarming sight. Joe Banker stood there, his back to the door, a hand on the Thunderbird's fender as if he were patting the shoulder of a long-lost friend.

19

Rob Wilder was tired. Bone tired. The bouncing around of his old pickup on the rural road helped to keep him awake but it was causing his remaining aches to act up, too. It had been two weeks since the disappointment of the Michigan race, better than three weeks since the big crash, but he still wasn't back yet. The day he was finishing had not helped one iota, either.

He had flown out that morning before sunup, spent most of the day at a sponsor appearance, and had landed with the sun at the airport. Still, despite the weariness from the long day and the lingering dull throbbing in his ankle, he really didn't relish going back to his tiny apartment and sitting there all alone on such a nice evening.

He automatically made the turn onto the highway that ran up to where the Billy Winton Racing shop was located. But as soon as he pulled the truck's old broken-off stub of a gearshift lever down into third, he knew that wasn't such a hot idea. Will would fuss and cuss about him being up and around on the ankle when he didn't have to be.

Michelle would jump him too if she found out. She had gone out of her way to clear most appearances and trips off his schedule for the last several weeks so he could mend more quickly.

He tried his best to tell them all that idleness might be just the prescription for a bum ankle. But all this lying around was, in fact, driving him totally insane. He had long since grown tired of the soap operas and talk shows, had rented every movie he thought he might like from the Cove Video-rama, had read and reread the news items from the Stock Car Fans newsletters on his computer, and had even managed to finish several of the paperback books Michelle brought him the last time she passed through. But he was quickly going stir-crazy.

He ignored the grinding of the mostly-shot brakes as he slowed going past Joe Banker's house. He actually planned on turning around in the driveway and heading on back home after all. But when he turned in, he couldn't help but notice a flock of familiar cars and trucks parked in the dim glow of the arc lights down next to the old barn beyond the house. Curious, he kept going down the drive instead, rolling past the house. He had no idea what could have attracted such a congregation at the dilapidated old outbuilding. Far as he knew, that ancient pile of kindling held nothing more than a few rats, chicken snakes, and maybe a scrap or two of farm machinery. Those would be remnants left over from a time when Joe's father had actually tried to work the hilly rock pile that was, only by the loosest definition, a farm.

He cut the engine and eased his old truck to a stop there in the midst of all the other vehicles. There was Joe's truck. And Bubba Baxter's pickup, too. And a couple of almost identical Lincoln Town Cars Rob immediately recognized as belonging to Randy Weems, his accountant, and Clifford Stanley, his lawyer.

Now what on earth could be the nature of this evening prayer meeting down at Joe Banker's barn?

As he stepped out of the truck, Rob could hear the men's good-natured banter coming from inside the old barn, and warm yellow light spilled out through missing boards and planks in its walls.

Rob didn't bother to knock. He pulled open one of the big double doors and walked right in, fully expecting to see a card game in full swing. But instead there was the stripped roll cage of a racecar sitting up on jack stands. Clifford and Randy were working at the back of the car, busily hanging the new body on the roll cage. The two huge men made quite a picture, sweating, red-faced, their overalls and work shirts soaked and dirty. Rob couldn't imagine these two fat old characters doing such precise work as hanging a body on a racecar. Or any manual work at all, for that matter. Although they tended to dress like a couple of rubes and acted even worse most of the time, they were as good a lawyer and accountant as anybody could want. But in Rob's experience, he had never seen either one of them do anything any more manual than lifting a Mason jar of their ever-present moonshine.

The flicker as the arc welder tacked the sheet-metal panels in place cast an eerie light against the dark walls of the old barn. The whole scene had an almost surreal quality about it, as if he had stepped into a cave full of sorcerers working their magic. The ancient racecars scattered around the big open room, the faded old posters tacked to the wall, and the odd lighting all served to make the scene seem almost unreal. Rob stopped and rubbed his eyes.

Then he spotted Joe and Bubba on their backs under what would be the front of the car. They appeared to be fashioning the new front-end suspension mounts to the frame rails. Joe spied him then, slid out from beneath the car, and sat up.

"Hey, young'un! Welcome to Uncle Joe's skunk works!" he called with a broad grin. "You gonna just stand there or you gonna grab a wrench and give us a hand?"

"What in the world is going on here, Joe?"

"We're rebuilding ourselves a racecar. What does it look like we're doing?"

"Okay, I'll buy that. But why here? And why in the middle of the night? Why aren't you over at the shop? And don't tell me those two are helping you rebuild a car!"

Rob pointed toward where Randy and Clifford were hunched over the quarter panel, grinning at him, each with a jaw full of chewing tobacco. Their faces and bald heads shone with perspiration. Randy and Clifford tended to make Rob nervous. There was something about their cornball sense of humor and rough-edged mannerisms juxtaposed with their obvious intelligence and ability to do what they did so well that kept Rob off balance somehow. He had spent plenty of time with the two of them in the last year, since he had hired them to handle his legal affairs and finances, and he knew they were actually harmless, but still, anytime they were around, bizarre things tended to happen. They were likely to say or do anything and it tended to leave the usually unflappable Rob Wilder crimson with embarrassment.

"You mean your two good buddies back there?" Joe asked with a nod toward Randy and Clifford. "I don't guess you ever knew that there was a day when they were about as good a body man and mechanic as there was to be found. I doubt they've lost much in their old age."

Rob looked wide-eyed at the two of them. At the moment they looked like a couple of hayseeds fresh out of the turnip patch, but as he watched, they went back to work with a vengeance, as if they might actually know what they were doing.

Rob looked back to Joe.

"So what are you doing?"

Joe held his answer while Bubba fired up a grinder and attacked a stubborn piece of metal with it. Sparks flew everywhere as the abrasive shrieked against the burr, and Joe smiled as if he were listening to a lovely tune.

"This is our little secret," he said once the noise had stopped. "I promised Bob junior a racecar for Talladega. I couldn't see no sense in him buying one when there were plenty of perfectly good ones laying around out here acting like chicken coops. I happened to remember having this one sitting out here, old Bubba stumbled in one night, then Mutt and Jeff back yonder got wind of what we was doing, and the next thing I know, we got us a race shop out here in the corncrib."

"Wow!" That was all Rob could manage to say as he marveled at how the shell of the car was taking shape. It just seemed so strange to see such a fine-looking racing machine sitting on jack stands there in the shabby old barn. "You're serious about this, aren't you?"

"Serious as the day is long! The hardest thing is going to be keeping this from Jodell, and for obvious reasons."

"You don't have to worry about me saying anything," Rob said seriously.

"I know that. But I meant what I said. We could use another hand if you ain't got nothing better to do. We got a lot of work to finish over the next month or so."

"Be glad to." He was serious about that, too. It still bothered him that Will and Billy most of the time forbade him to join the crew in working on the car. "Just one thing, though."

"What's that?"

"Well, I'm not about to tell Jodell what's going on here. But at the same time y'all can't let it slip to Will that I've been helping out, either."

"Deal. Your secret's safe here. Just be careful with that ankle or Will'll hang us all up by our toenails if you get hurt down here."

Joe steered him toward a set of wrenches on the workbench. Rob selected a few of them and then hobbled over to help hold the piece Bubba was working on. The wrenches and the metal part felt good in his hands. He had grown up working on cars. That and driving them had been the only hobby he had ever had. And besides, it was nice to be doing something productive for a change.

Soon he was whistling tunelessly but happily as he worked.

Slowly, over the course of the next few weeks, the racecar sitting in Joe's old barn began to take shape. The five men all worked late into the night every chance they got, hurrying to get Misty finished, ready for Bob to run. Still, because of all the other work they were doing to ready Jodell's car for the races each week, Joe and Bubba were only able to work a few nights a week. Clifford and Randy were busy with their day jobs, too, and Rob often found himself alone during the day with the project. He almost hated to leave for the races each Thursday or for the appearances he had to make, but he knew Misty would be there, waiting for him when he got back. He had grown as fond of her already as the others had.

The car had led to one other thing, too. Joe and Bubba had finally relinquished some of their duties at the Jodell Lee shop to Bubba's boy, Waylon, and to the other crewmembers so they could have time to work on the car at night.

If Jodell noticed anything at all, he never mentioned it. Not even when some of the others kidded Bubba about his sudden interest in fishing or accused Joe of running around on Sammie. Of course, it was likely not that Joe's and Bubba's sneakiness was so successful. Jodell was still maintaining the same blistering pace of appearances as he had for years. He only dropped in to the shop for a few moments at a time, and if he found everyone impressively busy and if the car was ready to haul away midweek before the race, then he was satisfied.

All the crewmembers agreed that the early afternoon quitting time appeared to be good therapy for Joe and Bub. The two of them seemed to have a new spring in their step when they were at the shop, a new vigor after forty years of racing. And frankly, without Bubba constantly looking over their shoulders, the members of the crew felt like they too could work better.

Still, there was good reason for everyone to be getting on everyone else's nerves. There had already been nine straight weeks of racing heading into the first of October. Now, there would still be four more races before the teams would have their first weekend off in three months.

Along the way, Rob was finally able to ditch the crutches and to get around with only a slight limp. He was driving well, still threatening, but only had a couple of top-fifteen finishes to show for it so far.

Meanwhile, in Joe Banker's barn, the racecar was just about ready. The primary tasks remaining were to apply the final paint job and install the engine. Nothing had been done on the paint because Joe and Bubba were still arguing over how, exactly, to do it. But finally they agreed it had to be the signature Lee Racing dark blue.

A week and a half before the racing weekend at the lightning-fast superspeedway at Talladega, they all gathered as usual around the car one night. But no one had yet picked up a tool. Randy and Clifford sat leaning against one of the other old cars, uncharacteristically quiet, sipping some mysterious clear liquid from their Mason jars. Bubba fiddled idly with his soda bottle, nursing its contents, for once not downing the fizzy liquid in a couple of gulps. Joe had pulled up an old folding chair within reach of a refrigerator he had dragged down from the house. Occasionally he would get him another cold one from inside the box, but he took it easy on the brew.

The four men were in a pensive mood this dark, moonless night and they talked quietly, reminiscing while they surveyed the car they had built. The truly difficult work was done. She still needed the power plant Joe had ready for her over at the engine shop. He had meticulously crafted what he was certain was the perfect engine for Bob junior. Now, all they needed to do was haul it over and bolt it in place.

They all agreed it had been a satisfying experience, the old team working side by side with Robbie's help, all working to get the car ready for Jodell's boy, just as they had once done for Jodell himself. And it had been fun. Hard work but fun.

Randy had just launched into a tale about something from the good old days when Joe suddenly raised up his hand to quiet him. Then they could all hear the tires of some kind of vehicle coming to a stop outside the barn.

"Rocket Robbie coming to see us tonight?" Clifford asked. He always used his pet name for Rob when he spoke of him.

"Nope," Bubba answered, cocking his head and listening harder. "He's off somewhere shakin' hands and autographin' stuff."

Randy's eyes got big when he asked the next question: "Jodell *is* out of town, ain't he?"

"Ain't supposed to be back till tomorrow. He'd

never dream of us using this old place for something like this anyway," Joe answered. But even he had a worried look on his face as he listened to the slamming of two car doors and the crunch of feet on gravel as whoever it was headed their way.

Bubba couldn't help but grin at the expressions on the other three men's faces. They looked like a bunch of teenagers caught smoking out behind the barn.

"Caught you!"

They all jumped at the sound of the voice. But it was a female voice. And it was Joyce Baxter and Catherine Lee who walked in through the wide-open doorway with big smiles on their faces.

Bubba Baxter jumped up and hugged his wife as he said, "Hi, honey!" But he still had the just-got-caught expression on his face. He had not exactly gotten around to telling Joyce the car he was working on so hard was not for Rex Lawford and Jodell Lee's team at all. That it was for Jodell's son so he could break into racing in a big way. Frankly, he didn't know how she might accept the news. She and Bob junior's momma had been best friends since before any of them had married. Waylon, their son, was near Bob junior's age.

Joyce tried to look serious but she couldn't help it. Bubba had a knack for looking guilty, even when he was actually up to nothing at all. Catherine giggled, too, but she had her eyes on the beautiful dark blue racecar sitting there, shimmering under the bright shop light. She carefully ran her hand along the car's smooth lines, inspecting the machine with what was clearly a skilled eye.

"You all did a fine job here. This car is beautiful!" she praised, then she stuck her head in the driver's window to check out the interior of the cockpit.

Catherine Lee knew what she was looking at. She had been at Jodell's very first race, there in the scraped-out cornfield on Meyer's farm. She knew her way around a racecar almost as well as anyone and she could appreciate a good specimen when she spied one.

Joyce Baxter too studied the freshly finished racecar. She quickly noticed that the dark blue paint job was still devoid of any of the usual sponsor stickers or decals. It was clearly perfect for one of the faster tracks, Daytona or Talladega. But where were the sponsor decals? And the number? Where was Rex Lawford's number?

"Whose car is this, Bubba Baxter?" she asked, hands on her hips.

"Yeah, Joe. Whose number you gonna paint on here?" Catherine chimed in right on cue.

Joe and Bubba looked at each other and shrugged.

"Well . . ." Joe started but Catherine stopped him with one finger to her lips.

"Let me stop you before you tell a lie. Bob's told us what you old grease monkeys have been doing out here most every night. Sammie's kept us up to date on the progress. Now Joyce and I have decided you need a woman's touch finishing her on out. What logo you plan on painting on there?"

Randy Weems cleared his throat.

"Ahem. I been meanin' to suggest that if it was up to me, I think we ought to paint the old Bubble Up logo on the side of that car like the one on the side of the Galaxie over there in the corner." He pointed to the old '64 Ford that was mostly covered in dust in the back of the barn. Through the powder of dirt a green logo could barely be made out. The local bottler of Bubble Up soda had been Jodell Lee's very first paying sponsor. "They were awful good to us for years and years. And I think it's one sharp-looking logo. Since we started this thing as sort of a old folk's project anyway, us workin' together to build the car—"

"That's right!" Clifford chimed in. "This deal is

kind of the start of something new for the family so it wouldn't hurt to go back and use something that was kind of special when the whole thing got started and it was new to all of us."

"I don't know," Joe said, his face all screwed up with doubt. "I thought we'd put Jodell's sponsor—"

"Randy and Clifford are exactly right," Catherine Lee interrupted. "The way all the other teams have been using nostalgia paint jobs on their cars over the last couple of years, I don't see why we can't." She smiled and closed her eyes as she remembered something. "After all, I worked awfully hard to get that sponsorship for Jodell in the first place."

Joyce Baxter shook her head up and down vigorously and grinned broadly.

"I agree with Catherine! That logo meant a lot to all of us back in the early years. Without all the help from the Bubble Up folks y'all wouldn't be anywhere close to where you are today. Bubba Baxter, you'd likely still be working at that old mill. Joe, you'd probably be working in a garage somewhere or raisin' rocks here on your daddy's farm." She turned to Randy and Clifford. "And you two? I expect you'd still be knee deep in manure in some old barn somewhere."

"She's right," Catherine added. She was already visualizing how her son's racecar would look, all painted up with the brightly colored logo on the sides and spread across the hood. "Plus Jodell will sure be surprised when he sees her and her new paint job sitting out there on the starting line." A positively evil grin spread across her lovely face then and her eyes sparkled with mischief. "I've already arranged for him to be out of town with the sponsor so he won't even get to the track until just before the race. I still don't know what he'll do when he finds out what's going on, but I want to make sure it's way too late to stop it once he gets wind of it."

"Then it's settled," Bubba Baxter pronounced, speaking slowly and deliberately. He stood and walked over to the car, carefully pointing out where he thought the logos should go and how big they ought to be so they would be clearly visible from the grandstands and towers at the massive Talladega track.

Then they all sat around the old table in the barn talking of the old days, laughing, telling and retelling well-worn stories. Finally, while the others talked, Catherine got up from the table and walked slowly around the barn, inspecting like a visitor to a museum the old cars Joe had stashed away there. The only thing was, though, that she had practically grown up with these exhibits.

She stopped next to the old Galaxie and, as she stood there, the memories flooded back to her.

All she had to do was close her eyes and she could almost smell the black, billowing smoke from the fire at Charlotte. She could come close to actually hearing the frantic voices of the announcers over the radio as they tried to describe the horrible crash. And she still felt the wave of relief when she finally spied Jodell and Bubba walking toward her across the infield from the awful conflagration, her husband with his helmet in his hand, his uniform singed and blackened from the fire, but apparently okay. Thank God, okay.

But her elation at her prayers being answered was quickly tempered by the fact that others were injured in the crash. Injured badly.

She still often remembered Fireball Roberts's handsome face and easy smile, his polite demeanor, his amazing skills behind the wheel of a racecar. She had not seen him alive again after the race began that day but she could still hear the lilt of his drawl.

And that brought other thoughts to mind. Were they doing the right thing, helping her only son to get himself into a racecar? Here she was, offering her tacit agreement, even her encouragement, to giving Bob junior an opportunity to do something he wanted to do so desperately. But she knew it was something that, at best, could be difficult and disappointing and heartbreaking, and, at worst, deadly. And she was, for the first time in her life, doing something substantial behind Jodell's back.

Nobody was more aware of the dangers of racing than Jodell Lee. He had seen friends killed, others banged up so badly they were never the same again. Little Joe Weatherley had actually been killed the very week Jodell had learned he was to be a daddy for the first time. That's the main reason he had discouraged his boy from taking up the game, why he had urged him to get as far from racing as he could, to go to school, to work in a profession that touched racing in no way whatsoever. She understood only too well why her husband had steered their son away from the sport.

Catherine Lee reached out and felt a roughly crumpled fender on one of the dusty, old racecars. Despite all that the governing body had done to make it as safe as possible for the sport's participants, driving a racecar was still a dangerous business. Jodell had been so happy when Bob went off to school, proud as he could be when he finished so high in his class, and when he took the job in New York City. Catherine had been glad, too, for mostly the same reasons.

And Bob had seemed perfectly content with his choices, showing no inclination to drift back to the gas fumes and the roaring thunder of racing. But now Catherine knew, as only a mother could know, how desperate her boy was to get back to his roots, to follow his heart instead of his head for a change. And she was determined that, if that was her son's dream, she would do everything in her power to make sure he had the opportunity to pursue it.

But as she listened to the others laughing at some

wild tale Randy Weems was spinning, she couldn't help but wonder how her husband would react to all this when he found out. Would he too realize the boy was only trying to catch up to and put a lap on his birthright? Or would he try to red-flag his son's pursuit of his own destiny? And how in the world would such a primal conflict play out? Would it drive a wedge through the middle of their family?

Those were only a few of the questions that she suspected would ultimately get answered on the high banks of Talladega.

20

The cars sat there queued up two-by-two along the pit lane. A large crowd was still filing in to take their seats inside the gigantic Talladega Superspeedway. The sun was high overhead already, the day warm for mid-October, and the flags that lined the pit road barely flickered in a gentle breeze.

There was plenty of activity in the pits, too. The crews swarmed around the racecars, their urgency obvious as they furiously finished their preparations for the upcoming race. The pits and garage were crowded, too, with most of the Cup crews still at the track, many of whom who were taking a short break from their own preparations for the afternoon's "happy hour" practice and the next day's big race.

An automobile race was about to be run. More than a few of them would watch, even if it was from their garage stalls or out of the corners of their eyes as they worked.

There was an especially vigorous bunch swarming

around the truck and trailer that had brought a certain gleaming, dark blue Ford to Talladega. Unlike some of the teams in this racing division who wore mismatched T-shirts and jeans and tended to be made up mostly of inexperienced youngsters, this particular group seemed as professional as any well-heeled Cup team. But it did include four men who were clearly in their sixties. And the rest of the crew was adorned in two different sets of team wear. It was a mix of members from the Lee Racing number "34" team and the Winton Racing number "52" team.

A brilliant red number "34" trimmed in white was painted on the side of the Ford. Above the driver's side door, the name Bob Lee was lined out in a bold block script. Someone with a good memory and an eye for detail might have noticed that it was precisely the name and style that Bubba Baxter had painted with shoe polish on Jodell's granddaddy's car the day they had raced it at Meyer's farm. The race that kicked off Jodell's long career. They had used that particular name to try to keep Grandpa Lee from finding out about their racing exploits, and keep from him the fact that they were actually driving his "whiskey car" in a slam-bang automobile race.

Bubba's boy, Waylon Baxter, and Will Hughes had decided to split up the over-the-wall duties for the race between members of their respective teams. Both were eager to help Jodell's boy make this historic run but they also intended to learn all they could from the day's racing and apply it to their Cup cars for Sunday's contest. They had already seen the "34" running in the brief practice earlier and knew it was a very good racecar. Both Waylon and Will wanted to see how the tricks Joe and Bubba added to the car would work out there. Bob Lee's new Ford was fast off the truck and had already qualified in seventh position for the afternoon's race.

Rob Wilder was in the middle of all the excitement,

too. He had taken as his job helping to acquaint Bob with the nuances of the big track, much as Bob's dad had done on Rob's first trip to this stunning raceway. Bob might have the "racing gene," Rob had announced, but he still needed a mentor. And that was a role Rob assumed with vigor and Bob accepted gladly.

Talladega was a simple but daunting track. The wide, high banking robbed from the drivers most of the sensation of raw speed. But at the same time, it allowed an abundance of swiftness. Three- and four-wide racing was not only possible, it was highly likely. Rob's advice was elemental: he told Bob to simply jam his foot to the floorboard and keep it there all the way around the place. Once he worked the car up through the gears, then the only way to drive was to keep the accelerator foot to the floor, never letting off the gas pedal. Crack the throttle even slightly, Rob warned, and the smaller carburetor that limited the amount of air the engine could suck into the manifold would choke off the power and it would take forever for the racecar to regain the momentum it could lose in a split second.

Bob Lee was there in the bunch, too, soaking it all in, relishing being there, being a part of it all. The first few laps of practice on the famed Talladega high banks were a bit unnerving. He had to fight the natural instinct to lift off the throttle as the car roared toward the steep banking of the turns. But it didn't take him long to get the hang of the place, to learn to stand on the accelerator and start mixing it up in the draft.

Drafting was a new phenomenon for him, too. He knew what to expect, but still he took to heart the practical advice Rob offered and he was soon drafting along with the rest of them as if he had been super-speedway racing for years.

Now, with the race only moments from starting,

the excitement coursed through him. He couldn't wait to get out there and mix it up, to prove that he had what it took to handle that heavy, powerful racecar among the others who were trying to confirm the very same thing. Only one thing bothered him. What would his dad think when he found out? How would he react to all this?

He would know soon enough. And right now, he couldn't worry too much about it. He had a race to win, then he'd face the old man. Still, somewhere deep inside he felt that that confrontation would go much more smoothly if he was carrying the winner's trophy at the time.

Catherine Lee and Joyce Baxter walked up just as the crew began to push the car off toward the starting line. Joyce carried a stack of carefully folded shirts and she quickly passed them out to the assembled crew. They were exact replicas of the Bubble Up route drivers' shirts the Jodell Lee team had worn in its early days.

Without a hint of modesty, Bubba Baxter peeled off his Lee Racing team shirt and pulled on the new one, modeling it proudly for everyone.

"You look like a million dollars!" Joe Banker crowed as he pulled on his own shirt. "Beautiful!"

Bubba seemed to have a sudden thought.

"Where's Jodell, Cath?"

"He just called. The plane just landed over yonder." She pointed toward the grandstands that stretched along the back straightaway. There was an airstrip back there, and on race weekends, it became one of the busiest airports in the country. "He'll be here in a few minutes."

"I hope he don't blow a gasket when he sees all this," Randy said as he slipped on his new Bubble Up shirt.

"I'll take care of him, boys. Y'all just worry about

crewing that car for Bob," Catherine replied with a wide smile.

Jodell could be difficult, stubborn, but if there was anyone who could handle him, she could. There was a good chance he would be angry when he found out what they had pulled, and he might be furious that Bob had gone behind his back to drive a racecar. But by the time he found out it would be too late to stop it.

Maybe, just maybe, the old racer would see how determined his boy was to follow in his dad's footsteps, how devoted he was. And maybe he would have enough fatherly pride to simply accept it and pitch in and help.

Maybe.

At any rate, the subterfuge had been complete and, it appeared, successful. Jodell Lee might just as well settle back and enjoy the race.

"You cats don't need to be worrying about old Jodell Lee," Joe chimed in, looking directly at Randy and Clifford. "We got us a race to win. We can take care of that grouchy old so-and-so after we do that."

The group slowly pushed the car through the garage, past the stalls of many of the old-timers. Several of them did a double take when they saw the dark blue car with the green logo. There was something eerily familiar about that car and the crew in their matching shirts. Something so strangely familiar.

The Bob Lee team had tried to keep their efforts low-key since they arrived at the track two days before. They worked hard at not drawing any attention at all, lying low for a couple of reasons. First, of course, they didn't want anybody wishing Jodell Lee good luck in his boy's big race. But they also wanted to shield Bob from what would certainly be a smothering amount of attention should word get out. The resulting media attention alone would have been dangerously distracting. To avoid such a thing, they even went so far as to wait until that morning to put the Bubble Up decals on the car, just in case somebody might put two and two together when they saw the throwback paint scheme. Several of the other cars trying to qualify were sponsorless, too, so nobody really noticed. So far, it appeared none of the crowd of motorsports reporters seemed to have caught on, not even when the anonymous "34" turned in the good qualifying run.

They were aided too by the fact that this particular division of racing attracted a broad mix of drivers and teams. Many were youngsters, getting their first taste of serious competition on the big tracks where their heroes ran on Sundays. Others were hangers-on, trying to keep a foot in the sport that had cruelly rebuffed their efforts so far. Some teams were well heeled, others obvious ragtag outfits with little hope. The Bob Lee effort was thankfully lost among them all.

High above the racetrack in the broadcast booth the long-retired, two-time driving champion who served as color man for the television coverage was scanning the pits with his binoculars, picking out the various cars he would want to keep an eye on this day. Then, something vaguely familiar caught his eye. What was it? That car over there looked like . . .

But then it was obscured by another car being pushed past it. He almost moved on up the line as the cars were being slowly pushed along, but then there it was again. The dark blue car with the green logo on its sides and hood.

"Oh, my God!" he whispered, loud enough that his partner heard him.

"What? What is it?"

The announcer swung his glasses over to peer off in the same direction.

"I am not believing this."

"Believing what?"

"That Lee bunch. Why in the world would they have a car in today's race?"

The announcer scrambled to find the entry list for the event.

"There's a car here owned by a 'C. Lee.' What do you think's going on?"

The former champ suddenly grinned as he looked closer at the group following along behind the "34" car. It still didn't make sense yet but at least he recognized most of the potential players. There they were, walking along behind the dark blue Ford. Joe Banker, Bubba Baxter, those two goofy guys who used to hang around Jodell's garage all the time. And there was Billy Winton and his crew chief, Will Hughes, and even a guy who appeared to be Billy's new hotshot driver, Rob Wilder. And to a man, they were all wearing Bubble Up shirts with the same logo as the one painted on the hood and rear quarter panels of their racecar.

"I don't know for certain what's going on, but we need to get one of the pit reporters over there to find out. They're up to something and it could be quite interesting."

A quick whirl of thoughts swirled through the retired champion's head as he watched the group roll the machine out onto the pit lane. Was this some kind of stunt? Were Jodell Lee and the boys having such a tough year that they were resorting to trying to cash in on the nostalgia wave and sell some die-cast cars to collectors? Or was the great Jodell Lee coming out of retirement? What on earth were they doing with that car all painted up and the crew dressed just like it was 1960 all over again?

But what the television man failed to notice was the confident young man walking purposefully alongside the car. Bob Lee wasn't the least bit nervous now. He breathed in all the hoopla, savoring the moment, tasting the excitement. Rob had urged him to take time to enjoy it all because there would only be one first time. Even as he walked along, even as he accepted the handshakes of a few of the old-timers who recognized him and guessed what might be about to happen, he tried to concentrate on the upcoming task. He understood the size of what he was trying to do. And he also knew that, with his name alone, he carried an enormous weight with him when he climbed inside that racecar.

But he knew something else, too. Joe Banker and the rest of them had given him a fine racecar to run. There would be no excuses. It was now up to him to prove to everyone, including himself, that he was truly up to carrying on the family tradition.

He grinned, took another deep lungful of the electric air, and stepped quicker to keep up with his racecar.

Not far away, just beyond turn three, Jodell Lee climbed from the airplane and took a deep breath of air. It was good to finally be here at this track. Although it had not always been kind to him, Talladega was designed for nothing but speed, and that suited Jodell perfectly. As he took in the distant blue mountains, the red clay of the broad fields around him, the climbing bleachers over there along the back straightaway, the sea of race fans wandering among the pine trees, he remembered his own first attempt at this place, how it had bitten him hard. But at that moment, he still would have given anything to be able to once again relive the numbing excitement, the breathless anticipation, when he cranked up and drove out onto those high turns for the first time.

Still, he was in no particular hurry as he left the plane, not particularly anxious to swim along with the crowd of fans still entering the speedway. He had been gone for four days, making appearances for his car's sponsor, and the last leg of the trip had them in the air since early that morning. When they spoke the night before, Bubba had reported the car was practicing just fine, and Rex Lawford had qualified it well, so he was really in no big hurry to get back, so long as they made it by "happy hour." But Bill Waller, the sponsor rep, had pushed him through breakfast and all the way to the airport for some reason, hurrying him as if they had a race to run today instead of tomorrow.

As they walked away from the plane, Jodell stopped to greet a few old friends who had landed just ahead of them. Bill turned and impatiently waved for him to come on.

"Jodell, we need to hustle on over if we're going to catch the start of the race," Waller urged. He had been the one who had conspired with Catherine Lee to get Jodell on the road and away from Talladega until the time was right. Well, the time was right now and it was his job to get Jodell inside the speedway.

"All right, all right. Hold your horses, Bill." Jodell slapped the old friends on their backs and told them good-bye. "Let's see if we can rustle us up a ride on over to the infield, then. I do want to check out some of the young drivers, see how some of those young guns do on a big, fast track."

Bill bit his tongue and suppressed a grin. There was definitely one young gun that Jodell Lee might have an interest in watching.

"Yeah, I hear there's a couple of young hotshots running this afternoon. It ought to be interesting."

"These kids'll put on a good show. I don't want to miss a lap of it."

Now he's in a hurry, Waller thought to himself and hustled to keep up with the much older Jodell Lee.

The prerace ceremonies were just wrapping up as Jodell and Bill passed their stall in the garage. Wes Wheeler was the only crewman to be found, either in the Lee Racing stall or the slot next door where Billy

Winton's Ensoft Ford sat all alone, seemingly abandoned.

"Where the blazes is everybody, Wes?"

"I reckon down there on pit road waiting on the start of the race. Bubba and Billy were looking for you. You may want to hustle on down there and see what they wanted before the race gets going and you can't hear yourself think."

"They better all be gettin' their hind ends back up here and to work on this racecar. I can't believe Billy's whole bunch is up there, too." Jodell shook his head. It wasn't at all like Billy or Will to allow their crews to take a break so close to "happy hour." Nor like Bubba Baxter, either. With the team still mired in a slump, they should be working twice as hard, not slacking off to watch some silly race.

As he and Bill hurried along the pit lane, Jodell cast an expert eye over the cars that were now lined up, ready and waiting for the command to start the engines. And then, up there toward the front of the line, he spotted a bunch of very familiar faces, all taking special interest in one of the cars.

"Who in blue blazes are they all looking at?"

"I don't know," Bill lied, straight-faced, as the national anthem was just finishing up over the public address system.

There was the giant figure of Bubba Baxter towering over everyone around him. And Randy and Clifford? What in the world were they doing on the pit road? Another couple of steps along and he suddenly stopped short. Catherine? Joyce? That was even odder.

What was going on here? Was somebody pitching a party and forgot to invite him?

Then, when he was five or six cars away, he finally noticed the shirts. It had been years since he had seen the bright Bubble Up route shirts, but it all flooded back to him then, so strong it almost bowled him over.

And the racecar. The distinctive Lee Racing dark blue paint job on the car. The Bubble Up logo on the side. The scripted name over the door that he couldn't quite read yet.

Bubba Baxter suddenly leaned in the window and gave the driver's safety belts a tug, just as he always had Jodell Lee before a race begun. Will Hughes was already sitting atop the Lee Racing pit box, surveying the scene. A thousand thoughts swirled around in Jodell's head and he felt almost dizzy as he took a few more steps closer to the car and the bunch gathered around it.

But before he could get there, one of the television pit reporters stepped in front of him and waved a microphone in front of his face.

"Jodell, tell our viewers how it feels as you prepare to witness your son's first race here at Talladega?"

"What?" Jodell asked, clearly startled by what he thought he had just heard. His hearing, long since diminished after all those years around unmuffled engines, had to be playing tricks on him. Had the reporter said "your son"?

"Your reaction to your son's start in today's race?"

This time Jodell heard the question for certain. Still, it took him a moment to collect his wits. Something had been up for the past several weeks. The business trip that suddenly materialized at the last minute. Joe and Bubba all of a sudden taking up fishing and leaving the shop well before dark each day. The virtual disappearance from the race shop lately by those two clowns, Randy and Clifford. Usually they were popping in most every day, causing some kind of mayhem.

He should have known something was up. Still, he couldn't quite figure out what it was.

"Well, you can imagine how I feel," Jodell said

confidently, his eyes serious and sincere, using his hands for emphasis. "You can imagine how anyone would feel in such a situation. And I'm here to tell you, that's exactly how I feel about it. Yessir, that's how I feel about this whole thing. Exactly the way any one of you would feel."

That said, Jodell stepped away from the microphone and on toward the familiar car and all the familiar people who surrounded it.

"And there you have it folks, directly from the man himself, racing legend Jodell Lee," the reporter said into the camera lens. "And he's clearly mighty proud of his boy as he does exactly what the rest of us will be doing this afternoon, witnessing the beginning of the competitive career of another driver in the family with one of the most revered names in racing."

"Gentlemen, start your engines!"

The command over the loudspeakers echoed off the high banks.

The officials were already waving everyone behind the pit wall as Jodell finally made his way to where the car waited. Bubba was already cinching up the window net so there wasn't even an opportunity for him to stick his head inside the car and see if what he now suspected was true.

But how could it be? How in the world could it possibly be?

Bubba almost stepped on him as he backed away from the car, flashing the driver a thumbs-up. Again it was something so simple yet so familiar to Jodell, a gesture the big man had given him hundreds of times before all those races down through the years.

Bubba winked at Jodell and eased him along to the wall and then over it. As he looked about him, he felt almost as if he had been drugged, as if he had suddenly awakened in the middle of a very odd dream.

There was the car with the logo. The crew in those shirts.

And the name over the door: "Bob Lee."

Bubba gently shoved him out of the way as Waylon hustled about, making certain everyone on the mixed over-the-wall crew was ready for the first stop, regardless of when it might come. The tools were ready, the gas cans filled, the first set of tires already lined up against the wall and waiting.

Rob Wilder had now climbed to the top of the toolbox and pulled on the radio headset. He was obviously talking to the driver now, giving him some last-minute tips even as the cars began to roll off pit lane. Bubba hurried up to claim his usual spot on pit road while everyone else moved to the back of the pits and clustered around a television monitor there.

"What on earth is going . . ." Jodell started to say as he stepped into the middle of the bunch of them. They all looked at him, most of them with odd expressions on their faces.

It was Catherine who spoke, straining to be heard over the rumble of the engines.

"Hi, honey," she said, and gave him a hug and a kiss. "Isn't this exciting?"

"Well . . . I guess. If I knew what 'this' was," he stammered.

Now the cars were away and he could actually hear her when she finally told him what was going on.

"Our son is finally doing something he's always wanted to do. Something neither one of us even suspected and that's a shame, Jodell. A real shame."

"You!" Jodell said, looking past his wife and pointing a finger toward his cousin. "Joe Banker, you're the one who's been behind all this. That's one of your motors in that car. I'd recognize that sound anywhere. I should have known something was up."

"Look, cuz—" Joe started to say, but Catherine cut him off abruptly.

"Jodell, we're all behind this. This was a family

decision and all of us here are part of the family."
She waved her hand around to encompass everyone
in the pits. "We've all worked awfully hard to make
this happen, including Bob, and now that it's finally
about to take place, you might just as well sit back
and enjoy it."

"But Cath, the boy's not been inside a racecar since
he used to fool around in some of mine before he
even learned to drive a regular car. He must've been
twelve at most. He'll get himself killed out there!"
Everybody laughed and he felt his face getting red,
even as the anger welled up inside him. "Have every
one of you lost your minds? You can't just one day
decide to climb in a car and go drive Talladega! Even
in a race like this one."

"Honey, listen to me. Bob's been racing for years
and keeping it from you. From us. All Joe did was
go up the week of Watkins Glen and help him with
his car like he asked him to do. And he watched him
win his first late-model race. Since then he's won six
more times at several different tracks up there. We
should've been there, Jodell. And when I found out
what was going on, I vowed then and there that we'd
see as many of his races from now on as we could."

"Seven races? My boy's won seven races. But
how . . . ?" Jodell Lee had a perplexed look on his
face but Catherine was now watching the pace car
lead the phalanx of racers down off turn four and
toward the trioval.

"Look, we can talk about the 'how' after a while,"
she said. "Right now, we need to watch him win his
eighth one."

Jodell walked slowly over to the pit cart. A radio
headset lay there. He didn't hesitate, pulling it over
his ears and dialing in the correct frequency. He could
hear Rob patiently explaining to Bob what he needed
to do on the start as the cars rolled by. Jodell almost

keyed the microphone to add his own advice, maybe ask some of the thousand questions he had. But Rob was doing a fine job, sounding for all the world like old Jodell himself. And besides, if his boy hadn't sought his counsel yet, there was no need to butt in now.

The cars coasted into the third turn, bunching up already for the start. The lights on the back of the pace car were already turned off. This thing was about to get the green flag.

"Good luck, son," Jodell finally called out over the radio net when there was a sufficient lull for him jump in.

Over the sound of the powerful engine, Bob heard the words loud and clear.

"Thanks, Pop."

He gritted his teeth behind the broad grin. Now that he apparently had his dad's blessing, it was time to make him proud.

Hardly three laps into the contest, Bob was already beginning to cautiously wend his way up through the pack. The car had plenty of power. No doubt about that from the instant he had taken the green. But the one thing that was holding him back was his lack of drafting experience. He planned to go to school for the first third of the race, studying the cars ahead of him, taking his time to pick up one spot at a time, not risking getting drop-kicked backward if he got too greedy. Slowly but surely he began to make his way toward the top spot in the field with Rob Wilder coaching him all the way.

Jodell hopped nervously from one foot to the other as he watched the lead pack shoot past their position on the pit road. As soon as the group with Bob junior in it disappeared from their sight angle off toward the first turn, he would wheel around to the television monitor and watch the cars there until they came around again. He whooped and hollered every time Bob made a pass for position. The rest of the bunch joined in with his celebration, dancing excitedly, high-fiving, pounding each other on the back as if it were the first time any of them watched their favorite driver move up through the field in a race.

For his part, Bob Lee was having the time of his young life. He was working hard, to be sure, sawing at the wheel, never lifting his foot from the accelerator as he and the other four cars in the front pack swept off into the broad first turn. The speed was deceptive as the cars ran so close together. They might just as well have been braving rush-hour traffic, heading homeward on a four- or five-lane interstate highway.

But in addition to having fun, Bob Lee was also learning. He was quickly getting a feel for the effect the air rushing off the other cars had on the handling of his own Ford. It was something he had never experienced on the small tracks he had raced so far. But with every lap, he became more and more confident, and that was only bolstered by his success in passing cars, marching relentlessly toward the leader.

Finally, he had the lead car's rear end filling his windshield and he patiently settled right in on the Chevrolet's back bumper, temporarily satisfied to hang with him as they both paced the field. It was early yet and it seemed to be the right thing to do to simply sit there and ride for a bit.

But soon, something else welled up inside him. Bob recognized it immediately. It was the desire to actually lead, to be in front of all of them. He decided then that there was no reason for him to settle for anything less than the point. As the field crossed the stripe marking the finish of the twentieth lap of the five-hundred-kilometer event, Bob suddenly dipped down to the inside and pushed his car out into the lead with almost casual ease. His had been a smooth, professional pass and now, ahead of him, there was nothing but clear track.

The feeling was amazing! Leading the race at Talladega! The calm, collected Wall Street financier let out a long, yodeling whoop worthy of any "good old boy."

Up on the pit box, Will nodded to Bubba, acknowledging their newly claimed spot. Bubba grinned and flashed him a thumbs-up before looking back to his clipboard where he was already plotting the strategy for their first pit stop.

"Good job, leader," Rob deadpanned once the pass was completed. "Now forget those guys behind you. We got plenty of laps to go."

His comments were met with silence. Bob still wasn't accustomed to using the radio. He had his hands full at the moment, anyway. The car bobbed and weaved on the bumpy track and Bob concentrated on trying to hold on to the thing, to keep the steering wheel from jumping out of his hands.

Jodell Lee was beside himself as he watched his son surge into the lead.

"That's my boy! That's my boy!" he kept repeating over and over to any and everyone standing near him.

Bob's mother shared his excitement. She stood there in her usual stance when Jodell had been driving, her arms folded over her chest, her fingers on both hands tightly crossed, pleading for the good luck to hold.

When the leaders disappeared from their view, Jodell turned to Catherine with the happiest look she could remember on his face. At least the happiest since the day the boy was born.

"Look at him, honey. Did you see that slingshot for the lead? Who's that remind you of?"

She only smiled back and nodded. The boy did

seem to be driving with exactly the same fluid, easy style as his dad once had.

The pit reporter caught up with Jodell for another interview just after Bob took the lead. This time there was no vagueness in his response. Anyone watching the telecast could see and hear the pride in the old racer's voice.

Green-flag pit stops came and went with Bob and the crew managing to keep the position at the front of the field. The fast work by the combined crews from the two teams kept him in the lead after that first stop. Over the next fifty laps or so the lead swapped back and forth among the top five cars, clearly the class of the field. Bob continued to get his share of laps leading the race as it wound down to its last fifty miles or so. A blown engine in one of the lapped cars slowed the field then and that set up the last frantic round of pit stops and a likely dash for the finish with the field once again tightly packed.

This time, Bob came out of the pits in second place. Rob cautioned him to be patient over the last twenty laps. It was a new race.

Michelle Fagan hung tightly on to Rob's arm as they watched the cars line up for the restart. Rob hardly noticed her there as he concentrated on calling the restart, on making sure Bob was calm and prepared for the mad dash toward the checkered flag.

Bubba Baxter and Will Hughes busied themselves figuring out exactly what they would do if there should be yet another caution period, calculating exactly what moves they would make. It was clear they were enjoying being joint crew chiefs for this upstart effort as much as they ever did their own respective teams.

Joe Banker fairly beamed. He was proud of the power Jodell's boy was forcing from the engine he had built for him. And he was totally confident of victory. Barring somebody up front getting overeager

and wrecking all of the leaders, or something breaking on the car, then Bob should be in a good position
to bring the Bubble Up Ford home with the victory.
He had already shown he had both the car and the
innate ability to get the job done. Only bad racing
luck could keep them from celebrating a win in just
a few minutes.

Time and again Bob sucked in big gulps of air as
the line of cars cruised down the backstretch behind
the pace, which was once again running with its flashing lights off, signifying they were already in the last
lap before the restart. The flagman awaited the cars,
green flag in hand, ready to once again set loose the
captured thunder of three dozen roaring racing machines. For the hundred thousand or so fans in the
stands, the finish promised to live up to all their expectations. They might be here for the weekend pri-
marily for the Winston Cup race the following day,
but they could appreciate good racing regardless of
the class. And since the word had spread around the
speedway, more than a few of them were pulling for
the legendary driver's son making his impressive de-
but in the dark blue Ford.

Bob twisted about in the seat, making sure the belts
were still good and tight as the cars rolled through
turns three and four coming down to the restart. He
tucked the nose of his car close up on the rear bumper
of the leader. He waited eagerly to punch the throttle
once more, hoping to follow Rob's admonition to get
a run on the lead car as the pack built speed heading
down into turn one.

Then the green flag waved high over the head of
the starter up on the flag stand. Simultaneously, Rob
was on the radio, yelling, "Green! Green! Green!"

Bob almost swallowed his tongue when the car
ahead of him made an amateur mistake, attempting to
brake-check the field before they all got on the gas.
He swerved downward and tapped his own brakes,

fully expecting to have half the field climb up onto his rear deck when he did. That one bonehead move by the driver in front of him could have caused a horrendous crash on such a tightly packed, late-in-the-race restart.

But somehow, everyone avoided piling into everyone else while Bob made sure he didn't actually pass the leader before they had crossed the start/finish line. Then he followed Rob's hastily called advice, got a good run on the hesitant leader, and moved up beside him on the low side as they shot across the short chute heading into turn one. Neither car carried enough momentum yet to push out into the lead as they raced through the corner, and the sight of the Ford to his inside had the leader now fully back into the throttle himself, fighting to hold on to the point.

They remained side by side down the backstretch as the cars behind them began to close in, forming a tight draft. Diving into turn three, Bob held the advantage on the inside. The car directly behind him tucked up tight, giving Bob just enough of an extra push of air to allow him to get a run down on the inside.

Bob pushed out into the lead as the cars came off the fourth turn and raced down toward the tri-oval, sailing along proudly in front of the long main grandstand and the soaring towers filled with cheering fans. If he had not been so busy taking the lead, he might have enjoyed the sight of so many spectators on their feet, wildly and noisily cheering him.

The spotter finally yelled "Clear!" over the radio. That meant it was okay for Bob to slide up slightly on the track and take his own line. Both he and the car that had given him the boost had moved ahead of the previous leader.

"Good job there," Rob praised. "Now don't worry about all that racing going on behind you. Just try to maintain the line you've been running. You have the fastest car out there. They'll have to run you down now."

Michelle had squeezed Rob's arm even more tightly as Bob made the pass. She couldn't believe how excited she was over a car without an Ensoft logo on it, but with the laps winding down now, she was totally captivated by how this race was playing out.

Most of the gang at the back of the pit kept one eye on Jodell and the other on the television monitor. None of them could remember seeing Jodell Lee so nervous. Even when his own car was running, he remained cool and calm, almost businesslike. But now, he was hopping up and down, dancing from the pit wall to the television, swapping high-fives with members of the crew with every good move out there by his boy.

The first pass for the lead almost did him in. Catherine laughed when she saw he was holding his breath until Bob finally moved into the spot. This last pass, Jodell was working an imaginary steering wheel, as if he were trying to drive the car himself by remote control. But Catherine also noticed a gleam in her husband's eye, a spark she had not seen there in a long, long time. She couldn't remember when she had seen him having so much fun at a racetrack.

Bubba and Will kept a close eye on the cars racing behind Bob. How those cars finally shuffled out would have a lot to do with their chances for winning. The early leader was still recovering from a bad pit stop during the last caution period, but now he finally completed a three-wide pass on the inside, pushing his car into the second-place position. Bob was running fifteen car lengths in front of those three cars, their side-by-side racing allowing him to pull away. But now, they dropped into line, nose to tail, and came after Bob in a hurry.

Bob risked a glance in his mirror as the Ford came

roaring off the second corner and onto the back straightaway. No doubt about it. Those guys had gotten their act together and they were closing.

Rob confirmed it.

"Here they come. Protect the inside line. They'll likely try to slingshot on by when they catch up with you. Let 'em push but don't let 'em past."

It appeared they would be at the end of the back-stretch by the time the three-car train caught him. Without having to be told what to do, Bob zigzagged back and forth on the track, trying to muddle the air coming off the back of his car so those coming up behind him could not latch on to the draft and shoot past him through the corner. Sure enough, they caught him as they were heading into turn three, but Bob kept his car pinned right down on the bottom of the track, his left-side tires tracing the white line down there. The cars farther back had been smart, too, lining up and running down the leaders so it was now an eleven-car lineup that thundered through the sweeping third and fourth turns and headed back around to the main straightaway.

Twelve laps to go.

Bob stayed low again into turn one. He was effectively offering up the outside line if the Chevy following him wanted it. Instead, its driver shoved the nose of his car directly behind Bob, following as closely as he could all the way through the turn.

It appeared, though, that the Chevy's pilot was getting impatient as they ran out of laps. He seemed to want to make a move to the front before he got caught up with some of the other cars racing for position. The lead was the place to be now and the dark blue Ford held it and showed no inclination to give it up without a fight.

The Chevy moved up half a groove to the outside as they powered through turn two. Bob caught a glimpse of the move in the mirror as they exited the corner. He noted it but kept his concentration on running the precise line he wanted to take.

"Be smooth. Drive your line."

Rob's words played and replayed through his head. There were now five cars lined up tightly at the front of the field as the leaders raced down the long straightaway toward the next corner.

This time, the early leader, the yellow Chevy, looked to the inside as the cluster of cars charged into the corner. He took a quick peek before thinking better of it. Whoever that guy was in the dark blue Ford was tough, and he seemed determined to hold that bottom line. Still, the Chevy driver almost ran his car onto the apron at the entrance to the corner before easing back up and tucking back into line. There was no other way around the Ford right now but high, and the outside just didn't seem to make much sense in the turn. Maybe the tri-oval. Maybe there he would find a way around on the low side.

The pack roared out of turn four. The Chevy again slid lower on the track, trying once more to draft past on the inside as they raced toward the center of the tri-oval. This time he caught the draft better coming off the Bubble Up Ford and got a fender alongside Bob Lee.

Still, Bob wasn't worried. The Chevy didn't seem to have the power to complete the pass and the cars behind them were now dicing it up again, racing each other. When the Chevy eventually dropped back behind him, they could work together and drive away, him to the victory, the Chevy to a respectable second place.

But the driver in the yellow car apparently wasn't willing to settle for second, even if he didn't have the car necessary for the win. He made an impetuous, impatient move and tried to force the issue. He ran the car all the way down to the track apron yet again as he tried to pull even with Bob. Bob had no choice but to move up slightly, giving the car to his inside a bit of room through the center of the tri-oval. He'd let the guy recover, then he'd power back to the clear lead and let the Chevy settle back in behind him.

But suddenly, the yellow Chevy ran out of room when its driver didn't take the extra bit of track that Bob was granting him. Before he realized it, his left-side wheels were on the apron, the right sides still on the banking, and he was immediately in deep trouble.

The Chevy driver's inexperience had just cost him mightily. As his racecar straddled the apron at over one hundred eighty miles per hour, control of the car was suddenly ripped away from him. He tried to correct with the steering wheel but the car shot to the right as if slapped that way by some great and powerful hand.

Bob could see nothing but clear track ahead of him out the windshield. He glanced quickly at the mirror, expecting to see the Chevy set up once again behind him. He was already planning how he would fend off the next pass attempt, likely coming in the middle of turn one.

But suddenly, something forceful and emphatic punched the back end of his car. He instinctively twisted back and forth on the steering wheel, trying to find an angle at which the tires would once again stick and propel him back into a straight line.

Come on! Bite! Go straight!

Will and Bubba watched the contact play out in what seemed like slow motion. Both saw it coming. Neither could believe the idiot alongside Bob would drive the car so dangerously low on the apron while beside another car. And neither was surprised at all at the car's sudden jerk upward on the track, at the quick puff of smoke when the yellow car's right front tire made contact with Bob's left rear fender. For an instant it appeared that Bob might miraculously be able to hang on to the car, get it straightened out after the rude shove.

But then, he lost it.

The beautiful new Bubble Up car spun around backward, looking almost comical, as if its driver had decided to whip around and run the race in reverse. Then the rushing air caught the spoiler, effectively turning it into a small airplane wing and lifting the rear of the car into the air in a broad, sailing motion. The car flipped nose over tail once, twice, and then a third time, then fell to its side, setting off another series of violent bouncing barrel rolls.

Catherine and Joyce both felt their hearts catch in their throats as they watched the car twist and tumble right there on the stretch of track directly in front of them. Catherine had closed her eyes before the first of the barrel rolls began. She never saw the rest of the crash.

Rob watched the whole thing unfold. He couldn't believe what he was seeing. He wanted to shout a warning to Bob but it all happened so fast that he never got the chance. He was so numb, so intent on watching what was happening out there, that he never felt the sharp pain from Michelle's fingernails digging deeply into the flesh of his upper arm.

All of them . . . except Catherine . . . watched as the car seemed to roll and twist forever. Parts and pieces were flying everywhere off the tumbling car. It seemed to be coming apart before their very eyes. Would it ever quit bucking and twisting and disintegrating?

Jodell watched with surprising calm. Like Rob, he saw it coming as soon as the cars rolled out of the corner. The Chevy seemed intent on forcing the issue and the result was inevitable. And he too thought for an instant that Bob junior might actually save the car before it spun around and got airborne. As he watched her flip and the pieces fly off in all directions, he kept his racer's mind focused. The car was bleeding off energy, doing exactly what it was designed to do. He only wished that he had had a hand in building it, watching it go together so he would have been assured in those awful moments that it was put together properly.

How much had Bubba helped? Had he had a hand in constructing the car? Lord, he hoped so.

Now he knew the next threat was one of the other cars plowing blindly through all the smoke and dust and crashing hard into the side of his son's shattered hulk before it finally landed. With the car flipping, it was most vulnerable to a bad lick from another car. And with all the sheet metal that had been shed already, such a collision could do a lot of damage to both driver and machine.

Finally, the Ford pirouetted one final time and landed on its roof just past the exit where the cars normally spilled out of the pits and back onto the track. Jodell walked calmly over to the edge of the pit wall where he could watch the smoking, steaming ruins of the shattered racecar. Now, he knew, all he could do was watch. Watch and wait and pray.

Michelle Fagan still clung tightly to Rob Wilder. Somewhere along the way, he had put his arm around her and pulled her close to him. He knew the driver had a good chance of surviving the crash. But how badly would he be hurt? And how would this affect his racing career just as it was beginning? Rob knew from experience how such an incident could cloud a man's mind, make him question his ability and desire.

He glanced down at Michelle. Her eyes were filled with tears as she stared out at the mangled mess that had been a racecar only seconds before. Her fingernails were digging so deeply into the bare skin on Rob's arm that they drew blood, but he didn't even notice as he tried desperately to raise Bob on the radio. Odds were it was busted but he had to try. And it gave him something to do as he watched and waited.

The safety trucks were on the scene immediately, the carcass of the car still rocking slightly as the first fire truck rolled up close. Several of the workers ran to the car, dropped to their knees, and peered inside the crumbled window of the upturned car.

There was movement inside. Thank God!

It was only a moment before Bob Lee in his blue driving suit could be seen scrambling out the narrow opening and crawling from beneath the car.

"He's out!" Rob called excitedly to all on the radio net. "He's standing up. Looks okay!"

A huge cheer came up from the grandstands as the crowd saw the driver squirm out from underneath the shattered car. Bob, in a move caught by the television cameras, walked once around the smashed car, gave it a good, solid kick of frustration, then turned to face the crowd in the nearest grandstand. He threw them a hearty wave of thanks for their continual and obviously sincere cheers. Only then did he consent to being led over to the ambulance for the mandatory ride to the infield care center and a checkup.

Catherine and Joyce started to head that way but Jodell's strong arm reached out and stopped them.

"The boy is okay. He won't want his mamma fussin' over him."

"I know," Catherine replied a bit sheepishly. For a moment she had acted like a mother, not like a *racer*'s mother.

"You forget who built that car. Joe and Bubba ain't gonna put a car out on the track that's anything but safe." Jodell made certain his words were loud enough for both of them to hear over the grumble of the slowed cars out on the track. "Now, let's lose all those long faces. We had ourselves a showing to be proud of today. And our driver came through a bad crash in fine shape. Once we get through with 'happy hour,' we're gonna fire up the grill and celebrate my boy leading his first race at Talladega!"

Catherine grabbed her husband and gave him a big hug. He kissed her, grinned and winked at her. There was disappointment there on his face, but no anger.

But when he turned to talk with the pit reporter one more time, she could feel her husband's hand where it still rested on her shoulder.

And it was trembling.

Darkness had long since settled over the giant Talladega infield and there was a slight chill in the air after the warm Indian summer day. Happy fans partied noisily as their crackling campfires sent sparks high into the black sky to mingle with the stars. Rob and Michelle walked slowly through the maze of campers, tents, and lean-tos, enjoying the cool night and the electric atmosphere that reigned over the excited throng that had gathered for the weekend's racing.

The party at Jodell's and Bubba's RVs in the drivers' compound turned into one of the best of the season so far. What started out as a small get-together for the Lee Racing bunch quickly grew to include many of the other drivers, crewmembers, and car owners who were parked nearby. Jodell became the proud host, holding court, cooking steaks to order, and keeping the tall-tale-telling as stoked as he did the smoldering coals of his barbecue grill. Several times people were dispatched for more meat, charcoal, drinks, or potatoes to bake in foil in the grill's embers.

It was hard to tell who was happier or prouder, Jodell or Bob junior. And it was amazing to all who knew him to see how quickly Jodell came to accept and actually embrace his son's interest in racing. For his part, Bob tried to tell everyone how fortunate he was to have a car and engine built by some of the best in the business. He also acknowledged his pit crew, one that could more than hold its own on any given Sunday, and reminded everyone he had one of the hottest young drivers on the circuit whispering advice in his ear all day. To waste those advantages he would have had to drive like a rookie on a short track.

The moonless darkness gave Rob the cover he needed to walk unmolested among all the thousands gathered around the campfires, makeshift tents, and RVs in the infield. In his jeans and windbreaker, he was just another skinny race fan taking a walk with his pretty girlfriend. The chill in the night air caused Michelle to snuggle up closer to him, so he wrapped his arm tightly around her to try to keep her warm. He often kidded her about her "California thermostat," her lack of tolerance for any variation in temperature. But tonight, he stayed quiet as they walked along. Neither of them seemed in the mood to talk much.

For some reason, despite the weekend's good qualifying effort and how well the car ran in the "happy hour" earlier in the afternoon, he felt almost melancholy. He finally realized that watching Bob's accident that afternoon bothered him more than he wanted to admit. When the first of the other crews began to drift away from the warm glow of Jodell's campfire, Rob used that as an excuse to slip away himself. Celebrating was not on his mind. He needed some time alone.

Still, when Michelle noticed his defection and caught up with him, he was glad to have her join him. He welcomed her company, her warmth, as she settled in next to him.

Without even thinking about it, he pulled her even closer to him. She melded up against his side, enjoying the strength of his arm around her, sensing somehow that he needed her there tonight.

Suddenly, Rob stopped in his tracks. She could feel a shiver run through him. But she remained quiet, wondering what he saw or heard. Some of the campers nearby had broken out in a raucous version of "Sweet Home Alabama," their singing only half drowned out by the country music blaring from the campsite next door. Off in the distance, some others were launching a barrage of bottle rockets and Roman candles to the cheers of the many who were watching.

But Rob cocked his head, apparently listening hard for something else on the soft, wood-smoke-perfumed breeze. Then, almost on cue, there it was. The distant sound of a race engine. The ghostly sound he had come to know so well over the last year and a half.

Oh, some might claim it was only the roar of one of the cars racing at the nearby dirt track over next to I-20. It was only about a mile from the speedway, over there beyond the third turn and past the building that housed the International Motorsports Hall of Fame with its own collection of ghosts.

But Rob Wilder knew what it was. He relaxed as he heard the sound peak then fade away in the blackness.

"What do you hear?" Michelle finally whispered when she felt the tension leave his body. She suspected what the answer was. She had heard Rob and Jodell talk about the ghostly voices they sometimes heard when they drove, the engine sounds that they claimed visited them at some of the deserted tracks. It always unnerved her. Why couldn't they have the usual innocuous racer superstitions?

But now, Rob was listening to the wind again.

"It's coming back around. Can't you hear it?"

It was her turn to shiver, and not from the damp chill that had settled on the raceway. At first, she heard only thumping music from a party across the way. She was about to dismiss it all as his overactive imagination, maybe kid him a bit about Halloween not being far away.

But then she too heard it. It *was* a race engine, echoing, growing gradually louder as if it might be approaching the darkened tri-oval out of turn four. But how could that be? How could there be a racecar out there running around on the track in total darkness? And why didn't the fans gathered nearby beneath the RV awnings seem to notice it?

A cold chill ran up her spine as the haunting noise faded as quickly as it had appeared.

"We'd better get on back," Rob said abruptly, turning her toward where the drivers' RVs were parked.

They walked in silence again, their arms still entwined. A dark figure was standing just inside the gate, leaning against the fence waiting for them when they got back to the compound.

"Jodell? That you?" Rob called.

"Just walking off some of that steak, that's all," came the reply. But then, as Rob and Michelle passed beneath the glow of one of the big overhead arc lights, Jodell could see the odd look on both the young peoples' faces. "Y'all heard it, too, didn't you?"

"Yeah, we both did," Rob answered, and Michelle nodded, too.

"It's a good sign. A very good sign. I got a feeling tomorrow's gonna be a good day for you, Robbie. Get plenty of rest. You're gonna need it come race time."

When they got back to Billy's motor home, Rob quietly excused himself and quickly settled into the main bedroom in the back. Everyone else was still at the celebration. Michelle, tired from the long day, claimed one of the narrow bunks up in front. She pulled the curtains closed and tried to fall asleep.

But sleep wouldn't come. She kept replaying the night's short walk over and over in her mind. She could still hear the ghostly engine noise ringing in her ears, the same apparition that also appeared to Rob. That was significant. Somehow, some way, hearing that sound had finally allowed her to connect with him. She had never known how it felt to be in a race-car at speed, never known the danger they must all sense out there, never understood what drove those men . . . and this young man in particular . . . to risk it all to win a car race.

But now it suddenly seemed clear to her. For the first time, she felt almost as if someone had sat her down and eloquently explained it all to her. It was all suddenly clear to her what made Rob Wilder hunger so badly for a win, why he drove through all the pain, fatigue, fear, and disappointment in a single-minded search for victory.

She smiled, pulled the blanket up tightly around her neck, turned to face the wall, and was asleep in seconds.

22

Rob awoke on his own, an hour before getting-up time. That was highly unusual for him. Normally it took an alarm clock and a couple of wake-up calls to rouse him. But this morning things were different. He felt as rested, as healed, as he had in weeks. Stepping out of the stateroom, he found Billy asleep in one of the chairs, the obvious victim of too much of Randy's and Clifford's finest corn squeezings. Michelle was still sleeping soundly, too.

Rob moved quietly through the motor home, waiting until he was outside to pull on his sneakers and jacket, careful not to wake the others. Shoes tied, he started his usual early morning walk around the race-track. He crossed through a gate with a wave to the guard there and walked briskly out onto the edge of the pit road, then pointed toward the towering banking in turn one. The ankle felt good, with the limp mostly gone. There was no more pain in his rib cage, either. His breath came easy and free and fogged in front of him as he double-timed toward the sloping turn.

Rounding the corner heading out of turn two, he saw the familiar figure of Jodell Lee outlined by the rising sun, standing there, staring at a spot on the backstretch as if looking for something. Rob hurried on down the way to join him.

"Mornin', Jodell."

"Robbie. Sleep well?"

"I sure did. Like a baby. I don't know what it was but as soon as my head hit the pillow, I was out."

Jodell grinned then motioned for him to follow him as he walked slowly down the back straightaway. They talked quietly as they often did on these race-day walks, Rob mostly listening as the old driver offered him small bits of advice mixed in with the man's own unique philosophy. But still, along the way, the old driver seemed to be looking for something he might have lost on the track.

Suddenly Jodell stopped and stared at a seemingly nondescript spot on the pavement. Rob stopped too and watched him for a moment. Jodell had an odd look on his face.

"What is it?" the kid finally asked.

"It was right about here, I think. Yeah, right about this spot here," Jodell said, pointing. "That's where Tiny got T-boned."

He was talking about Tiny Lund, one of the sport's most popular drivers, and the accident here back in 1975 that had taken his life.

Rob felt uneasy. Talk of the bad accidents was usually off limits among the drivers, and especially on race mornings.

"They never seem to forget the bad ones, do they?" Rob finally said.

"No, those never go away. Wrecks like Bob's yesterday fade, but the really bad ones, the ones that snuff out a bright-burning spirit, they stay around forever."

"Well, Jodell, to tell you the truth, on a day like today when we'll be racing three-wide out yonder for five hundred miles, I'd just as soon not think about any of them."

Rob shuffled uncomfortably from one foot to the other, anxious to move on from this spot.

"That's exactly why I brought it up. We all know the worst can happen to us. But if you let it eat at you, haunt you like a ghost, you'll never have what it takes to win here. Today, this afternoon, you can't afford to be afraid of anything. You've got a fast car. You have the ability. You can beat anybody out there. The only person who can beat you is yourself, and that will happen if you let it."

"I don't plan on that happening," Rob replied confidently.

"I know you don't. That's why you got to have a clear mind and be willing to run wide open." He looked up then from the patched spot on the asphalt. "They'll all be ridin' with you, you know."

"Who?" Rob asked instinctively, but by the time he had said the word, he knew precisely who Jodell was talking about.

But the old champion had turned and was already walking away. If he heard Rob's question, he didn't acknowledge it. The rest of the stroll passed mostly in silence.

23

The second the driver introductions were completed, Rob headed straight for the racecar. He was ready to escape the crush of people milling around where the cars were lined up on pit road. It always amazed him how many people managed to get garage or pit passes. The last couple of hours had been nothing but chaos. He must have signed more than a hundred autographs since he climbed into his driving suit a little over an hour before. He hated to turn anyone down, but he also needed a chance to think, to focus.

Michelle finally gave him some cover from the all the people wandering around the cars. Bob was with her, taking in all the prerace activities. He had been showing everyone the color photo on the front page of the Sunday editions of the Birmingham paper. It showed Bob's car, flipping, coming apart. He admitted he was a little sore but the crash had clearly not damaged his enthusiasm for racing. Rob had gently teased him about leading the race with ten laps to go but then finishing twenty-seventh. Still, Bob ran a good race, better than anyone could have expected. And everyone was confident he could make it in this sport if he truly wanted to, if he was willing to make the sacrifices necessary.

Will and the crew congregated around the car, checking everything one last time. Donnie was making a final check of the tape on the front end, making sure it was stuck exactly where they had decided on, its location based on the day's weather forecast.

Joe Banker took a moment from his own team's preparations to stop by and give Will an appraisal on the final tune he had personally put on the motor earlier that morning. He spoke to Rob on his way back to his team's car.

"Ain't puttin' pressure on you, kid, but you got the engine to win this thing. You just have to believe you can get it done."

He gave Rob a slap on the shoulder.

"I'm ready. I just wish they'd finish all the singing and parading and let us get down to business."

"There you go again," Joe Banker snorted. "Doin' your best Jodell Lee impersonation."

Billy and Jodell showed up not long after Joe left. Billy still looked a bit ashen.

"Billy, you okay?" Rob asked.

"If you ever see me accept anything again from those two rascals, you run me down with the Ford, okay? Them and their firewater. That stuff'll slip up on a fellow."

Billy held his head with both hands for emphasis.

"Now Billy, Randy and Clifford assured me that stuff was medicinal. That it cleanses the soul."

"Well, I can testify that it pickled mine!" Billy said with a groan.

Jodell stood back, grinning. He waited until Billy had walked over to chat with Will before he spoke.

"Remember what I told you this morning. Patience is the key here. Get impatient, step out of line at the wrong time, and you'll get shuffled to the back in the blink of an eye. Then you'll spend half the race trying to make back up the track position."

"I've got a few dancing partners lined up I can draft with already. I'll be okay."

"Just drive smart. When the time comes, you have to be willing to put the car where it needs to go. At that point, if you're timid, you'll lose. That simple. Understand?"

"I understand. I won't let you down."

"Even though I've got a dog in this hunt, I got a feeling this one is yours, kid!"

"Thanks, Jodell."

As Rob swung a leg in the open window, Michelle stepped near. She appeared to want to say something, but stopped short. Instead, she suddenly and without hesitation leaned over and kissed him full on the lips. The move caught Rob completely off guard, but surprisingly, he didn't resist. Somehow, he actually managed to return the quick kiss, then nonchalantly dropped down into the seat.

He was ready to go racing. It was time to win. This time, there would be no second place for him!

Michelle quickly walked away, heading down to their pit. She didn't want to be hanging around when she knew he would be readying himself for the race. She didn't know what had gotten into her, why she had felt the need to give him that kiss. But she noticed he gave none of the usual resistance, that he had actually returned it. And she also knew without a doubt that today was Rob's day to finally find his first Winston Cup victory.

Will helped Rob buckle in as they got closer to the command to fire the engines. Paul Phillips inspected the generator that was humming away in the background, warming the oil in the oil tank. Donnie Kline was already in the pit making sure everyone knew exactly what he was supposed to be doing. Tires were stacked and ready. The tire specialist was double-checking his work, making certain every set had been meticulously matched up. Every member of the team was ready. They too were prepared to go racing.

Rob finished a last-minute, mike-through-the-window interview with the network, his voice muffled by the full-face helmet but his confidence coming through loud and clear.

"We'll be talking later in victory lane," he wound up.

"It seems we have one very confident young man starting here in the fifth row for this last of the re-strictor plate races this season. I guess we'll all see when the checkered flag finally falls if Rocket Rob Wilder can back up his bold prediction."

"Gentlemen, start your engines!" echoed around the packed speedway and the sudden roar of the engines mingled with the expectant bellow of the massive crowd, nearly two hundred thousand strong.

"How's everything look, Robbie?" came Will's voice on the radio.

"Oil pressure's good, fuel pressure is perfect, and the volts are straight up."

"Okay, they just radioed down from the tower and said they're going to run three pace laps before they let y'all go."

"Ten four."

The officials began to wave the two-abreast rows of cars off the line. When the orange and white car ahead of him began to move, Rob eased out on the clutch, careful not to slip it. He knew it was easy to burn up the tiny clutch pads they used on the speedway cars they brought to Daytona and Talladega.

The cars slowed considerably on the next pace lap so the drivers could get a reading on their tachometers to designate the pit road speed for the day. Rob noted the RPMs on his own tach before radioing it to Will so he could remind him each time he pitted during the race.

"Okay, one to go, Cowboy. Green next time by."

"Ten four, Will. Green next time," Rob answered, punching the mike button on the wheel with his right thumb.

"Temperatures still okay?" Will asked.

"Coming up nicely. Everything looks good."

"Great! Now, go get 'em, Cowboy."

"See you in victory lane," Rob called back, and he believed it as strongly as he had ever believed anything in his life.

24

The crowd had been on its feet for a good fifteen minutes already. They were primed for racing. So was Rob Wilder as he twisted the Ford's wheel back and forth. He and the racecars around him were just hitting the long backstretch for the last time before taking the green. They were ready to give the fans who packed the stands and who were watching on network television exactly the show they wanted to see: truly frightening side-by-side racing, inches apart at near two hundred miles per hour.

Rob twisted the car side to side to clean off any lingering debris that might have stuck to the tires on the warm-up laps. He checked the mirrors for the fifth time, making sure they were still set correctly. The field behind him had already begun to tighten up as the cars rolled into the steep banking of turn three.

Two by two, the field exited turn four. At the last instant, the pace car dived onto pit road, leaving the tightly bunched field on its own to decide the contest.

The starter used his upturned hand to keep the field at bay until he was satisfied that everyone was properly lined up in the correct position. He then tapped the ceremonial starter on the shoulder, signaling him that it was time to wave the green flag. The leaders, anticipating the start, were already hard into the gas as the racecars came down toward the start/finish line. The sound of the engines soared from an annoying buzz to a full-fledged crescendo of rolling thunder as the forty-three powerful machines all accelerated at once.

Rob Wilder stomped on the throttle pedal. Even as the car accelerated, it seemed like something invisible was holding her back. The restrictor plate beneath the carburetor was doing its job, robbing the powerful machines of some of their acceleration. For a racecar driver accustomed to explosive acceleration, it seemed as if it took forever for the RPMs to build up, for the cars to finally reach speed. They passed the start/finish line with the field slowly rumbling off toward turn one. Everyone stayed in line as the cars came up through the gears. It would take more than one complete lap for the cars to finally get up to full race speed.

Rob tried to look everywhere at once as he watched the cars in front of him, behind him, and to his inside bounce over the slight ripples and bumps in the track. Nobody at the front of the pack dared jump out of line before the cars had built full speed. This was a tricky time for the drivers. With the cars all stacked up tightly together, one ill-conceived move in the front of the pack could leave half the field more suited for the junkyard than for victory lane.

The racers had all been urged in the drivers' meeting to take it easy early, especially on the restarts, that it was a five-hundred-mile race. So far everyone seemed to be heeding the advice.

Rob stayed tucked in tightly to the inside, ready to

make a move to the front when he spied the inevitable opening. He didn't want to be the first to jump out of line, though, as it could mean a quick drop to the back of the tightly packed field if no one followed him or allowed him to tuck into the line. Instead he decided to be patient and let someone ahead of him make the move first. Once they started mixing it up, he would use the power he knew resided beneath the Ford's hood to push him forward.

Finally the black number "3" jumped down to the inside line only two cars in front of him. It was exactly the move Rob was looking for. He pulled out of line, using the draft off the car directly in front of him to push his bright red Ford forward. Once down to the inside, he immediately sensed the vacuum in the air coming off the "3" car. That was exactly what he needed to allow his own car to suck right up onto the rear bumper of the black Chevy.

Joe Banker's hand-turned engine wasn't all Rob had going for him. Will and the crew crafted the machine to take maximum advantage of the new shock and aerodynamic rules. Unlike some of the others, his car could pick up the draft from another car while still twenty or more car lengths back and quickly close right up onto the back of him. Many of the other teams were still struggling with the new handling packages, sprouting headaches trying to get their cars so they could close in tight on another car from a distance when picking up the draft.

Rob and his new partner, the "3" car, gained several spots down to the inside of the line of cars even before their spotters could call out that they were there.

Their move left the field three-wide coming off the turn. Rob expected the cars in the middle of the sandwich to shoot quickly toward the back of the pack as they normally did here and at Daytona. This time, though, those racing in the middle seemed to be able to hold their ground and ride along with the cars to their inside and outside. That only made things more nerve-wracking for the drivers.

Rob dreaded having to race this way for five hundred miles but it looked like a good possibility. Regardless of how the drivers felt about it, the wild, three-wide racing was a crowd-pleaser. They still had not settled back down into their seats after the rip-roaring start, and the fans cheered the tight knot of cars each time they passed by.

Shooting down the backstretch, Rob caught the hand signal flashed at him from the black Chevrolet's driver. The subtle wave told Rob to follow closer. Then, a fraction of a second later, the Chevy pulled out of line, making it four wide on the broad straight-away.

Rob followed obediently, tucking in tightly, giving the other car a propelling push of air while accepting a welcomed tow, and that enabled the two of them to claim another spot together. The leader was now in sight, but so was the mad scramble for position behind him. Cars were darting and diving everywhere on the track even as they approached two hundred miles per hour. They were even running up to five wide as everyone tried to draft his way to the front. Less than a second and a half separated the cars from first place to forty-third.

Rob and the "3" took a shot for the lead as the pack thundered through the tri-oval. They were three wide as they raced through, but Rob never hesitated. The guy in the car he was trailing was the owner of many championships. The kid was only too happy to follow and trust the savvy of the veteran.

He rode inches off the black Chevy's bumper, instinctively trying to push his foot a little farther into the floorboard all the time, attempting to coax an extra horse or two out of the engine. That's all it seemed it would take to push the two of them out into the lead. Just an extra horse or two.

The cars in the middle, struggling to hang on and keep their line, pushed the "3" car and Rob's "52" Ford downward toward the track apron as all six of them closed in on turn one. Rob stopped breathing. He knew they were rapidly running out of track on the inside.

Still he didn't dare let up on the gas.

He was determined to follow the "3" anywhere he went on the track. If the black Chevy had made a sudden dart to the outside wall, Rob was bound to plow in right behind him. With the cars packed in as tightly as they were, there was simply nowhere else to go.

Will Hughes looked down as the pack left his view heading to turn one. He watched on the television monitor at his feet as they all raced for the corner, so close that the camera made the half-dozen cars appear to be a single machine bolted together somehow. He could see Rob and the "3" stuck all the way to the inside and running way too low, not far from green grass and sure catastrophe. The flat part of the apron that marked the start of the banking was coming up fast. It was frighteningly similar to the spot where the car racing next to Bob Lee had gotten into trouble the day before. If the Ensoft Ford and the black "3" got caught on the flat of the apron, they were both likely to spin, experience and talent and desire would mean nothing, and they would trigger the major calamity everyone was always predicting when the engines roared at Talladega.

Will fought to keep his eyes open. He didn't want to see it but he felt compelled to watch.

Inside the RV, Michelle, Catherine, and Joyce all squealed in unison as the whole thing played out on the television screen.

Rob didn't have time to think about it. The corner

was coming up quickly but there was nowhere for him to go. If he let off the gas, he ran the risk of wrecking the other three dozen cars charging directly up behind him. The only thing he knew to do was exactly what he had been doing. Follow the former champ and hang on for dear life!

The cars in the middle hit a slight bump as their front tires reached the beginning of the banking. That caused their cars to jump up the track, but only a quarter of a racing line.

For the champ, that was all he needed to see. He bulled his Chevy back upward and barely onto the banking. There was just enough room for the width of the Chevrolet to fit between the roaring beasts to his right and the treacherous lip of pavement to his left. Still, the right front of his car touched the left front of the middle car, the driver who still held the lead, but only by less than two feet. A brief puff of smoke from the tire touching sheet metal verified the contact.

Rob never flinched. He couldn't even see the rear end of the "3" he was so close to him. But he did see the touch, the smoke. Somehow his own car stuck and didn't go skittering sideways as they hit the beginning of the banking. The driver in the car to his right side had moved up just a bit, too, giving Rob enough room to race.

Amazingly, all the cars made it through the first turn without causing the "big one." Rob finally breathed again, but his foot was still pushing hard on the accelerator. He realized then that he had never lifted throughout the brief but harrowing dive into the first corner. Somehow he had known to keep pushing, that hesitation in the situation in which he had just found himself would have cost him hard-won track position at best, and certainly could have caused a tragedy.

The laps began to wind off and there remained a

constant shuffling of positions at the front of the field. One lap, a driver could be sailing along happily, leading the race. The next time by, that same driver could be back in ninth or tenth position, digging, wondering what had happened. The cars simply didn't have enough power to break away from the rest of them for long. Cars in line could run faster than two vehicles side by side could manage. But once the cars stopped racing alongside each other and slid back into line, they would usually run down the lead cars quickly.

After fifty caution-free laps, Will was busily plotting their first green-flag pit stop, likely coming between laps fifty-five and sixty. The cars could run another couple of laps farther, but at this point, nobody was going to risk running out of gas. It would also give them a good read on their cars' gas mileage in case they needed to stretch it farther later in the race.

"Donnie, we need to get four tires ready," Will called down. "Go down and talk to Waylon and make sure we plan on stopping on the same lap as Rex does. Tell them we plan on stopping with the leaders. Make sure Rex isn't planning on coming in early."

A car needed to pit with other drivers under green-flag stops or he would run the risk of getting back out onto the track all alone, with no one to draft with. If the driver lost the draft, he ran a good risk of quickly going a lap down, and laps were hard to make up here. All up and down the pit lane, crew chiefs were making arrangements for someone to pit with them.

"Gotcha, Will," Donnie rogered. "Four tires coming up. Guys, let's be ready!"

Then the big man hustled down to the Lee Racing pit where Waylon and Bubba Baxter were holding court over their own crew. They were running three spots behind Rob at the moment and were only too glad to see Donnie so they could seal the deal.

At lap fifty-five, cars began slowing, peeling off for their first stop. The leaders stayed out as long as they could, none of them eager to give up the track position so early in the race, hoping against hope for a caution flag. Rob wasn't even thinking about pitting yet. All he wanted to do was retake the lead position that he had held unofficially twice already. He had made passes going down into turn one to pull ahead of the leaders on two occasions, only to get himself slingshotted again seconds later going into turns three and four.

"How is it, Cowboy?" Will called as Rob hit the backstretch.

"Good. Maybe a tiny bit tight in the center of the corners."

That meant the car's nose wanted to head outward, toward the wall, in the turns.

"Ten four. We'll do a quarter round of wedge on this stop. Watch the fuel pressure. If it drops at all, bring her in. Otherwise, come on in when the '3' or the '88' does. Rex is going to follow you so you'll both have a dancing partner."

"I got an eye on the fuel pressure," Rob said quickly, his hands suddenly full again as the car was about to climb the banking off the third turn. The tight racing kept him from doing much chatting on the radio.

Abruptly the front three cars began to make the turn toward pit road. Rob first resisted the urge to slow at all. Everything had been working so well he hated to risk tainting the magic. But then he knew it was the right thing to follow the others onto pit road. And he also knew that Will would kill him if he didn't!

He finally cracked the throttle for the first time in over fifty circuits of the giant speedway and tried to follow the leaders in their left-hand turns. But immediately he realized he was going much too fast. He jumped on the brakes so hard with both feet that the gimpy ankle protested with a sharp shot of pain running up his leg. The tires smoked a bit but somehow he managed to avoid a spin and got the Ford slowed by the time he hit the line where the officials began clocking the cars' speed.

"Watch your speed! Watch your speed!" Will yelped after Harry informed him that Rob was heading to pit road. Luckily, he wasn't able to see him jam on the brakes and come close to spinning the car out onto the grass.

Rob didn't reply. He was now straining, trying to pick out their pit sign among all the others that were bouncing up and down as the cars came charging down pit lane.

Where was the dadgum sign?

It looked like hundreds of floating signs and logos being waved around down there. Then, he listened to the calm, steady voice of Harry Stone, singing cadence as he called him down to the correct stall.

"Ten . . . five . . . four . . . three . . . two . . . one!"

Donnie stood on the top of the pit wall holding the big jack in his hand. The others were ready to come across the wall, holding either tires or the air guns. The gasman already had the first of the heavy cans up on his shoulder, ready to step over the wall and begin dumping the fuel into the car's left-rear fill spout.

When the car was still two stalls away, Donnie led the charge over the wall, he and the front tire changer jumping almost directly into the path of the Ensoft Ford. Rob had finally picked out the swinging sign with the Ensoft logo on it and guided the car in to a stop, perfectly hitting the L-shaped area that had been duct-taped on the pavement. The brakes smoked from the friction of dragging the 3800-pound car to a stop from one hundred and ninety miles an hour.

As the car came in smoothly to a stop, Donnie

thrust the jack beneath her and raised her right side off the ground with two mighty pumps on the handle. Paul attacked the lug nuts on the left rear, sending them flying in every direction. He yanked the old smoking tire off the spindle and placed it on its side on the ground. The tire carrier slid in a fresh Goodyear and, with balletlike moves, Paul cinched the new lugs up tight. As soon as he finished the last one, he was up, on his feet, racing around to the left side, making sure to swing the air hose wide around the car to keep it from becoming tangled. The gasman was finished with the first can of fuel and now hefted up the second one. Paul was already ratcheting off the lug nuts on the right rear wheel.

Will watched the whole process carefully. He knew that the slightest slipup would translate into a huge deficit they would have to somehow make up once they were back out on the track. Every second lost in the pits would mean a distance equal to a football field in track position. He also didn't want to lose the draft of any of the cars he came in with once they exited the pits. He watched anxiously as the tire changers finished up their work without a hitch.

Donnie stood there, holding the jack handle, waiting for the catch can man to signal that the gas tank was full. At the first hint of fuel spilling out the overflow, he nodded to Donnie and the big man gave a quick twist on the jack handle, dropping the car down hard. Rob took that as his signal to go and was already releasing the clutch as Will's redundant call came over the radio: "Go! Go!"

Rob jammed on the gas once he felt the clutch engage, careful not to burn it up or have it catch too quickly and snap an axle. It happened all the time, and to drivers far more experienced than Rob Wilder. But Rob was away cleanly, blending in with the same bunch of cars he had come in with once they hit the line at the end of pit road.

"Good stop, everybody. Sixteen point two," Will called, checking the time on the stopwatch he held in his left hand. "Let's make all the rest as good as this one and we got a shot at this thing."

Everyone in the crew was slapping each other, whooping, dancing. They took pride in what they contributed to a race effort and they knew to a man that they had just completed a good stop.

The field sorted out again into three basic packs. A front group that consisted of about ten cars, the next pack of about twenty running two and a half seconds back, then a third slower bunch about ten seconds behind them.

Rob ran in sixth place in the middle of the lead pack that had sorted itself out in single file. While all the cars in this group were clearly fast, none of them seemed to have the ability to dominate. Rob was determined to change that. He caught the draft off the car ahead of him, boldly pulling out of line as they all roared off the fourth corner. His momentum pushed him ahead of the Ford that had been running in front of him, and, once he realized he had been bettered, the other Ford's driver immediately jumped down behind the red Ensoft machine.

The two cars running together on the inside began to make a run on the front four. The cars behind them broke into their own scramble for position as the single-file line of cars quickly split up into side-by-side racing. At the same time, the third-place car took the opportunity to make an outside run on the two leaders. That move gave Rob the break he needed and he brazenly pushed his car to the front.

He could almost smell the lead and it was a heady perfume.

As he dove into turn one, the spot was his while the trailing Ford chased futilely in his wake. Rob held his car down low through the turns, loving the empty track stretching out ahead of him, the mass of cars chasing behind. But he had been in this spot before, only to have the point rudely ripped away from him before the group could cross back to the finish line, putting his lap at the front into the books. Now, Rob could care less what was going on behind him. He kept the car pinned to the low line, trying to protect the short way around the track. Pacing the field back to the start/finish line, the lap belonged to him and his red "52."

Twenty laps later Rob was still leading. With the race approaching the halfway point, he was making a statement to everyone else out there. Not only did he have a car capable of dominating the event, he was proving that he was now fully recovered from his injuries at Indianapolis two months before.

In the pits, Will Hughes wore a very uncustomary smile. Normally he never allowed himself this luxury until the race was actually theirs, checkered flag and all. But today it was a case of "so far, so good." They were going to need some flawless pit stops and they didn't want any more yellow flags to bunch up the field.

But just when Will had that thought, a car blew an engine right in the middle of the tri-oval. From where he sat atop the pit box, Will saw the line of thick, black oil laid down by the smoking car after it went coasting by. An instant later, there was the yellow flag waving from the flagstand and the yellow lights were flashing all around the track.

"Caution's out," Harry radioed from his spotters' stand.

"Yeah, he dumped a load of oil right in the groove running through the tri-oval," Will added. "Take the high line through there and watch out."

"Ten four," Rob called quickly, watching his mirror to see if anyone was going to try to get around him on the way back to the caution flag.

But apparently the news about the oil was passed

to the other drivers, as well. Everyone backed off as the cars rolled into the tri-oval, all of them looking for the slippery mess so they could avoid it.

"Pits are open next time around. Some of these guys are going for two tires but we'll make it four," Will proclaimed.

"Your call, Will. I just drive this thing," Rob responded. Will had just confirmed his confidence that Rob could make up the time it would take to put on the two additional tires. And the kid was sure, too. "Make sure they pass me a cold towel," he added.

"You okay?"

"Yeah, I'm fine. It's just gettin' a little hot in here, that's all."

Will was correct. Several drivers opted to go for two tires only, picking up the first four spots in the field in the process. Paul had trouble with one of the lug nuts on the left rear, costing them an extra second in the pits. That put them in eighth on the restart, riding to the outside of several lapped cars that were lined up down below him. There would likely be many pressure-packed laps before the field would get sorted out again. But Rob knew the cream would rise to the top yet again. All he had to do was be patient, drive smart, and he'd rise right along with the other contenders.

The first accident came well past the halfway point in the contest. Three cars locked horns coming off turn three, sending one hard into the wall and the other two spinning wildly off into the infield. That brought out the caution once again, of course, and set up the promise of a wild forty-lap dash to the finish.

Rob actually welcomed the caution period this time. He was getting hot and tired. The vibrations in the car were causing his left leg to go numb. The slower speeds, riding along behind the pace car, allowed him to stretch and move his leg around to get the blood circulating. There was a dull ache at the

point where it was broken and it radiated up his leg
to his thigh. He worked to put it all out of his mind.
There were other things to be concentrating on, things
he could actually have some control over.

As before, several cars only changed two tires during the stop in an attempt to gain track position. After
everyone pitted, Rob sat in seventh position with fast
cars ahead of him, including the "3," the "88," and
the "24." It would be a tough run to make it back up
to the front and then stay there. Those guys ahead of
him carried plenty of victories at Talladega among
them. They certainly had no intention of allowing an
upstart rookie to get past them again if they could
help it.

Bob Lee was thoroughly enjoying his time in the
pits. He alternated between watching his father's team
and standing behind Will and the gang as they sup-
ported Rob Wilder. Things had not gone well for Rex
Lawford and the Jodell Lee Racing car. What started
as a promising run had gone sour when a right front
shock broke and they were forced to make the change
under green. That left Lawford two laps down to the
leaders and no real chance of contending for the victory. With Rob still very much in the hunt, Bob finally
gravitated down to the Winton Racing pit. Whatever
the outcome for Rob, this was clearly going to be an
exciting finish to watch.

But there was one emotion welling up inside Bob
Lee that he recognized immediately. It was envy. He
would have given anything to be out there mixing it
up with those guys, the sport's best.

"And someday I will," he vowed out loud. No one
could hear him over the roar of competition, but that
didn't diminish his determination one bit.

Back in the motor home, Catherine Lee was having
trouble containing her excitement as she watched the
final laps play out on the television screen. She had
been around racing long enough, understood the game

well enough, to know that Rob Wilder had a real chance at winning. Talladega's penchant for first-time winners only added to her conviction. She now knew him so well that Rob seemed almost like another son to her. Even though he was competing against her own husband's team, she was openly pulling for the youngster, as surely as she would have if Bob had been out there racing.

Michelle Fagan was so worried as she watched the breakneck pace and close-quarter racing that Rob's chances for winning were not even being contemplated. She had even stopped noting how often the Ensoft logo was highlighted on the network telecast or the company name mentioned by the commentators. All she knew was that there were still forty laps to go, forty treacherous laps, and it was much too early to be thinking about victory.

The laps began to wind down. Rob somehow managed to get himself bottled up by several of the slower cars. He found himself boxed in on the outside with a half-dozen cars slipping by to his inside before he could manage to free himself. Harry Stone casually informed him that he was in fifteenth place with Rex Lawford and several other lapped cars separating him from the rest of the other top twenty.

Will could tell from his clipped words on the radio that Rob was getting frustrated after being shuffled back so far in the field. The lead eight cars were stretched out in a long, straight line and were starting to put some distance on the second pack, the bunch that included Rob and his bright red Ford.

"Easy now, Cowboy, we got plenty of laps to sort this out. Let's don't be the one who causes that caution flag."

"These guys act like they want to cause the big wreck. I got to get away from them," Rob shot back.

"Just take your time and pick your way. You know

you can run with those boys once you get loose again."

Rob didn't reply. Instead he yanked the wheel to the left, taking the car all the way down to the apron as he attempted to zip past several cars. If he didn't get to the front of his pack quickly, the leaders would be gone without him. Will watched the move unfold in front of him. He could only shake his head. There was no way he could be mad at his driver, though. He knew Rob had had a taste of the lead and that he wanted more. What driver worth his salt wouldn't?

Now, with twenty-five laps to go, Rob was leading the second group of racecars, three seconds back of the nine-car lead pack. Several of the cars behind him finally lined up and, together, it gave them their only hope of chasing down the front-runners. Suddenly, one of the leaders jumped out of line, trying to make a move to the front. That one maneuver, getting the leaders running side by side for position, gave Rob and the racecars trailing him a chance to close the distance between themselves and the last car in the lead pack.

With twenty laps to go, Rob finally caught the draft off the lead group, pulling up onto the back of the last car in the bunch. He tried to focus on nothing but the track and the cars around him but there were still powerful distractions. The throbbing in his left ankle was more than a nuisance now. His face was covered with sweat and his fingers ached from the tight grip being maintained on the wildly jerking steering wheel.

Still he refused to allow any of that to bother him. He drove like a man on a mission. Second place wasn't going to cut it today. The leader was now in sight and Rob Wilder was finally within hailing distance of where he knew he belonged.

Now, feeling the time was right, Rob took the high line around the track, trying to get a good run at the cars ahead of him as they all came up off the corner. He used the built-up momentum from the high line to swing low coming out of the turn, zooming past several cars with surprising ease. Coaxing every ounce of power he could find from the powerful engine, he pushed toward the front.

The front was the only place to be now. Jockeying around back there in the middle of all the other challengers ran the risk of getting shuffled out of line and sending the Ensoft Ford sailing to the back once again. If that happened, there were likely not enough laps left to work his way back to the lead yet again. Or, if the dicing around led to a wreck, it would be much better to be ahead of it, not blundering right into the middle of the mess at a hundred and ninety miles an hour.

Somebody jumped in behind Rob to draft off him. That helped him maintain his position on the inside as the front group raced for the corner. Rob sat in sixth place now and it might have made sense for him to remain there, to ride there for a while until things at the front shook out some more.

But not to Rob Wilder. He wasn't content to ride anywhere but up front.

Now he pushed his car down to the inside. Something deep down inside told him it was time to go, not a time to hesitate. Drafting partner or not, he was determined to race his car to the lead. This time, no one dared to pull out of line and go with him. But Rob didn't care.

He was tired of chasing. It was time to be chased!

"What do you think?" Billy Winton asked Jodell and Joe.

They were all standing together on top of Jodell's hauler as the leaders flashed past their position. The scoreboard showed seventeen laps to go.

"Kid's got a good chance, but the way those guys

are shuffling things up in the draft anything can happen," Joe said.

Both men turned to Jodell for his opinion.

"Billy, you better be planning your first victory speech as a Cup car owner," he said emphatically, never taking his eyes off the cars circling the track.

Back out there in the middle of the melee, Rob was determined not to give an inch as the cars hit the backstretch and he held on to third. Suddenly, the black "3" jumped in behind him, giving him the extra boost he so desperately needed. The lead car tried to move over and block him but Rob caught the draft off that car and pulled up even.

Side by side, the two cars raced through the corner, heading back around to the front stretch so the bulk of the frenzied crowd could see firsthand their battle for the point. Rob slowly gained on the leader with the "3" locked tightly on his bumper. Heading toward the tri-oval, the "3" actually tapped Rob in the rear end. Instead of spinning him, the tap gave Rob the push he needed to clear the pass before they hit the tri-oval. The "3" darted in behind Rob as soon as he cleared the former leader and now the two cars took over the front two spots.

He was leading at Talladega!

They were fifteen laps from the checkers but Rob was not thinking that far ahead. He was taking things one lap at a time. It was a thrill to have nothing but clear track in front of him. But all he had to do was glance in the rearview mirror to see a dozen racers waiting for him to make even the slightest of mistakes so any one of them could make him pay dearly.

With four laps remaining, Michelle was already on the way to the pits. It had been Catherine who urged her to go on, that Rob was about to win his first Cup race and she might want to be there when he got to victory lane.

Rob still wasn't quite as sure but he was beginning

to feel it. He stayed hard in the throttle, never lifting his foot even slightly. The black "3" was still there, looming threateningly in his mirror. But he was not the only one. The "88," the "24," the "6," and the "40" were all back there, too. Each of them was convinced he had the car that would win. Even if Rob managed to hold the lead over the next three laps, the end would still be a shoot-out.

Through the tri-oval the cars lined up behind Rob began to shift around impatiently, checking out different lines on the track, each of the drivers beginning to plot his final move. Time was running out. If they were going to make a move, it would soon be time.

Rob began to stretch the gap to second, pulling out to a three-car-length lead.

"Drive smart. You can outrun them."

The voice was loud, distinct. Rob reached a thumb for the mike to give Will a response, but it had not been Will or the radio that he heard. The voice had the familiar broad Virginia drawl.

Rob grinned, gritted his teeth with determination, and said, "I will. I will."

The cars hit the backstretch and the drivers seemed to all lose their patience at once. One car went high, two others dived to the inside to try to catch the draft. The cars seemed to scatter everywhere in Rob's rearview mirror. He steered his car in a serpentine pattern trying to upset the air behind him so nobody could get a good clean draft on him.

Rob hit the low line through the corner in an attempt to leave no opening for a pass. With all the racing going on behind him, there was a good possibility the wily driver in the "3" car could catch the drafting partner needed to make the attempt to pass on Rob. If they got hooked up just right behind him, Rob and his hopes for victory were done. And, possibly, so was even a top-ten finish.

From the vantage point atop the pit box, Will

fought his nervousness. This was the position any crew chief wanted to be in, the spot he had always dreamed of. His driver and his car were leading the race with only a few laps to go and they had a real chance to win. The work back at the shop, in the garage, in practice, in the pits, was done. It was up to his young driver to bring it home now.

Billy's knuckles were white as he gripped the railing that ran around the top of the truck. He was thrilled to have his car leading but he also didn't like the prospects of the black Chevy riding the rear bumper of his machine. He was probably the toughest driver in the business. He would hold nothing back. Rob would have to be ready for a rough-and-tumble last lap. At least, if Rob could hold on for the win, there would be no doubt he had beaten the very best.

Michelle shuffled her feet nervously as she studied the monitor on the back of the pit box. She didn't notice the smiles on Randy's and Clifford's faces when they saw the cars behind Rob getting three wide in a frantic attempt to move closer to the front. That would work in Rob's favor.

Jodell's face carried a broad grin, as well. This close to the end of the race, there was no doubt in his mind as to what the outcome would be. He'd seen it in the kid's eyes that morning, just as he had that very first night two and a half years before. That's when he had watched a gangly young racecar driver show amazing talent winning the feature race. The promise Jodell had seen in the kid was about to burst into full bloom in only two laps.

Rob came racing back around to take the white flag . . . one lap to go . . . while eight cars still fought desperately for position behind him.

One lap to go for the victory. A hundred and eighty thousand cheers merged with the thunder of the racing machines as the field went by for the last time.

Rob never even considered lifting his accelerator

foot. He glanced in his mirror, watching and waiting for the challenge he knew was coming from the "3" and likely from some of the others, as well. Any pass would have to be on the outside. There was no way for anyone to get any lower on the track than where Rob Wilder kept the red "52" planted.

Still, down into turn one, the black Chevy took a look at what sliver of daylight there might be to the inside. Nope, nothing there, so he moved high in an attempt to get some momentum coming off turn two. There was a frantic rush for third with three cars racing side by side followed by three more doing the same directly behind them.

Next, the Chevy tried to get a run to the inside on Rob going down the long back straightaway. But the kid took the veteran all the way to the grass, determined not to let him by. The cars touched briefly, both vehicles skewing slightly. Despite the jolt, Rob never lifted. He would have sworn he simply closed his eyes and held on, but somehow, the car stayed straight and Rob drove it hard one more time into turn three.

One mile to go to the checkered flag.

The driver of the "3" desperately tried to close up tighter onto his bumper, to get one last shot at him as the cars raced for the start/finish line just past the tri-oval.

The flagman stood ready, the checkered flag already in hand.

Rob allowed the "3" a bit of the inside now. With a five-car-length lead coming off the corner, Rob's job was to simply hold his ground and hope the engine and the tires stayed together until they got to the line a final time. Now it was clear that without a drafting partner the black Chevrolet just didn't have what he needed to push him on by and the cars racing behind him were too busy trying to capture better positions to help the Chevy challenge for the win.

With a flick of the flagman's wrist, the checkers were waving as Rob sailed beneath him. It was a feeling he would never forget. His first checkered flag in the big leagues. And to claim it, he had outdueled the very best in the business all the way down to the line.

The "52"s crew spilled out onto the pit lane in a spontaneous yet jubilant celebration, their high-fives and hugs captured live by the network cameras. Michelle literally jumped on Clifford, nearly throwing out his bad back. Randy was doing one of his wild hillbilly jigs. Donnie Kline had a tire changer lifted up on each shoulder and was giving them a ride down pit road. Back in the RV, Catherine and Joyce only sat back and grinned at each other, too exhausted to do more.

Will watched the ending in disbelief. He always knew they would win, certain they had the driver, car, and crew to eventually score, but now that it was actually happening, it was too much to believe. But before he even had a chance to think, someone stuck a microphone in front of him.

"How does it feel to get your first win as a crew chief?"

"We have the best driver in the world. The kid put on one whale of a show. And the best crew. And the best sponsor . . ."

He had silently rehearsed that first victory interview a hundred times but all he could do was babble when the chance finally came.

Maybe the second-best moment of the day for Rob came just after taking the checkered flag. The black car, the one that initially helped him then, at the end, chased him for all he was worth, pulled up alongside him. The victory salute the driver gave Rob made him beam with pride. It was something to have earned the respect and good wishes from this particular driver.

Rob coasted around to pit road where one of the officials flagged him to a stop to check the angle on his spoiler. Noting it was within spec, he waved him on to victory lane.

And that was a problem. In Rob's excitement, he had completely forgotten how to get there. A long file of crewmen from the other teams lined up along pit road to salute him, to congratulate him on a very popular first win. That meant a lot to him, too. Plus it gave him a clue as to where he was going. He simply followed the line of crewmen until somebody stepped out and waved him in to what was apparently victory lane.

Only when he finally parked on the checkerboard cement floor of the victory circle did he realize the toll the tense five hundred miles had taken on him. His left leg was numb. The ankle painfully reminded him of the recent break. He was exhausted, yet exhilarated. The safety belts were unsnapped and the helmet tossed to the floorboard, then he dutifully pulled on the sponsor's hat someone had tossed in to him, and finally, he tried to climb out of the car to the waiting microphones.

But he quickly saw he couldn't summon the energy and slumped back into the seat. It took the strong arms of Donnie Klein gripping his shoulders to yank the tired but happy driver out of the car. Donnie stood him up and held him erect next to the car until he could find his legs.

A grateful Will grabbed him then, unashamedly giving him a hug. Rob managed to maintain his composure throughout the interview, just as Jodell Lee had taught him.

"Act like you been there before and plan on going back a whole bunch of times," he had counseled.

Then it was Michelle Fagan who came charging through the crowd and embraced him, much to the delight of the network cameras and news photographers. Without even thinking, Rob accepted her long, hard kiss on the lips, wrapping his arms even more tightly around her.

After the celebration, and while Rob sat for still more interviews, Jodell, Billy, and Joe walked together back toward pit road. Bubba Baxter met them halfway and immediately picked Billy up and gave him a massive congratulatory bear hug.

"You finally got you one, you old redheaded son of a gun!"

"Put me down, you lug head!"

"And just think, if I hadn't of picked you up that rainy night when you was hitchhikin' . . ."

Both men smiled at the memory of their first encounter, Bubba on the way home from some race somewhere, Billy Winton hitching across the country after his last tour of duty in Vietnam.

"And just think, if I hadn't of been there to save your butt from that bunch of hippies . . ." That fight too had been a key part of their meeting that night. "We've come a long way since then, though."

"I'd say we all have," Jodell added. "And I'd say we got an awful lot to be thankful for. And you, Mr. Winton, still have some more celebratin' to do."

"Nosir," Billy said sharply. "We *all* have some more celebrating to do. Now come on before they run out of confetti and fireworks!"

Jodell Lee grinned and slapped his old friend on the back.

"Billy, I think they better be makin' a lot more confetti and fireworks for this whole bunch. We're gonna need it!"

Almost two thousand miles to the west, Christy Fagan punched the button on the television remote control, a swirl of emotions coursing through her. She was so proud of Rob Wilder, proud of how well he had done in the race and during the interview afterward. Proud that he had just realized a dream he had carried since he was five years old. A dream he recounted for her many times.

She had cheered out loud and danced around the tiny apartment where she had watched the race all by herself. But she was filled with regret that she couldn't be there with him at this most important moment. Right now she couldn't even remember what vital bit of work it was that kept her from flying back to Alabama. Rob practically begged her to come, but she told him she would make it another day.

The joy on his face when he was pulled from the car only made her feel worse that she wasn't there to hug him, kiss him, tell him how proud she was of him. Then, there was her sister, emerging from the crowd in full gallop, her face glowing with the excitement of the victory Rob had brought to her company.

Then, Michelle and Rob were hugging and sharing a deep kiss, relayed by the TV camera all the way across the continent and into Christy's living room.

She brushed away a tear. A tear of happiness for the man she loved and the wonderful thing he had accomplished this day. For her sister, who had talked Ensoft into embarking on the racing sponsorship in the first place and had dedicated herself, night and day, to fully realizing the investment's potential. A tear of joy for the two people she loved most as they shared their own joy together there on the television screen.

But before Christy could stop them, more tears followed.

Jodell Lee sat there all alone on a stack of used-up racing tires as the darkness claimed the racetrack's infield. He was surprised the kid's win that afternoon left him in such a reflective mood. But somehow, as he rocked gently back and forth, the last forty years seemed to rush past like a racecar at speed.

Then, from a distance, he heard it . . . the sweet song of a high-powered racing engine, building RPMs, seeking velocity.

Eerie as it was, there were no chills up his spine, no ghostly dread. The sound seemed to grow closer and then, just as quickly as it had approached, it faded again, eaten up by the hazy mist and the gathering darkness.

And the old driver could clearly hear riding on the soft breeze the wicked laugh of Little Joe Weatherley, the smooth voice of Fireball Roberts, the easy drawl of Neil Bonnet. They might just as well have been down the way there somewhere, telling lies, swapping stories.

Jodell stood slowly, ignoring the creaks and aches that were left over from his many racing crashes over the years. He eased back the sponsor cap on his head and grinned.

As soon as they got back home, there would be a gigantic celebration, no matter what time it might be. A celebration the likes of which hadn't been seen in Chandler Cove since the first time he and Joe and Bubba had won their first big race at Darlington and the whole town was still up to welcome them home. A party that would make Little Joe Weatherley or old Curtis Turner proud.

He wanted to talk with Billy Winton, too, about an idea or two he had been mulling over lately.

Then, first thing tomorrow, he and his son would have themselves a little talk of their own. A talk that was far too long overdue.